Nick Christofides

The right of Nicholas Christofides to be identified as the author of
this work has been asserted by him in accordance with the
Copyright, Designs and Patents Act, 1988.
Copyright ©2015 Nicholas Christofides
ISBN. 9798377450122
All rights reserved. No part of this publication may be reproduced,
stored in retrieval system or transmitted in any form or by any means
electronic, mechanical, photocopying, recording or otherwise, without
the prior permission of the publisher, except in the case of brief
quotations embodied in critical articles and reviews.
This work is a work of fiction. Names and characters are the
product of the author's imagination and any resemblance to actual
persons, living or dead is entirely coincidental.

For you Tors

ONE

He was suffocating - faces and limbs came from all directions. The raucous chatter and sweltering heat from the packed room brought the walls inwards, stifling his energy for this sham.

Mobbed by his party members. They hugged him and kissed him, shook his hands eagerly and slapped his back. His own face beamed back at him from a sea of placards adorned with his picture and the words *The New Way: The New Socialist Order*.

Ben Baines clawed at his collar and rubbed his brow. He knew that it was too early to leave, but in conversation he felt his eyes glaze over, and he found himself lost for words; these politicians and party busybodies were not *his* people. He maintained a frivolous grin, waving all the way and accepting their praise, as he backed out of the room. He jogged up four flights of stairs to the calm of his office.

He had won. He had brought the NSO to power. Pushed to the fore by his peers, he had defeated The Establishment, Big Business and the Media.

Lucas Dart was waiting for him there. He lounged in Ben's chair, a bottle of beer in his hand and his feet on the desk.

'Fancy something stronger than that?' Ben asked as he flicked the switch for the strip beam lights – he hated them, the incessant hum they emitted – and the office was left draped in shadow.

Lucas took a long, deep breath and exhaled loudly, exaggerated and bullish, 'why not…'

Ben poured two glasses of whisky, delivered one to Lucas and then wandered over to the window.

He stood at the sash window and rested his forehead on the cold glass. He studied the revellers milling in the street below, like bees in their hive.

'And they thought leaving Europe would give rise to fascists...' he said absently, without looking away from the window.

Lucas smacked his lips after knocking back his drink, 'what did you say?'

Ben walked over to the sofa and slumped into it, he looked at his friend with a broad grin, 'how the hell are we going to do this?'

'Ha, same as we've always done it... belief! Commitment to the basics... and no quarter for...'

'Don't say it Lucas, you sound like that lot downstairs, division is not success...'

'Come on, we must fulfil our mandate...'

Ben shook his head as he watched Lucas huff and puff as he rose to pour himself another drink at the sideboard. The clink of cut glass and the groan of aged wood was calming.

'We must do the right thing.' Ben mumbled.

'You couldn't last any longer downstairs? They'll be disappointed...'

'No, I'm afraid I find very little more annoying than our party membership.'

'A necessary evil...'

'An evil nonetheless,' he laughed, picked up the remote control and pressed the little plus button and the sound from the street below filled the room via the television's speakers.

On the screen, they watched a sea of faces: young, old; men, women; all sorts of people. He saw colourful knitwear under dreadlocked heads alongside families dressed in well-kept brightly coloured hiking jackets, Roadmen and students, chavs and fashionistas, all beside blue-collar workers. His eyes were caught by a little girl on her father's shoulders playing with the helium balloon she was gripping tightly. Then a couple in work wear skipped across the foreground, a bottle of champagne swinging from her outstretched arms. He felt tears in his eyes momentarily as pride welled within him.

Ben looked at his colleague, who looked down at the screen, grinning. His stomach tightened as he shared this moment with his deputy. He shook his head but couldn't shake out the thought: that never had he felt so detached from the people.

'Our names will go down in history,' said Lucas, dreamily.

Ben got to his feet and crossed the room. 'Not yet.'

'Where are you going now?' he shouted after him, but Ben didn't answer.

Left alone again, Lucas sat down in front of the television screen. The ecstatic outpouring of joy continued as the shot panned around to a chubby-faced reporter, whose hair refused to cooperate with gravity, it drifted upwards in the breeze.

Lucas straightened up now. He gulped. As he watched the crowds in the mayhem of release, he realised suddenly who he was looking at.

'You bloody madman…' he whispered.

There behind the reporter and on the shoulders of the people was Ben Baines, the new leader of England. His fans carried him like a footballer who had just won The World Cup, while he cheered and reached out to every hand that tried to touch him. There was no acting now.

'Thinks he's the fucking Messiah,' Lucas mumbled to himself with a chuckle.

Then he got up and marched to the window. He stood where Ben had been only minutes before. A shiver ran down his spine as he thought about doing what his friend had done. Then, through the window, he saw the crowd put him down. He turned quickly to the TV screen again as Ben appeared next to the journalist. He scrambled back to the sofa and turned up the sound.

The young reporter's voice was raised against the noise of the revelry. Excitement animated his face, and his vocal cords were raw after hours spent covering the celebrations. There was something of a northern lilt to his accent and he performed like a seasoned correspondent.

'I cannot quite believe this, but standing next to me is Ben Baines.' He turned to the leader. *'Hello sir!'* he shouted awkwardly.

'Hello!' screamed Baines.

Dart shook his head as the reporter looked purposefully into the camera.

'If you wondered what was different about our new leader...' He looked at Ben and gestured with his hands at him being alone amid the jubilation.

'What would you like to say to the people?' The reporter was evidently struggling to find the words as he passed the microphone to Ben, who took it from him and looked around, sucking in the energy of the crowd.

Lucas could see the solemn figure of Pierre, Ben's bodyguard, standing at the leader's right shoulder.

'Over past decades,' Baines boomed into the microphone, *'we have watched economies crumble! We have seen Terror threaten the western world and we have endured the right-wing backlash! All the while corporations and politicians have profited! We have seen the might of the USA destroy itself from within!'* His voice cracked a little as he fought against the noise of the crowd. *'Now, we are making history – together, we are stronger!'* he looked around him, wide-eyed and pumped with emotion.

Dart snorted at the screen.

'And together,' Baines screamed, *'we will make this world a better place for all of us!'* He punched the air, pointed to all the people surrounding him then raised the microphone in the air, screaming in jubilant celebration,

unreserved and at the top of his lungs. The journalist watched him, mouth wide open.

Lucas stared at the screen as Ben passed the microphone back to the speechless journalist, the crowds around him went crazy. He was jostled and bumped; Pierre appeared to climb on Baines's back in an attempt to protect him from the revellers, but Ben was in his element and his face radiated pure joy.

Lucas took a huge gulp of whisky and slammed the glass down on the table.

As Pierre ushered Baines away, the camera remained focused on the journalist, who finally gathered himself,

'Can you believe that?' he said, before getting a grip. *'...As you can witness from the crowds around me, the mood here on the streets of the capital is jubilant. Today's results are overwhelming. The Peaceful Revolution has been sanctioned! Capitalism is dead! Collectivism is our future... The Baines era of politics is upon us. At least for tonight, the NSO and Mr Baines evidently, can enjoy their victory.*

'But it is now, that Ben Baines will need to make good his promises with action. Yes, his support is unquestionable, but Baines, the dissident revolutionary, has inherited a country on its knees, bankrupt financially and at loggerheads with its neighbours.'

The journalist now stared soberly into the lens.

'While everyone cheers in Socialism, what of Land Reform, a policy that is integral to our leader's dogma? The policy that is causing unrest – even violence. How long can this charismatic man persuade those generations born of Capitalism that his ideology will work? What we know for certain is that only time will tell. This is Rory Henderson for News –'

As Lucas turned off the television, he leaned back in the sofa and rested his arms across the back of it, he rested his head back and smiled to himself.

Ben fell into the rear entrance of their building and whooped with pleasure. He looked at Pierre, who evidently did not share the rush that he was experiencing.

'This was dangerous…' he said with a stern expression.

'Come on, if I am not the same as everyone else – if we can't stand together – we have nothing.'

'It was dangerous, Ben.' Then the corners of his mouth curled. 'But we are okay, so we do not need to worry. *Veinard!*'

Ben put his hands on his knees and caught his breath.

'No French…' He looked up at Pierre.

Pierre shrugged and tutted, 'how do you say… er lucky bastard!' He put a hand on the leader's shoulder, and they shared a laugh.

Ben walked straight to the sideboard when he came back to his office and poured himself a Scotch.

'D'you want another one,' he called over his shoulder.

'No, I've had enough.'

Ben, surprised, turned to look at his deputy, as Lucas leaned forward, the lamp caught his meaty face, creating dark shadows across his features. 'That was stupid. One day, your ego will catch up with you!'

Lucas stood up and looked at Ben as if he was about to speak, but instead he simply bowed his head, tapped the surface of the desk a couple of times and headed for the door. As he was about to leave, he turned to Ben. 'You are the leader of the NSO, and you have to act appropriately. Your cavalier attitude may work out there…' He pointed to the window. 'But leadership is about image. There are a lot of ambitious and powerful people who have invested in you.' He looked at him sternly, a finger raised towards him. 'They're your primary concern, and stunts like that make you look reckless. You are the Leader!'

'Not you as well Lucas! The only people that matter are the people out there and we will need every one of them to believe if we are going see this through…'

'I will make your policies work, trust me, I will see them through, you do not need to take those risks. Give me credit!'

Ben felt his shoulders sag, 'I trust you. Go downstairs, have a good time Lucas, make sure all those people who have invested in me know how much I care.'

TWO

Esme Bell looked at her hands poking from the ragged cuffs of her husband's jacket. Her hands were chapped and red, a testament to hard work. She straightened her fingers from around the steering wheel. Her fingernails were short, the skin around them was tough and jagged. Her mind returned to the road ahead and she stamped her foot hard on the brakes.

'Shit!' she cursed. The dogs' heads shot up from the flatbed as the old Land Rover squealed and shuddered to a halt on the roundabout that crossed the border road. Esme looked at the traffic in front of her. She was fifty miles from the border. The queue of vehicles crossed her path; it stretched back towards Corbridge and on towards Scotland. People and their possessions filled the vehicles to their limits. Belongings were in trailers, strapped to roofs, and stuffed on laps.

Esme scanned the queue blankly; she'd never seen so much traffic. She ran her hand through her hair before gripping the wheel with more conviction, transferring her foot from brake to accelerator, the vehicle lurched out onto the junction. Steering the Land Rover, the wrong side of the roundabout, she u-turned back in the direction of home.

Carlins Law was a grand old farmhouse, stoically facing the full force of the prevailing winds that swept in from the southwest. The farmyard and outbuildings on either side protected it from the ferocious northerly winter gales. To many, the old house standing atop its rugged hill, engulfed by the infinite sky would be a lonely, desolate place to live.

To Esme, it was home. The truck bumped and jolted as it climbed the long straight driveway. She watched her sheep flee the racket of the grunting engine to either side of the track. Thick matted fleeces wobbled on their backs as they ran.

As the tyres hit the gravel of the parking area, the Land Rover skidded to a stop. Esme jumped from the cab and the two collies followed swiftly behind and then darted away to the farmyard behind the house.

The wind tore over the oranges and browns of the rugged hillside to the lush green farmland on the valley floor. Shaped by this persistent wind, the trees swayed and arched like claws tearing at the ground and the clouds in the endless sky sailed towards the farmhouse perched on top of the hill.

The rain was falling across the valley and closed in on the Bells' home with every passing minute. Esme paused for a moment. She turned her face into the squall and her hair whipped behind her back. She breathed in the weather, her eyes closed for a moment until she felt the first spats rain on her face. Then she turned and strode towards the house, her husband's green military jacket flapped around the knees of her muddy jeans and her work boots kicking up gravel with every step.

The latch on the door clunked as she burst into the kitchen, which was awash with a golden hue from the fire that crackled on the far side. A steaming brew, lengths of wire and a shotgun lay on the huge oak table, at which sat Amber, cutting and shaping the wire with pliers. She raised her head sharply, her explosion of auburn curls bouncing around her face and her intense green eyes locking onto her mother's.

'Mam! Ye frightened the life out of us. I'll not be a minute here…' She said nodding at the wire traps on the table. 'You weren't long… everything alright?'

'Put the radio on, love,' Esme said. 'Where's your da?'

Amber pushed herself up and away from the table and turned on the radio. It fuzzed and crackled to life;

she turned the dial until she found the dreary tone of a newsreader.

'Where's your da, Amber?' Esme asked again.

'He said something about the tarp... What's happened now?'

Esme looked out of the window which looked over the farmyard. The darkness of the storm had enveloped their hillside. The wind was gusting and there with his heels grinding into the dirt was her husband. Nat gripped a rope attached to a tarpaulin, which each gust of wind billowed like a parachute, lifting it off the haystack and high into the air. Nat was near horizontal, and the dogs barked around his legs, enthralled by the action. Esme watched him confront his problem head on. That was what he did best. Then she focused on her own reflection in the window.

'They're all leaving,' she said. 'You should see the cars at Errington. Hundreds o'them. All heading north.' Out in the yard, Nat was winning his battle with the tarpaulin. Hand over hand, he hauled in the rope as it closed in on the haystack.

'Will the Scots let them in?' asked Amber.

'Aye, probably. They'll take all the good un's, I expect – leave us with all the nutters.' Esme watched Nat tie off the rope. He took a lazy swipe at the dogs with his foot, and they scattered. Then he turned into the squall, jutted his chin into the wind and allowed the deluge to beat down upon his face. Esme rubbed her hands and turned to her daughter, they looked at each other momentarily.

'He'll know what to do,' Amber said. She sat back at the kitchen table and picked up her pliers.

'I hope you're right, lass,' Esme said. 'But you cannot solve every problem with your hands...' She left by the door she had entered.

Nat's eyes were closed as the rain lashed his face. Esme put her arms around his waist and rested her head on his back. It was plenty broad enough to form a capsule of calm against the wind.

'There's hundreds leaving for the border, Nat. They're all going.'

She felt his body stiffen.

'What'll we do?' she asked.

He turned in her arms and his piercing eyes captivated her, then she saw them soften briefly. She cupped his face in her hands. As she looked at him, she could see the struggle inside. His teeth clamped tight, and his jaw became rigid; rage bubbled under the surface like molten lava. She stroked his face to exorcise his demons. It seemed that his eyes searched for words that she knew would never come.

'We better go and get that feed, Mam...'

Esme heard Amber call and Nat looked over Esme's shoulder and his face softened.

'Maybe Scotland?' Esme whispered faintly up at Nat.

His eyes darted back to her, determined. 'Over my dead body,' he spat.

She tugged the front of his old wax jacket as though to straighten it. Then she slapped her palm into the middle of his chest and patted him there. 'This is our home. Go to that meeting with Rowell, eh?'

'Aye.' he said through gritted teeth.

Turning she ran to catch up with Amber, who was walking to the Land Rover.

'Hang on, Amber! I'm coming with.'

Esme hurried to the Land Rover, flung the door open and climbed into the passenger seat. It creaked as she slammed it after her. Standing in the lashing rain, Nat wiped the back of his hand across his jaw and winked at her. She smiled at him before he turned back towards the farmyard.

Twenty minutes later, the Bells' Land Rover arced into the warehouse yard. Amber performed the manoeuvre precisely and routinely, as though she had done it a thousand times before. They crossed the yard together. Amber, a head taller than her mother, bent down to stroke a scruffy dog that ran to greet them. She recoiled as it went for her with teeth bared. Recovering her composure, she feigned to attack it and the hound scurried away. She looked at Esme. 'New arrival…'

'Aye. None too friendly, though.'

As she looked back towards the wide-open doors of the warehouse, Esme noticed half a dozen figures appear from the shadows. One of them approached – a stranger. He needed a good bath.

'Where's Jon?' said Amber.

'Jon's gone,' said the stranger. 'I'm here now.'

'Gone where?'

'Scotland probably. That's where they all run to isn't it?'

'*They*?' Amber's back straightened and her eyes narrowed.

The man stared right back at her. 'The hidebound bastards that'll not reform.'

Esme edged in front of Amber, squeezing her forearm surreptitiously as she did so. She fixed the stranger with a stare of her own. 'Go and fetch the feed, Amber,' she said, without looking at her daughter.

Amber was silent for a while before she exhaled loudly. 'Aye, okay.'

'No need love – just you relax!' The stranger gave a gap tooth smile. 'There's ten of us here now. A collective, y'see? Worker-ownership!'

'Jon's family built this business from nowt,' said Esme. 'What happened to them?'

'You'll find it's all cheaper.' The stranger ignored her question. 'Everything's changed for the best... unless you're one of *the few*…'

Three men came out of the warehouse with a sack on each shoulder. 'Six enough?' their boss asked Amber.

'Aye.'

Amber followed the men to the Land Rover and lowered the tailgate. She grabbed the first sack from one of the men. The others waited impatiently, standing in silence as the rain continued to fall. Amber worked fast, showing little effort as she stacked the sacks neatly in the back of the vehicle.

The man in charge gestured for Esme to follow him as he ducked back under the cover of the warehouse. 'I need to fill out some papers...' he said.

'What papers?' Esme followed through the dusty building with its familiar smell of animal feed and sawdust as the rain drummed on the roof. She glanced behind her. Her throat was dry.

The office was a tip: there was paperwork everywhere; old product boxes, twenty to thirty years old, full of junk; more paperwork stacked against every wall; an old office chair with the felt all patched up and worn through again, foam bursting out of the holes; thick dust on every surface. This was nothing new; it was Jon's mess, the man who had supplied them goods for the last forty years, the man whose father had done the same for Esme's. A sad reminder that Jon had gone – disappeared.

The man sat at the desk, almost invisible below the papers and junk that covered it. He searched hurriedly through piles. Esme felt her stomach knot as the man rushed to find his ledger. Finally, with a grin and a sigh of evident relief, he pulled out a formal looking book that Esme had not seen before.

'Name?' he said.

Esme rubbed her forehead. 'Bell'

'Address?'

'What *is* this?' Esme rubbed her palms against her jacket and coughed to clear her throat. 'I pay in cash.'

'Just a record of our business...'

She fixed a stare at him, but he didn't hold it, choosing instead to bury his head in the ledger.

'Six bags, feed.' He flashed a brief smile at her as if he wanted to put her at ease. She did not reciprocate. Instead, she scanned the ledger where she saw the previous customers' details: address, acreage, employees, crops, livestock, machinery all listed there.

'We'll come back to the address...' He smiled again.

'Can you tell me the acreage of your f –' 'No!' Esme exclaimed.

Suddenly a grubby, well-worked hand slammed down on the page and ripped it from the book. The man sat back, startled.

'You want to look at how much we've got,' said Amber, 'you better come and see me dad on the farm.'

Esme watched her loom over the man, face flushed, and fists clenched, the right one crumpling the page from the ledger.

He regained some composure as his colleagues appeared from the shadows on the warehouse floor and surrounded the office. Esme saw hard faces and snide grins.

'Amber…' she said quietly, '…come on Amber… let's go.'

The rain hammered louder on the roof as she tugged gently on Amber's sleeve, all the while her attention darting between the men who were behind them and her daughter. Amber was stock still, simmering, anger glinting in her eyes. The man, still seated, gazed upwards, saying nothing. His face was blank, but droplets of moisture beaded on his forehead. 'Amber. Let's not buy more trouble.'

After a few unbearable seconds, Amber seemed to relax. She looked at the piece of paper in her hand. She ripped it up into little pieces and threw them at the man in the chair.

'Looks to me like change is harder to accept for some of us,' the man said.

Amber seemed to tense again, but Esme had hold of her jacket and hauled her away from the office. 'Come on, it's not worth it.' Amber ran a hand through her curls and shot a last venomous glance at the man before following her mother.

'The old system's gone... you best get used to it.' he taunted.

The women walked between the workers on the warehouse floor. Esme jogged a few steps to move beyond the men, but Amber walked slowly, staring at every one of them. About to pass the last, who showed little sign of moving aside for her, she dropped her shoulder into his chest. It was enough to knock the man back a step. He recoiled with balled fists and a vicious grimace. Amber stood ready to fight, staring him down. His eyes flickered around the other men and back to Amber. He broke into a nonchalant chortle, but the violence remained in his eyes.

Amber did not budge. She stared him down, committed to physical confrontation. Long after his chortle had been swallowed by self-doubt, Amber remained.

'Now, Amber, leave it!' barked Esme from the truck.

Amber turned her back grudgingly on the man and followed her mother slowly back to the Land Rover. Esme took a deep breath as Amber climbed into the safety of the cab.

'You can't swim against the tide, you people!' shouted the man in charge. 'There's no place for Hidebounds in Tynedale!'

Amber started the Land Rover and begun to pull away.

'There's too much of your father in you, Amber Bell. Rage is a circle - you'll only end up back where you began.'

Roland stuck to the wall of the gymnasium like a barnacle in the rising tide. The crowded room hummed with a mix of excitement and bravado. He watched as a group of people nearby bumped into others they knew, with loud expression they hugged and clapped hands. Roland looked at the floor. 'Didn't come here for socialising anyway,' he said to himself.

'What did ye say mate?'

Roland started, the voice belonged to a scrawny kid who was standing right next to him, although he had been completely unaware of his presence, until now.

'Oh, er, hi! …just mumbling to myself,' he said, gazing out at the crowd, 'seems lots of people know each other…'

'Aye, or they're good at talking,' said Scrawny with an awkward chuckle, 'I'm Davey.'

Roland grasped his extended hand and shook, 'I'm Roland…' He was desperately wracking his brain for something else to say to this guy when he was saved by another anxiety inducing racket booming from the opposite direction.

'Oi Oi! Roland me old china!'

He spun around to see a familiar face, 'Oh, hi Gerry, how are you? Didn't think I'd see you here…'

'Jesus, I haven't seen you since Parliament Square,' Gerry turned to the two men he was with, 'oi lads, this here is the NSO's own little boffin, he'll be top brass one day.'

Roland looked at the two men with Gerry, they were big and scary - military, he thought.

'That's Steve and this fucker's Conor, bad boy Bootnecks, out to cause mayhem for the money men up North,' said Gerry with glee. 'C'mon you stick with us…'

He didn't wait for an answer, instead he grabbed Roland's arm and dragged him along. The big men pushed through the crowds towards the front of the school gymnasium in Hexham. All Roland knew was that this would be home for the next six months as he performed his active service to the NSO.

'He'll be on in a minute…' said Gerry as he nudged past a woman.

They stopped when the crowd became thickest. The other people in this area were as eager to be at the front as Gerry and his mates, so passage forward became more of a brawl. As they waited Roland felt swamped, he looked around him, everyone appeared excited and happy to be there, full of energy and jokes, he felt like he was physically shrinking. When he glanced behind him, the scrawny kid, Davey was there at his shoulder. Davey gave him a smile and then nodded towards the front of the room.

Roland turned back to see a man had appeared, he climbed up onto a bench so that he could be seen by those further back. The man was dressed in black fatigues, and his presence swept over the crowd by silencing the chatter.

'My name is Bill Ludlum. I know you must be wondering what life holds for you going forward,' his opening salvo resulted in a shiver running down Roland's spine. 'Today you become reformists for the New Socialist Order. You will soon realise the honour attached to our work.'

He looked searchingly at the men before him. Roland looked at the floor to avoid the chance of eye contact.

'Never forget… we are here to make this country better for every person who calls it home. None other than Ben Baines himself has bestowed this honour upon us. We must go forward with determination to complete our duty to the NSO. We cannot fail to enforce reform! Our job will be one of the most difficult of the revolution. We will not be working in a field or a factory! We will be bringing change and ensuring a fairer future for everyone! But we must be hard… we must not bend to the capitalists will, just as history shows, they took no pity on us!'

Roland watched as Ludlum absorbed the energy from the floor, and the chant of 'N-S-O! N-S-O!' rumbled to a thunder from the crowd.

The five men walked silently towards the cheap plastic seats and hard-wearing table in the cafeteria. The five of them now made up the NSO's Northern Division

Enforcement Squad Two. Four of them were gripping cans of fizzy pop. The other, Roland, had a bottle of water.

Roland sipped his water and watched Davey gnaw his nails to the quick.

'So, how'd you know Gerry?' Asked Steve out of the blue.

'I met him in London when I was protesting, must be five or six years ago now,' he gave Gerry a smile.

'There was a bit more to it than that,' said Gerry, 'I was seen out of Afghanistan by a roadside bomb in Helmand Province the first time we were there.' Gerry's hand involuntarily brushed the scar that stretched across his face.

'What regiment was you in?' Asked Conor.

'First Battalion, *the Old and the Bold*. Long time ago now, though,' Gerry said with a distant pride. 'Anyway, I struggled back on civvy street and when this guy met me, I was living rough. Cut a long story short, he was protesting, we started talking and before I knew it, Roland had put my name down and I was in the NSO system, within two weeks I had a roof over my head and a place in society, you know.' 'Got that right brother,' said Steve.

'After that I joined the protests, we got up to some adventures,' he said; Roland enjoyed the thought of that time of excitement and romance, everything had seemed possible, 'this one,' Gerry pointed at him, 'he was organising protests, recruiting and beating the streets, all while doing a degree - the brains!'

'I don't know about that, I just felt so strongly about it... and look at us now, eh?'

Steve and Conor nodded their respect to him. Then all eyes turned to the other man, fidgeting at the end of the table. Roland noticed Davey's leg bounced under the table as the attention moved to him.

'Alreet, me name's Davey. I've never had a job in me life... wahey!' he said, with a broad smile and an insecure chortle.

'Are you simple, son?' asked Conor.

Davey took a moment, then realising the big soldier was serious, he sniggered to hide his embarrassment. 'Nah am fuckin' not. Divn't ye worry, man.' He shifted in his seat. The other men looked at one another blankly. Roland gave Davey what he hoped was a reassuring smile.

Conor leaned towards Steve with a smirk. 'That's cannon fodder right there.'

THREE

A bright winter sun bathed the land. It glistened through the pines and criss-crossed branches of the deciduous trees in the woodland. There was not a breath of wind. The acres of wild land high up on the hill at Carlins Law were peaceful. There were no fences or tracks up there. No buildings, crops or wire. The Bells left this land to nature.

Nat and Amber burst from a copse of oak trees, sprinting, the grass whipping around their thighs. Heading east, the silvery line cut into the pasture ahead of them transfixed their eyes. The buck had dashed a straight course across the opening and into the woodland half a mile distant. Judging by the tracks it had passed through only minutes before they picked up the trail. Its belly had flattened the grass as it passed through, creating the track the hunters now followed.

Once in the open, Amber edged ahead of her father, moving with staggering fluidity. Nat sucked in the cool air, he felt as though he could run forever. His bow was strapped tightly across his back. A quiver of arrows on one hip and his hunting knife on the other. He watched his daughter hurdle a fallen log, almost invisible in the long grass. Her curls bounced around her shoulders as she landed. She didn't break stride and showed no sign of slowing. Nat pushed on, trying to keep up.

The trees enveloped her ahead and Nat followed her into them a few seconds later, ducking under the boughs and shimmying around the tree trunks. Then he stopped as suddenly as an arrow hitting a target. At his daughter's shoulder, he stood in silence, saving only the distant caw of a crow and the faint breeze rustling through the trees.

Nat peered across the sun-spattered woodland. He nodded at Amber in a northerly direction, then secreted himself into the brush.

Amber swept the hair from her face. She was flushed from the run, so she calmed her mind to settle her breath. She bent to remove her boots, then placed them neatly together and slipped silently away into the undergrowth, in the opposite direction of her father.

The roebuck stood in a small clearing. His head lowered as he nibbled moss from the forest floor. As she moved, Amber visualised her muscles as they gave traction against the forces of gravity; allowing her weight to spread gradually and slowly. The result was silence. She stiffened mid-step as the buck's head rose and he sniffed the air. Amber's eyes darted upwards. She was downwind – she was sure of it. Was it swirling in the trees? Then the deer's head returned to the moss and Amber edged closer.

Nat lost his daughter and the buck in the woodland. Majestic trees towered around him as he stood waist deep in the undergrowth, scanning for a clue to their whereabouts. Moisture dripped from the canopy in an otherwise silent haze. He felt the hairs on the back of his neck stand up. A fly buzzed around his brow, and he swiped at it with a gnarled hand.

Suddenly Amber erupted from the undergrowth. Nat's heart skipped a beat. She was some thirty yards away; a broad grin crossed her face.

He watched her wipe blood from the steel of her knife on her jacket sleeve. Nat shook his head and ran his fingers through his hair.

'You've got a gift lass!'

They dressed the animal where it lay, leaving its entrails as carrion, and set off in an easterly direction until the trees gave way to a rocky outcrop, atop a sheer valley side. They looked down into the gorge fifty metres below them where Esme sat under the bare branches of the giant oak tree that dominated the meadow below, arching over a winding burn.

Nat and Amber made the precarious descent as they had done so many times before. They approached Esme, who was enjoying the last rays of the sun. She had pulled her jacket tight against the chill. Despite the sun, there was a seasonal nip in the air.

Amber heaved the kill off her shoulders onto the grass.

'That's a beauty,' said Esme.

'It is. She's quiet, when she wants to be.' Nat gave Amber a wink, before turning to prepare the meat.

Amber sat down next to her mother, resting her hand briefly on her shoulder.

'You kept him out the way then?' Esme said.

'Aye, miles away.' Amber crossed her legs and pulled her sleeves over her hands. She raised her face to the breeze and closed her eyes. Esme pulled a bottle of beer from the pack at her feet and tapped it on her daughter's shoulder. Esme lazily held another bottle in the air, and gave a short, sharp whistle.

Nat looked around at the women, then back to the deer that lay on the ground in front of him. He laid his hunting knife softly on its body and ran his hand across its pelt. Then pushed himself to his feet. After taking his bottle, his eyes danced around the trees, then he raised his bottle to Esme and Amber with a contented grimace.

Ben took the spanner from his belt, it was a fiddly job as he was suspended by rope and carabiner clips, but he was managing ok, he thought. He loved the view down the line of the rows of solar panels. This farm covered three hundred acres in Kent and Ben could proudly attest to personally fitting at least an acre of them.

'Can you leave us.' Ben heard Lucas's voice below, he arched his back to look below and there looking up at him was his deputy. The other workmen were wandering off.

'Have you done your work?' He asked.

Lucas waved his hand, 'not now Ben, we need to talk…'

Ben relaxed in his harness, like a puppet stored after the show. He was sick of this, and exhaled loudly, 'it's vitally important; you have to work like everyone else, four hours a week, that's all I asked of you.'

'Later, later. Why haven't you signed off on my defence spending?'

Ben sighed, and reached for his harness, he let the rope out and he slowly descended to the ground. He unclipped the rope and removed his gloves.

'We have powerful allies. And we have bigger issues to sort out at home, the money is not there Lucas.'

'You're mad! Scotland's independence has left our back door open and our allies in Southern Europe are so aggressive they are pushing the Scandinavian Arc…'

Ben watched as Lucas huffed and turned away from him, he was aware of all this. Then Lucas turned to face him again imploring, 'you know all of this! I don't understand why you'd allow us to sleepwalk into a war that other powers will fight on our shores!'

'It won't come to that; The Arc will not fight on two fronts and the Russians are not going to pull back in the East…'

'Ha! The Russians would love to fight a proxy war on British soil…'

'Is that why you're asking them for military aid?' Ben watched Lucas closely, he saw the flicker of surprise.

'We need to do more. Otherwise, everything we're working for will be lost to foreign players, there are too many people in Scotland who want England back, let alone the Scot's themselves who are after revenge for a millennium of hurt.'

He couldn't help but smile when he heard Lucas spew the very same rhetoric that those who sort to control had spewed for all of time.

'I'll fear things when I have a reason to. Now, I tell you what; you do your four hours labour and I'll sit down with you and have another look at the defence spending.'

Ben watched as Lucas's face flushed, 'don't treat me like a child.'

He chortled and patted him on the back, 'c'mon, I'm sorry, we'll look at it, I promise but one step at a time. Have you had lunch?'

'No, I haven't actually…'

'Great, I've got some sandwiches, you can share.'

'Jesus Ben,' Lucas said with a sigh, shrugging Ben's arm from around his shoulder, 'keep your sandwiches, I'll get something when I get back to the city - I thought you were going to take me somewhere!'

'Oh, well, we can go somewhere, I'll get it organised.'

'Don't worry, I've got stuff to do.'

'Your four hours?' He said with a wink.

Lucas flung his arms in the air and trudged away to his waiting car.

The last rays of the day were filtering through the trees at the top of the valley. The Bells were out of the sun now, though, and the coolness of the evening was creeping through the gorge. Esme had countered the chill with a roaring fire, while Amber helped Nat prepare the animal for eating.

As the Bells ate as the darkness drew in. Now and then the moon would wash the valley with a silvery light, then the clouds would close once more, or Esme would stoke the fire and the orange glow would brighten the vicinity.

With full bellies, they drank their beer and, with the fire to keep them warm, they enjoyed the calm, crisp evening. Nat nudged a log into the fire with his boot, sending sparks showering upwards into the darkness. Esme was leaning against him watching, his arms wrapped around her.

He did not speak, but Esme felt him stiffen. Something sparked Nat's attention out in the gloom. 'You expecting anybody, Amber?' asked Esme out of the silence.

'I heard it, too,' Amber said.

The dogs had now sensed something out in the trees. Looking to Nat they stood, wagging their tails and whimpering in excitement. Nat gave a sharp whistle and they dropped to the floor in silence. He looked up into the trees as though he smelled the air for scent. Esme felt him tense; about to get up, when Amber whispered,

'It'll be Matty. He said he'd be calling for me.'

She put a finger to her lips with a conspiratorial grin, and they waited in silence listening to the soft rustle of footsteps in fallen leaves.

'You better be readier than that when the NSO come for yer!' The voice came from the top of the cliff.

Amber smirked at her parents. 'Aye, you're like a ghost, Matty! Wait there! I'm comin' up!' She picked up two bottles of beer from the pack and glanced at her mother. Esme nodded, and Amber tucked them in her pockets before disappearing out of the fire light.

'Hey Nat!' Matty's voice echoed through the woods.

'You gonna join us against the reformers?'

'Seen no trouble here!' Nat called back.

'Not yet...'

'I'll not be buying trouble for mine and my farm by joining your gang, son!'

'They're coming, man! Call them *Enforcers*, I heard.'

'Enforcers, eh?' Esme called out. 'Don't believe everything ye're told, Matt! Something'll give. This is England!'

There was a pause, a distant owl offered its chilling hoot before Matty responded. 'Sorry Es, but you're wrong...'

'We'll see who comes,' growled Nat. 'Until then it's all words!'

Esme turned in his arms and wrapped her own around his neck. She squeezed him to release the tension that so easily coiled in his muscles.

Amber reached Matty at the cliff top. Handing him a bottle, she smacked him on the back. 'Howay, doom merchant! We'll miss last orders at this rate. And don't wind me dad up. He'll knock you out!'

Matty popped the cap with his keys as the pair disappeared into the darkness. 'He'll have to face facts at some stage,' he mumbled.

'Stay out of Hexham!' came Esme's call from the valley. 'Don't start anything with the reformers!'

Esme listened for a moment, but the pair had gone. She lay back down on Nat and lifted his spade-like hand. 'You need a wash... fancy a dip?'

'Hadaway, we'll freeze, woman!'

Raising her head off his chest, she swigged her beer.

'We could keep each other warm,' she suggested.

"We could, eh?"

She leaned forward to kiss him.

FOUR

It was a wet, grey morning in North London. Jocelyn Waterman stepped out of the taxi; her security detail stood to either side of her as she approached the restaurant. Though Baines had banned all government cars for ministers, he had stopped short of banning security, and for that she was thankful.

She entered the cheery little eatery on Green Lanes. Jocelyn had never been to the area, but she liked the vibrant, bustling street, although if it hadn't been for Ben Baines, she certainly wouldn't have been there then.

The restaurant was jammed with people. She spotted Ben immediately in the centre of the melee. He waved her over and then caught the attention of a passing waiter. A place had been set for her by the time she reached the table.

As she sat down, she leaned close to Ben's ear, 'so, what's this one all about?'

Ben looked at the faces around the table.

'Small business owners. They had some worries and fears about the future…' he said to her as quietly as the racket would allow.

'So, you thought you'd come down and educate them,' she couldn't help but smile her admiration.

'I prefer to call it a chat. A bit of give and take.'

'How'd it go?'

'Alright, I think. I haven't been lynched!'

'*Yet*,' she laughed, before leaning in closer. 'Can we have a chat?'

She watched him look around. The restaurant was full; there were people in every corner.

'C'mon.' He said as he stood up and made his excuses to his lunch guests.

She noticed Pierre now. He got to his feet at the same time as Ben and joined them as they made their way between the tables to an office at the back of the restaurant.

Ben offered Jocelyn a chair, but she chose to perch on the edge of the desk. Ben stood to the side of the room, while Pierre closed the door and waited in the corridor outside.

'How are you? How's the new house?' she asked.

'Ah I'm good, you know. I haven't really thought about the house. It's just a house. No wife, no kids to fill it with life. Can't see me spending much time there anyway.' She knew the look he gave her. Taking the cue, she cut the small talk. 'The Scots have just announced that they've ceased all diplomatic relations with us – with England.'

Ben was silent for a moment. 'Don't fret. It's not the end of the world. Any idea why?' He was calm, and she felt it wash over her.

'I know exactly why... Lucas Dart and the Southern Bloc. We are aligning too closely with the Southern Bloc. Scotland is our back door, and I don't need to tell you about the threat we pose to the Scandinavian Arc, and they to us! Our Socialist allies across the Southern Bloc will fight the war on our shores, not on the continent... The French bankroll the economies of our comrades in the south; Iberia, the Balkans, Italy. Those Jacobins have a two-hundred-year-old tradition of exporting revolution, and they've got their sights firmly centred on the Scandinavian Arc. Dart is doing deals without consulting you...'

'I wouldn't go that far.' She saw it in his eyes. 'We had to pick a side...'

'Stop winging things, Ben! We've been through too much for you to bullshit me. You need to keep an eye on Lucas. The military implications of his dealings are scary. I don't think you have any real idea; you're blinded by friendship and loyalty - too trusting!'

'He is one of us. From the beginning, he shares our dream, and our goals.'

Jocelyn blew air through her lips stood up and turned away with her head shaking. 'You don't believe that any more than I do. He's in it for himself and you damn well know it.'

Ben nodded and smiled at her; she could see he was irritated.

'Look, I'm not saying you should get rid of him – just be careful, okay? I'm hearing pretty scary chatter.'

'We have over twenty years of history together. And, anyway, I'm not sure he's capable of *that*.'

Jocelyn felt he was trying to persuade himself. 'Trust me, time means nothing when temptation comes calling. I was with my first husband for twenty-three years, but it didn't mean much when that pair of legs from Chelsea came along!'

'Well, I could've told you *he* was an arsehole.' Ben chuckled.

'Don't!' She tried to suppress a smile and felt herself blush before she continued. 'Power changes people.'

'I hear you; I do. But the truth is I need him more now than ever. He is a great organiser. He is bullish and blinkered. He is the facilitator of our vision.'

'Yes, don't get me started on his reform enforcers…'

'Now, come on, the only people against my reforms are the one percent, sometimes force is necessary to facilitate change.'

'The one percent and all those who worked for them.'

She could see him contemplate this quirk, 'but they will still have their jobs, and probably better pay…'

She waited for the penny to drop, 'forcing sorry dictating change makes you a…'

He smiled and nodded, 'very good,' he said, 'I understand.'

Jocelyn laid her hand on the desk in front of her. She wanted to reach out to him, to support him – even comfort him, but then the steel reasserted itself as she leaned forward. 'Get him on a leash! And if you can't hold it yourself, get him tied to something that will not give!'

'We must make some unpopular decisions right now. I know he's heavy-handed...'

Jocelyn crossed her arms. He had always irritated her when he ran on instinct. But things were so much more critical now. 'You're not spearheading a movement anymore. There is no gravitas in ruling through fear. That is not you, for God's sake! Only individuals reap the spoils of division. Governments fall!'

'I get it, Jocelyn, I get it.' He smiled wearily. 'Do I need to ask how you're getting on?' he added changing the subject.

'Of course not. But you may.' She leaned back on the desk again. 'We are in a golden age of employment. Class sizes halved. Care for the elderly, and England is building stuff again. Your ideology can work, Ben...'

'It *will* work. Have no doubts about that. And I'll sort Lucas out – you're right, I need to pay attention. I know it really. I've always thought of him as a big child. Maybe I've underestimated him.'

'I better let you get back to...' She gestured to beyond the door. '...whatever it is that you call this.' She could never hide her admiration for him for long.

As they walked along the corridor, she nudged Pierre. 'I bet you'll be watching the football tonight?'

'Oui, madame.'

'Don't get him started,' Ben interrupted. 'Most of the time he doesn't speak – but mention football and I've been known to spark my own security incident just to shut him up!'

'Well, if there is an incident tonight, you are on your own,' said Pierre, smiling at Jocelyn as they walked back into the restaurant.

It was the middle of the afternoon when Nat saw the black estate car pull off the road, cross the cattle grid and drive up the track that led up the hill to his farm. There was no fence either side of the track and the sheep scattered as the car passed. Nat stood in the middle of the gravelled parking area to the front of his home and awaited their arrival.

He had heard the rumours: the NSO moving from farm-to-farm assessing, planning, documenting; the first step of reform. The last was the appropriation of his property by the government. With every day that passed without this visit, the Bells had lived in hope.

Gerry slowed the car as he turned into the drive. After they crossed the cattle grid, they were travelling at a respectful ten miles an hour. He noted the farm's potential. 'Check it out, lads! This looks like a goer!'

'Christ Gerry, this is someone's home, let's try and treat them with respect whatever their politics.'

'Fuck off Roland you soft bastard, property's theft pal, and if you don't start towing the line, we'll have to give you some re-education.' Conor smirked, looking over at Steve across the back seat.

'Don't be silly mate,' said Gerry looking at Conor in the rear-view mirror, 'ignore him Roland, he's not here for his brains.'

Conor smacked the back of Gerry's seat.

Davey sat in the middle of the backseat. He rested forward, leaning each arm on either side of the two front seats, tapping his fingers and bouncing his leg uncontrollably.

Conor gave him a dig in the ribs.

'Ah, howay, man!' Davey exclaimed in pain. 'Look!'

As they neared the top of the hill, a lone figure stood waiting. White hair whipped across his face. He didn't move to clear it from his eyes but stood unwaveringly in their path. Gerry likened the man to the surrounding countryside: windswept and hard-bitten.

The farmer's right hand gripped a long-handled felling axe, which hung menacingly by his side.

Gerry noticed Roland and Davey sit back in their seats simultaneously as though they were trying to put as much distance between themselves and the farmer as possible.

'Oi, oi! Look at this geezer!' said Gerry. 'Lock up your daughters…'

'Fucking yokels!' Said Steve.

When they hit gravel ten yards from the farmer, Gerry slowed the car to a crawl and pulled past him, he stood unmoved. Only his eyes followed the car. He offered a slight turn of the head as they passed behind him. The enforcers craned their necks to see what the farmer would do.

'What's he doing now?' asked Gerry urgently, his eyes darting between his mirrors and what lay ahead of him.

'Nothin',' said Davey. 'His head's bowed… like he's listenin'.'

'Okay, let's be sensible here,' said Roland. 'This guy looks crazy. I'll do the talking. Keep your distance. We don't want trouble. If he doesn't want to cooperate, don't start anything. Steve… Conor… you guys stay in the car – let's not be too intimidating.'

'Nah,' said Conor, 'you stay in the car, leave this to the grown-ups. Me and you Gerry, and Davey you can come too as the human shield.'

The skinny enforcer looked at him, wide eyed.

'You keep away from that axe now,' Conor whispered.

Gerry looked at Roland who was staring at him with questioning eyes, his stomach churned, but he just shrugged at his friend and opened the door.

Gerry, Conor and Davey stepped out of the car, crunching feet on gravel. The farmer stood with his back to them, head down, listening.

Gerry took the lead; the other two fell in a foot or so behind him. They stopped a good six feet behind the man, who at close quarters proved to be as colossal as he was menacing. He stood stock still.

Gerry and Conor glanced at each other, then Gerry cleared his throat. 'Are you Bell?'

There was no reaction.

'Oi! We talk, you answer…,' shouted Conor.

Gerry flashed him a look to say *my show*.

The farmers stony hand constricted on the shaft of the axe and then his head began to turn slowly to the left until his chin met his shoulder and one dragon's eye fell upon them.

'You raise your voice at me again, boy…' he uttered with a low, calm growl.

Gerry stared hard at Conor, who conceded with a shrug. Davey took an involuntary step backwards as the spectral figure turned to face them. The farmer's gaze was determined and relentless; Gerry felt it, Conor must have felt it and Davey looked ready to run.

They stood face to face for long moments before Gerry gathered his thoughts.

'Were you expecting us?' He asked.

'Aye.'

'Do you know what we are here to do?'

The farmer shook his head, faintly.

'Can I explain? Or are you resistant?'

The farmer said nothing, his piercing blue eyes burned holes in Gerry's psyche communicating everything he needed to know.

But he persevered, 'the NSO is the new government. We want to improve the –'

'Save it.' He said as the breeze whipped his white main across his face.

Gerry felt his stomach turn - he was in control here, not this farmer.

'I'm sorry?'

'Save your bullshit. You take this place off your list and save me the trouble.'

He cleared his throat. 'We want to know what you are producing here. Then, we'll look to improve it. After that, we'll calculate how many people the farm could employ. How your produce will fit the jigsaw of self-sufficiency for the Hexhamshire Collective.' Gerry took a breath and looked the farmer in the eye. 'You and your family… you'll come under the umbrella of the collective or you'll be made to leave.'

The farmer's grimace hardened as he stared at them, then he turned and walked away.

Conor blew out his cheeks and shook his head, before following the man. Gerry followed suit.

The farmer walked calmly to his house and in through the back door. Conor skipped a step and hurried after him, disappearing through the old wooden door.

Gerry looked at Davey, who shrugged, and he pushed the door open; he stepped in through a boot room that wafted animals and mud, then through to a kitchen. It smelled of wood smoke and oil and dirt from the fields. It was a warm and inviting space with a rich glow from the open fire bouncing off the earthy colours of the flagstone floor.

As his eyes became accustomed to the dull light, he noticed the farmers axe lying on the kitchen table, and there on the flagstone floor lay Conor, unconscious or dead, his face bloodied. The farmer towering over him with fists clenched and eyes betraying a whirlwind within.

'Take us off the list.' The farmer hissed. He stepped closer now with leathered palms and knobbled fingers raised aloft, 'do these look like the hands of the bastard privileged?'

As Gerry opened his mouth to speak, the farmers hand darted with the speed of viper, grabbing his throat, he choked and tried to back away, but the farmers strength was too great; his Adam's Apple was trapped in a vice like grip.

'Be careful what you say next,' snarled the farmer calmly.

Gerry felt panic spread through his body like a freezing chill, he couldn't answer.

Davey stepped forward, 'alreet, alreet,' he pleaded, 'we'll leave, we'll go, please let him go!'

Gerry saw the farmer's eyes, he tried to nod agreement through spluttered coughs, and just as quickly as it had begun, the farmer let him go.

Gerry bent double, resting his hands on his knees as he caught his breath.

'I-is he still alive?' Asked Davey, pointing at Conor who remained on the floor.

The farmer looked down at the body lying on his kitchen floor, then back towards Davey. His face, weathered like a lump of oak, it gave away no semblance of worry or fear.

'Either way, you'll be getting him off my floor...' he said.

As they moved Conor to pick him up, he began to come around, they helped him out of the house with his arms around their shoulders, but his knees were buckling with every step, like a boxer fighting the results of a knockout blow.

When they rounded the corner of the house and their car came into view, Gerry's heart sank once more; two women stood on either side of it, each armed with a shotgun pointing at the occupants of the vehicle. They staggered on; Gerry felt Conor's head loll in his direction.

'He won't be so lucky next time... caught me surprised...'

'Yeah mate, I'm sure, you just keep it down now.'

The women said nothing to them as they put Conor into the back seat. Davey jumped in quickly after him and Gerry had a long walk around the car, the women were a mass of hair blowing in the wind and wild eyes burning down the barrels of their guns.

As he opened the driver's side door the three farmers stood in a line, the guns no longer trained on him but resting on their shoulders; this was not what he had imagined.

'Take us off the list' the farmer said again.

'You know we can't do that.'

'You'll not take our home.' Said the older woman.

'Then co-operate with the reforms, you won't be moved on then…'

'We'll never be moved on… know it!' Spat the other.

He ducked into the car and turned the engine on. He looked at Roland who was white as a sheet.

'Don't ask.'

'Jesus Christ,' said Roland as the car pulled away.

They watched the car leave their property in silence, as it turned right out of the gate Nat turned to Esme.

'So?'

'Nothin' good'll come of this that's for sure,' she said.

'Aye…'

'We need to prepare for worse to come.'

'Agreed,' he grunted as he turned back towards the house.

Ben Baines took a long swig of his water. Night had drawn in hours before, but the other two men were still drinking coffee – much to his bewilderment. The boardroom was hot, the lights bright and the silences were becoming unbearably frequent and painful. Baines fiddled with his pen, it kept dropping from his fingers and bouncing on the desk. Lucas Dart leaned against the wall to the side of the room. After sitting for hours, now, even he had to stand.

The Police Commissioner sat on the other side of the table from Ben and Lucas with his arms and legs crossed, his grey hair arced around a bald crown. He sat straight, and his face showed irritation. His uniform was faultless and probably the cause of the beads of sweat on his brow. The Commissioner was still addressing Ben. He had barely allowed his eyes to fall on Lucas since the meeting began hours before.

'I am sorry. I admire you – really, I do. I believe if there's anyone who can bring about the changes you are instigating it's you.' His face was heavy with emotion. 'But I cannot sanction police support for *his* actions.' He pointed at Lucas.

Ben allowed his head to fall momentarily before he flashed an irate look at his deputy. Then he looked back at the commissioner as he committed to roll the dice in Lucas's favour. 'As I have said, his actions are my actions – the actions of the NSO.'

'Oh please! I don't think you know. Or don't want to know. You need to make yourself aware of his –'

'It's regrettable. But we will see our policies through with or without the support of the police.' Ben interrupted.

'It will make life complicated.'

'We have moved greater mountains already and you are offering no alternative.'

Lucas pushed himself off the wall. Resting his knuckles on the table he leaned on it, his frame dominating the space. 'What happened to the police force carrying out the will of the elected government?'

The Police Commissioner's sharp eyes found Lucas. His face showed no emotion. 'I have always seen policing as a duty carried out for King and Country, but then you've seen to it that *he's* out the way now. Politicians like you, Mr Dart… well, you come and go like a common cold, and we usually recover from those.' He smiled a thin smile. 'I will not do your political bidding. You'll have to find others to carry out your... work.' The Commissioner's eyes lingered with distaste on Lucas Dart before he turned to Ben. 'I understand your position... you are trying to figure out the right plan for an almost impossible task. But in that man there, you are backing the wrong horse.' He stood without waiting for a response, straightened his jacket and looked down at Ben. 'Sir, my position is untenable. I resign. I will have no further part in this mayhem, and I have no further words.' He turned abruptly on his heels and walked out of the room.

Ben threw his pen onto the table. Lucas straightened up and paced to the side of the room where the Commissioner had been seated. 'Good riddance,' he said, triumphantly.

'What the hell?' Ben stretched out his arms.

'Come on, he's one of the old school! He just doesn't want to turf his mates out of their country piles! We knew this might happen. Leave policing to me. I'll sort them out.'

'I've given you great responsibility, Lucas...'

'Yes... yes...'

Ben watched that familiar smirk appear on Lucas's face as he nodded his assurance. 'I mean it.'

FIVE

Esme stepped out of the bath, and she paused as the heat from her soak and her sudden rise made her light-headed. She leaned on her fingertips on the edge of the bath while the pulsating in her temples faded. She enjoyed the feeling. She padded through their bedroom, pausing at the full-length mirror. She stopped and moved back to look at her reflection.

She walked over to her dressing table, enjoying the feel of her hair as she ringed it out over one shoulder. She sat down and looked at the photo under the glass on her dressing table as she always did. On a hazy summer evening, Nat sat with a six-year-old Amber. His face looked earnest as he explained something to his daughter. Amber's head was cocked to one side, she listened in wonderment. Esme adored the picture. It reminded her of the man who had arrived on her parent's farm and of the man he had become.

She started, as the heavy bell at the back door clanged. *Shit.* She grabbed the first piece of clothing that came to hand – one of Nat's heavy woollen jumpers – and she pulled it over her head as she ran downstairs.

She rushed to the back door, her hair dripping. The steel latch clunked as she drew it back. 'I forgot all about you coming, I've just got to throw on some clothes, have a seat and I'll be back in a minute…'

The man entered without speaking and sat down at the table. He looked confused, but she didn't think anything of it - everyone looked confused now. The NSO had changed everything, now even the oil delivery was a bureaucratic nightmare.

Esme dressed quickly and then returned to the kitchen.

'Coffee?' She asked as she flicked the switch on the kettle.

'Err, black coffee, thanks.'

She picked two mugs out of the cupboard, 'so come on then, how complicated will this be now these fuckers are in charge?'

'Um, I'm sorry but there's been some misunderstanding here…'

Esme stopped, the coffee cups stood in front of her, and the kettle began to rumble, it was suddenly overwhelmingly loud. She turned to look at the stranger sitting at her table.

'Who are you?'

The man looked down at the table. He tapped his finger on it a couple of times. The air became heavy. Esme felt her heart beating in her chest.

'Bill Ludlum,' he said. 'I work for the NSO.'

'Get out of my house!'

'I just want to talk…'

'We have nothing to say to you, as we said to those who came the other day; take us off the list.'

'We can't do it…'

'You can, just wipe us from the records, whose gonna come checking?'

He smiled and nodded, 'if there's one thing a nationalised work force can do, its check - we have so many people and they all need something to do.' He looked up at her, 'if it was up to me, I'd let it slide.'

Esme walked over to the table, she rested her knuckles on it, 'you're not hearing me. We will not hand over this land to anyone…'

'Then stay and work within the system!' He implored.

'Tssst, you're joking,' she pushed away from the table and turned away, her blood was broiling, she walked towards the back door.

'You can't win, you've had your time,' he stood up and turned to face her. 'I can only reason with you for so long. You've already broken the law. We'll use force where necessary. Please don't let it get to that.'

Esme looked him in the eye as she smiled. He smiled back, until he noticed that she had picked up the shotgun which was leaning against the wall next to the back door. She watched as the warmth slipped from his face.

He laughed, 'Fuckin' hidebound' he said.

She drew the shotgun across her front, 'if it has to be this way, then you'll pay dearly for this land.'

He raised his hands casually, and walked towards the door, 'you people, still giving the orders…'

As he opened the door, Esme saw outside, several men, all armed, and she caught her breath. Ludlum gave her a look with a smile, and she felt herself step backwards.

'I'll have your land. And the rest, whenever I want it.' He said with a wink.

Gathering herself again she slammed the door behind him. She leaned against it for a couple of breaths then ran through the house and up the stairs to Amber's bedroom. There she looked out of the window and watched the men as they talked to each other. They were pointing up towards the top of the hill. They were animated and laughing. She felt the stress press against her temples, the violation of their presence burned deep in her gut.

After agonising minutes, the men casually climbed into two big trucks and pulled away from the farm. Esme turned away from the window, she slumped down to the floor, still gripping the shotgun, she wished Nat and Amber hadn't gone to meet Rowell.

The wild North gave no respite to the hardy souls who called it home. The wind felt like it was howled straight from Siberia, sweeping over the coastal plain and into the Border hills, biting flesh with icy fangs. The stooped figures of men battling its fury appeared from the gloom as they trudged up the hillside.

'Why's he brought us all the way out here?' said one, fighting for voice over the gale. The question was lost to the wind and none of his companions heard him as they approached a lonely stone byre. The rain fell like daggers to rap on its tin roof.

They were southwest of Wooler, close to the Scottish Border, and the Cheviot Hills loomed in the darkness. The howling weather battered the already beaten barn, but an orange glow radiated from lights within; like an inn on a long remote road, it offered sanctuary.

The heat from the assembled men appeared like smoke, rising from rain drenched coats inside the confines of the shelter. The haze escaped from the building and expanded into the air briefly before the wind whipped it away.

There must have been a hundred farmers rammed into that byre, their ruddy faces glowing in the orange light. The smell of silage wafted through the space, and a muted hullabaloo spilled from chattering mouths, bravado cloaked the fear.

Old Man Rowell farmed near enough four hundred acres outside Hexham. Almost eighty, the passage of time struggled to age him, he was rotund and red-faced but, like a packhorse, was built for hard graft. He was flanked by his three sons, all stern and upright. Two of them shared the old man's build; the third was a foot taller.

Slamming his fist repeatedly into his open palm, he paced with a broad bow-legged gate back and forth across the makeshift stage they had cobbled together from hay bales and planks.

'...We've farmed this land... toiled, sweated blood and shed tears!' he boomed. 'The soil is grafted into our skin!

This land that our fathers passed down through blood to hand, it's our right...'

The crowd drowned out Rowell's voice with cries for revolt.

'...We must resist the government's treachery,' he continued, to rapturous cheers. 'We must fight this robbery!'

The men in the barn stamped their feet and bashed whatever they could that would make a noise. The racket overwhelmed the howling wind and dust fell from the roof as the building shook at the mercy of the farmers' energy.

As the clamour ebbed, Rowell roared out: 'What they're saying is a 'new beginning' for some is the end of the world for us! If necessary...' The crowd fell silent. 'If necessary, we must *fight* the men they send!'

Again, fever gripped the room, which bristled with physical electricity. Rowell stepped back to allow the assembly to voice their rage. As the reaction to his words died down, he stepped forward again.

'Those bastards will not beat me.' He turned to look at his sons. 'And I'll not let it be the end for you.'

Rowell craned his neck and shaded his eyes to investigate a dark corner of the barn. There, Nat sat bent forward; his eyes fixed on the floor. Steam rose from his sodden clothes and his hands were clamped together, elbows resting on his lap.

His head rose slowly to look back at Rowell; years of squinting into sun and gales had wreathed wrinkles around his eyes.

Rowell implored him to say something, but Bell just appeared to grind his teeth and pick at a scab on his hand, drawing a red trickle from the wound. As he smudged the blood across his skin, his eyes met the expectant crowd once more. For a long moment he appeared on the verge of delivering the words Rowell wanted to hear, but instead he stood up, silent. He didn't raise his eyes again but simply masked his grimace by pulling his hood over his head. Bell turned without a word and threw the heavy door aside.

The violence of the weather silenced the room. As the freezing wind filled the void that Bell left, Rowell watched him vanish into the deluge falling like shards of glass across the open doorway. The old man forgot about his audience. His shoulders sagged, and his hands hugged his arms and rubbed against the chill while he waited for men to heave the door closed. When he snapped back into the present, he saw the spiritless faces staring back at him.

Nat climbed back into the Land Rover. Amber sat in the driving seat.

'So?' She asked him.

'Aagh, riling 'em all up to start some sort of revolution!' Nat looked at his daughter, 'I don't know, I feel like a fish and the net's closing in…'

'Mam'll not have the government at Carlins Law… That farms been Nixon land for centuries… there's generations buried in that soil.'

'Aye, true.' He tapped the dashboard, 'c'mon then love, let's get back home.'

SIX

As Nat and Amber walked into the farmyard the wind was howling and the rain came down in sheets. Through the deluge they saw Esme, pickaxe in hand hacking a track across the yard. Nat saw behind her the coil of demolition fuse he had been using in the quarry. She didn't stop when she noticed them, instead she worked like a metronome swinging the tool over and over.

'What're you doing woman?' He shouted over the squall.

She ignored him, and so he grabbed the axe. As she looked up at him, he saw it in her eyes. She tugged at the axe to take it back and he let it go. She turned back to begin digging again.

'I'll burn it…' she screamed.

'You'll what?' He exclaimed.

She stopped again and looked him in the eye, 'if they come again, to take it, I'm going to burn this place to the ground.'

'You've gone mad!'

'No, I haven't, we'll live up there,' she pointed up the hill.

Nat looked into the darkness, suddenly aware of the water pouring off his face.

'Call Matty, as we discussed,' she instructed him. He paused briefly but knew there was no bending her will. She was already back to hacking at the dirt. He could see the hole punctured in the side of the oil tank, with a rag stuffed in to stem the flow.

'That won't go up easy you know.' He spoke.

'Diven't worry Nat, I know how to light a fire,' she briefly paused and nodded towards three jerry cans, 'they'll do the trick.' She stared at him with wild eyes, 'the fertilizer I've chucked down the cellar'll help too…'

He looked back at their home, then looked at his wife once more, he did not understand but this was a decision she had made, and he would not attempt to bend her will.

As he stepped into the back door, he stamped his feet and flapped his wax jacket to shake off the water. He found Amber in the kitchen, warming her hands on a fresh brew.

'Can you get Matty on the phone?'

'Now, why?'

'I want to talk to him.'

Amber pulled her mobile phone from her pocket.

'Not on that! Turn it off!' Nat said. 'Use the house phone!'

'Come on, man…' She grumbled but put her phone back in her pocket.

'Don't need a bloody satellite watching me…' Nat muttered.

'Jesus…' Amber rolled her eyes as she crossed over to the house phone. She dialled Matty's number from memory and twisted the cable around her finger as she waited for an answer.

'Matt, hi! It's Amber!' She smiled. 'Yeah…' She twisted the cable some more and slumped slightly – then her back straightened abruptly as she laughed. 'Don't, man. We've had a nightmare here!' Her voice was suddenly richer, softer than normal, Nat felt his stomach knot with exasperation, he towered behind Amber, waiting. Amber leaned over the phone as though she were about to divulge important information. 'Yeah NSO…' Her curls bounced as she nodded. 'No, nobody hurt…'

'Give me that!' said Nat, impatiently. Amber jumped as he snatched the receiver.

'There's four bales on the quad. Take it to the horses, lass.' He said to Amber before putting the phone to his ear. 'Matty? that you? You local?'

Nat spoke on the phone as Esme bowled past him, he saw her out of the corner of his eye, soaking wet and covered in dirt, stinking of oil, she was pulling the end of the detonation fuse through the floorboards from the cellar.

'Is he coming?' She asked when he put the phone down.

'We'll meet him at the Errington.' He watched Esme, the steel in her eyes, she would not be bent from this course, he turned away and called out, 'come on Amber! We've got to go!'

He picked up the phone again and dialled a Scottish number. He waited as the ringing tone resonated down the line. He pictured his old friend sitting in his kitchen listening to the phone ring, thinking *Who's that?* and *If I leave it long enough, they'll go away.* But Nat knew he didn't have an answer phone and it would just ring eternally if necessary, so he waited it out. Finally, someone lifted the receiver. There was no *hello.* Only silence.

'Stuart, it's Nat. I need your help.'

'Ah, Nat, it's you,' said Stuart in his Borders drawl. 'What's happening down there? The news says it's a fucking riot in the countryside - for landowners. There's a big debate up here whether we should intervene or leave you English to kill yersels.'

'Well, they've been, and they'll be back.'

'It's all fear up here. The Arc think we're going to war. You've got that nutter running the army. They think he'll attack Scotland when he's done enough deals with the Southern Bloc – strengthened the military and that.'

Nat looked at Esme. She stared at him, eyebrows raised, questioning. He couldn't think straight with everything he had just heard, so he shut it out, 'aye, well I know nothin' about any of that, but I need your help, okay?'

Nat drove fast. The village of Great Whittington was quiet as his truck passed the stone houses and village pub – a little too quiet for this time of night. There was an eerie orange glow in the middle distance to the southeast. It was too close to be the lights of Newcastle, and he guessed that it was the paper factory in Prudhoe, burning.

As he approached the roundabout where the Errington Arms stood, Nat saw the flash of headlights from Matty Rowell's truck. He took the first exit and turned into the car park slowing to a stop next to the verge.

The pub was closed and boarded up and the road was quiet. As he stepped down from his truck, the deathly silence made his skin crawl. He thought about picking up his rifle, but Matty was already approaching so he left it in the foot well.

He nodded to Amber in the passenger seat.

'Ready?'

'Aye.'

'You go with Matty, now. Meet Stuart. Help him sort a few things and then come back with him, okay?'

'Aye, Dad.'

Nat's gaze lingered on his child, usually so full of fight – so fearless. His stomach turned with anxiety. He had no idea what the right thing was to do – he just knew he had to do something.

They walked towards Matty, his blonde Mohawk hanging wet around his temples. He was dressed in black, and he carried an SA80 assault rifle.

'Where'd you get that?' Nat, nodded at the gun.

'I told you. We're getting organised. A present from the Scots.'

'That's a red flag to the government that, son. They catch you with it they'll arrest you on the spot.'

'They have to catch us fir –' Matty started to bluster but checked himself. 'We're beyond that now, Nat,' he said sombrely. 'They catch me, they'll probably shoot me…' He looked around urgently. 'Howay, we better get off,' he said to Amber softly.

Nat shook his head, he couldn't believe the speed that everything was moving, 'how did we get to this…' he mumbled.

Amber walked over to Matty. She looked back and smiled at Nat. He tried not to show the cocktail of fear and love and helplessness that made him want to fall to his knees and burst into tears. His grimace tightened and he stared in their direction. He struggled to find any words.

'Go on then, I'll see you,' he said, finally. As he turned away, he remembered what Stuart had told him, 'forget the Carter Bar, Matty. Stuart'll wait in the woods north of Kielder. Take the Kielder Road, skirt the reservoir. At the head of the water there's an old stone bridge on a right-hand turn. Park up there and follow the burn north. It leads straight over the border and under a wooded track. Follow the track east. He'll find you.'

'We'll be okay, Nat.'

'You better had be, Jess. Please, son… nowt daft. Just get up there, find Stuart and do as he says, eh?' Nat looked up into the sky and then across in the direction of Carlins Law. 'I have t'get back. Go now,' he said to Amber with his best attempt at a smile.

He watched the youngsters climb into Matty's truck. As they pulled away Amber looked at him through the passenger side window. She smiled and raised her hand. He waved back and watched as their red tail lamps disappeared over the roundabout.

Matty's truck entered the dark void heading north, a lone vehicle in the vast expanse of the Northumbrian night. Amber watched Matty as he drove. He had changed so much recently. A couple of years before, she was taller than him; he was just the skinny kid with the blond Mohawk. Now he had a couple of inches on her, was broader, and he carried a machine gun.

'What?' he said.

She chortled, embarrassed. 'Nothing, just looking at the army man.'

'Rebel insurgent. *please*.' He laughed. 'They scared you, haven't they?'

'Me mam, I think. She'd never let on to me though. It *is* scary though, isn't it? It's not all talk anymore.'

'Been telling you for weeks. Your da needs to realise that.' The truck sped over a blind summit, and she felt her stomach in her mouth. 'Don't tell him I said that mind. Nobody scares me like your da!'

'Give over, man... He just doesn't like you.' She grinned. 'D'ye think we'll win?'

He hit the brakes as they raced up behind a steady stream of vehicles heading North. The silver fans of headlights and red dot eyes of the taillights wound over the undulations of the straight road for miles ahead. 'There's hope – that's all, I reckon.' he said. 'Hope the border's still open for all these poor bastards too.' 'You plugged in?' She asked 'Me?' He looked at her briefly.

'Well, you, the rebels?'

He chortled, 'not me, no one I know.' He looked at the road ahead, 'I'm sure someone keeps an eye, but...' He drifted away, 'but what?' She asked.

'Well, you plug in, AI strips your digital imprint, better than any torture for information gathering, and then feeds you what they want you to know anyway... what's the point!'

'What the fuck...'

'Ha! Then ten minutes later there's a knock at the door... no, I'm not plugged in and you neither, never again, ok?'

Amber folded her arms tight and hunkered down in her seat, the squeak and whoosh of the wipers and the pulsing of the white lines flashing into sight only to disappear under the truck were making her drift off, but for the wrinkles in the road that whipped her back into the present.

The straight ribbon of lights ahead of them shortened momentarily as they headed up the hill just east of Otterburn, but reappeared in all their glory as they crested the rise and headed down towards the village. The line stretched off for miles over distant hills towards Carter Bar and the safety of Scotland. Theirs was a different route: they turned left out of the traffic and over a narrow humpbacked bridge towards Bellingham. They were alone now and would lose themselves in the dark wilderness of the Border Country.

The night had been black as death, but the rain broke as they now headed west, and Amber could see some stars penetrating the churning cloud cover. This was a good omen, she thought; it would be drier and lighter for the walk ahead.

Soon after, Amber sensed the looming emptiness of Kielder reservoir on their right. She opened her window. The cold air, heavy with moisture, was fresh and invigorating. She took long deep breaths.

After a few short minutes, she saw the lights of a house on the left, and the shadowy outline of the stone bridge on the right. Safely short of the house, Matty pulled into the side of the road and turned the headlights off. 'This is it. C'mon.'

She nodded and opened her door with a crunch and a creak. Matty jumped down from the driver's seat. As he moved around to the front of the truck he suddenly disappeared.

Amber scrambled from the truck and around to where Matty had been, but she lost her footing and skidded down a steep short bank. When she found him in the dark, he was chortling to himself. He had also slipped into the ditch at the side of the road. His hand extended up towards her.

'Well, help us up then. I'm in this clart like a plug in a bath!'

She shook her head and laughed; clapping her hand tight to his, 'God help us,' she said.

She watched him as he wiped himself down, then took the pack from her shoulder. He smiled at her, then they set out in the cold night air, at home and in control. Their eyes were now making use of what light there was, and the world of shadows unravelled in front of them step by step.

The road continued straight for about two hundred yards then veered sharp right over the old stone bridge. Ahead was a rough track that led past the house. Its lights were on.

Amber grabbed Matty's shoulder and pulled him back gently, 'head up the track, but stay in the shadows,' she whispered. 'We don't know who's home, and if they're nervous, we could end up shot.'

As they jogged along the track, Amber nudged Matty and pointed to the fence on the right. The field dropped away, enough to hide them from view, and they hurried into it.

The wind swirled as they moved swiftly through the ankle high grass. They followed the burn beneath the bridge under the rough track that they had just left. The burn skirted the edge of a thick conifer forest, but they stayed out of the trees; there was no need for cover and the going was much easier on the grass. The silence of the night was all consuming, broken only by their own breath and the swoosh of their boots in the grass.

As they turned north once more, the trees ended, and they were running in the open. Amber felt a change in the symphony of the night, sensing an alien presence.

Out of the black, loomed a shadow against the sky. Amber slowed and walked up to a concrete pillar rising up at least three metres. She felt the cold concrete, as if to convince herself the thing was real. She thought for a minute then looked to her right. She could see nothing in the dark, but she strode out into the darkness with her hand in front of her. She counted *one, two, three...* and at five strides she hit another pillar.

She had heard the rumours about a wall. Whispers the NSO were planning to close the border. As her hand drifted over the cold masonry, she realised that concrete slabs would fill the gap between each of these pillars. Then, nobody would be crossing the border.

Amber thought about all those cars heading towards the Carter Bar. She didn't fancy their chances of getting through the night.

She looked at Matty, 'another wall built to keep the Scots out.'

'Or to keep us in…' he replied.

A chill ran down her spine as she thought of home.

They ran over open ground now, occasionally startling livestock, which kept their hearts pounding. After another mile, they hit the dirt track, which cut across their path, and Amber tugged Matty's sleeve to confirm that this was where they turned.

The track was about ten feet wide and ran through thick mature coniferous forest on either side. It was clear, but there was no light getting past the giant firs. They moved forward slowly, their eyes had become used to the dark, but they could see almost nothing at ground level. The going was rough and they stumbled and tripped step after step.

Amber began to worry that they were on the wrong path, and they were heading away from Stuart into a thick forest. There was no sky, no view and no way to find her bearings, so they just kept on.

Suddenly, the forest burst into bright white light, and they fell to their knees, shielding their eyes. Amber instinctively dived into the undergrowth for cover. Matty followed, throwing himself over the fallen tree that she had hidden behind. He crawled behind the trunk, next to her. She squinted into the alien light, with wet moss between her fingers and wafts of peaty foliage filling her nostrils. Amber was aware that Matty pulled his weapon off his back. As they heard a car door open, she heard the click of the safety catch.

Amber saw the whites of Matty's eyes shining in the dark. He seemed unable to catch his breath. She reached out and rested her hand on his arm. He turned to her, and she smiled. She slipped her hunting knife from its sheath.

'Wait here!' she whispered.

Matty shook his head vigorously and tried to grab her arm, but she slipped his grasp and eased her way through the undergrowth towards the vehicle.

'Whit the feck are ye dein' ye pair o'chebs!' The exaggerated Scottish wail barked through the trees.

Amber slumped in the dirt and growled at the cruel joke. Then she jumped up, ran to Stuart and punched him in the arm. 'Ye daft bastard!'

She wrapped her arms around him in a warm embrace. The big man put her gently back down and looked at Matty.

'You alright son? Stayin' safe, eh?'

'Aye. Doin' my best…'

'Much trouble?'

'Some.' Matty looked up at Stuart. 'You know Young over Whitfield?'

Stuart nodded. 'Aye, I know him.'

'He's dead. Tried to resist. They bloody well killed him, his wife and four hands – including Sammy Clough, who was two weeks off eighty! Young's grandson saw the whole sorry mess. He hid in the grain silo. They took the bodies, looted the house. It's the Wild West! They're running us off our properties or worse, and saying we plotted to flee to

Scotland or to destroy our crops and livestock.'

Stuart looked at his boots and shook his thick head of hair. Matty glanced at Amber. 'Carlins Law's a target now…' Amber's stomach churned at the stark statement – the reality of it put into words for the first time.

'We're talking to the Scots though,' Matty continued, 'and they're getting us weapons over the border. We're gonna fight back. It'll be alright…' His eyes shone with the grit and determination that fuelled him, but his expression looked desperate.

Stuart nodded. 'Well, dinnae you waste any time now, son. You get back, an' be careful. Come on, Amber. we've got shit to do.'

Amber hugged Matty tight and kissed his cheek.

'Thanks,' she said, quietly.

Matty smiled sheepishly then nodded a goodbye to Stuart. He turned back down the track, and he set off at a run into the darkness.

After climbing back into his truck, Nat sat quietly awhile, relieved by the silence and peace of the night. He gazed at the darkness and tried to make sense of everything.

He switched on the radio. Nothing had changed. The stations were the same, the songs were the same, and the presenters sounded the same. The NSO's influence only became clear with the news bulletins. Nat listened, frustrated by the good news stories: how the NSO was funding new industry, new schools, more doctors. There was no mention of the land appropriation or the chaos in the countryside.

He rubbed his temples. Was the rest of society really so content with this regime? Could he really fight all this? *Should* he fight it? Perhaps co-operation was their only option. Perhaps they could work with the NSO. If they were allowed to stay on the farm, it might work – better than this mess. This uncertainty. The vice-like pressure on his temples eased. He concluded it was time to push the subject with Esme and approach the NSO with an attitude of compromise.

He turned on the ignition and pulled out of the car park, heading home. He felt relief at the thought of an end to this worry. He had to persuade Esme, but the thought of working the land, of preserving their way of life in the outdoors – of *normality* – would surely make her see sense.

As he turned onto the single-track road leading into Great Whittington he noticed the car immediately, slewed across the road, blocking his path. He managed to stop fifty yards or so short of it and slammed his truck into reverse, but as soon as he began to move, a van pulled into the turning behind him, blocking his exit back onto the main road.

Nat's truck stood idling in the road. He remained quiet as the minutes ticked by. There was no movement from the vehicle in front or the one behind. He looked down at his rifle in the passenger foot well. *Really?* Had it come to this? Was he seriously contemplating a shootout – and after all his thoughts about being more conciliatory? He shook his head at the madness.

The van was about thirty yards behind him, the car about the same distance in front. He waited, but nothing happened. There was no option but see what they wanted, so he got out of his truck.

The door swung open with a loud creak. Nat stood with one foot in the vehicle, the engine still running. 'What d'you want?' he shouted at the car blocking the road in front of him.

He heard a soft electronic whine as the car's window slid down and a voice came back at him.

'You. We have to arrest you…'

'Why's that?'

'Dunno. But if we don't its trouble for us. Come on, Nat! It'll only get worse if you don't…'

Nat ducked his head a little and squinted into the gloomy light.

'That you Bob?' He stiffened. 'It is, you little bastard! You had my business for thirty years!'

'Not anymore.'

'Damn right not anymore!'

'You haven't got a bloody business. You're finished. So come on… don't make this difficult.'

Nat looked at his rifle again, but as he did a sickening thought occurred to him. His leg gave slightly, and he had to grasp the door of the truck to steady himself. He looked up the hill to the north. Somewhere in the dark was Carlins Law, his home.

'How did y'know where I was?'

When she saw the headlights approaching Carlins Law, Esme ran to Nat's gun cabinet. She grabbed a shotgun and cartridges, filling the pockets of her jacket with them hurriedly. She ran back through the house and out into the cold night.

She waited on the driveway; two vehicles were speeding towards her. She thought about shooting out their headlights – *maybe they'd spin around and disappear… no. No one was going to intimidate her here.*

As she waited, she loaded the gun. She closed the break action as the men stepped out of the vehicle. She caught her breath when she saw their guns.

'Leave!' She screamed as she raised the shotgun.

The men kept coming at her fast, she sensed their voices and their guns. The familiarity of her home was overwhelmed by this alien threat. The threat moved as a unit and held no stock in words, like a wave they inundated the space, and her mind.

She threw the gun to the ground and raised her hands, backing away. But still they came, she had no time to absorb the vitriol spat in her direction, no time to register anything, except the savage blow to the side of her head.

Of course, they knew where he was! Nat ducked back into the truck. 'Fucking watching us…' he mumbled.

He slammed the truck into first and stamped his boot to the floor. It lurched into action. Nat stared at the car blocking the road ahead. His truck slammed into the side of the car. Before impact he saw a pale face with a scream etched across it. In some corner of his mind, he realised it was Bob as the truck bore down upon him.

The truck ground to a halt after a hundred yards or so; the mangled NSO car was jammed under the bull bar. Nat reversed and with a scream of metal he was free, but the NSO van smashed into him from behind. His neck jarred, showered in splintered glass and for an instant, dazed.

When Esme came to, she was lying on the table. The world was different now; dark, tainted and intangible. Her mind was bleak, and her pain was deep, gut wrenching and personal.

She watched the man who had sat at the kitchen table the day before leaving her.

'You' she heard him bark 'get in there while it's still warm…'

As the door closed behind him the sound became stifled and, she listened to a muffled exchange that began to get heated, she rolled off the table, falling to her knees, she spat blood on the floor and crawled over to the corner of the kitchen, behind the door. She pushed herself up to her feet and as her hands felt for purchase amongst the boots and coats, she fell upon hickory.

As the door opened, the man who stepped into that suffocating space said, 'you can blame your old man for this…' but as he registered her disappearance, he turned quickly, and she saw his bruised and battered face.

His eyes widened as she brought the felling axe over her head, but he had no time to cry out. The steel of the axe met the enforcers neck at the cusp of his shoulder. The angle of her swing drove it through his flesh and bone, breaking his neck and showering her in his blood. He crumpled to the floor, and she reached out for the machine gun that had been hanging over his shoulder.

She looked at the door, before turning quickly, she grabbed a lighter from the fireside and ran into the house. She found the small white end of the demolition fuse. She had pushed it between the floorboards from the cellar below. The lighter sparked but wouldn't ignite, she looked over her shoulder and shook it violently, before trying again.

Finally, the fuse ignited, and she watched the flame fizz down below the floor, then she swivelled again and as the door began to open. She raised the gun and squeezed the trigger, peppering the kitchen with rounds.

Between the splinters and smoke, she had no idea whether the soldiers had entered the room, but the magazine was empty in seconds, so she ran down the hallway, she picked up a chair and threw it through the window, allowing her to climb through and into the freezing night air.

As she stood in the yard, she could see smoke billowing up from the cellar already and the Gerry cans of petrol were ablaze, shining a bright yellow flame which was licking the oil tank. It was only a matter of time before something exploded so she ran as fast as she could for the safety of the barn.

Nat rolled his head to ease his jolted neck, while he checked the van behind him – no movement.

Suddenly, to the northeast, the sky lit up like a supernova. The first fireball rose into the night. It was followed by another in quick succession. Then an almighty inferno grew like a black, orange and yellow mushroom belching upwards and outwards and engulfing the skyline.

Nat's foot slipped from the accelerator. His arms fell limp, and his mind numb. The truck drifted across the road while he watched the explosion. As the vehicle bumped up onto the grass verge, he was shaken from his thoughts. He grabbed the wheel, slammed back into gear and stamped his boot down on the accelerator again. The truck leapt forward and smashed the NSO car out of the way.

With the big tyres and soft suspension dogging his control at every corner, he struggled to keep the vehicle on the road. He managed to get within a few yards of his gates when a white car sped out of his driveway. As Nat's headlights flooded the car with light, he saw five ghostly faces, faces full of menace and adrenalin, faces from Hell. Nat shuddered. He recognised the ones sitting in front: the scarred man and the scrawny one who had hidden in the shadows.

Once again, he pressed the accelerator to the floor, clipping the back of his truck on the old stone gate post as the truck fishtailed into his driveway. He watched his house burn as he approached. Misjudging his speed, he slammed on the brakes and skidded on the gravel in front of the house. He crashed into a blue hatchback parked in front. He didn't recognise the car. Realising there were still intruders there, he grabbed the rifle from the foot well of the truck.

The wind fanned the flames that twisted upwards, and Nat shielded his face from the inferno, the farm diesel tank and oil tank had both been ignited and caused the explosions. Sparks flew like burning rain. The house was already a ruin. Roof timbers protruded like the ribs of a huge burning carcass. The rest lay as rubble. The heat blistered his face, but he couldn't stop looking. Surely Esme ran. Surely, she was in the barn or, better still, the top wood. He knew she was – he just knew it! He ran around the collapsed flank wall into the farmyard. The scene hit him like a juggernaut.

At his feet, a man had been shot at close range. The bloody mess of his chest was visceral and horrific. Nat stopped for a second digesting this new reality. He glanced around and there, just outside the back of the house, lay a charred corpse. The explosion had engulfed the person. He started over to the body with his stomach in his mouth. He was working on instinct now. That the body wore trainers revived his hopes instantly, but he gasped at the horror of those hands mummified by the flames, the melted sinews pulling fingers into claw-like remnants. He couldn't turn his eyes away from the blackened face, the flesh melted tight into a satanic scream.

He staggered towards the barns now. He would look there first, then head to the top wood. *Surely Esme would agree to leave for Scotland now.*

Then, out of the corner of his eye, he saw something – the wheel of the tractor almost hid it from view. The blaze caught the colour and it shimmered again. A brief flash of auburn blowing in the wind. He burst into a sprint.

Behind the Massey Ferguson Esme lay on her side in the dirt. Mud, blood, and soot matted most of her hair, but there'd been just enough of it blowing in the wind to give her away. Nat convulsed and threw up. He fell to his knees and crawled the last ten yards to his beloved wife, his tears already soaking his face and chilling it in the night wind.

Esme was alive, but part of him wished she wasn't. He didn't know whether her injuries were life threatening but the blood pooling under her back was horrifying. Her face was pummelled black and blue, and her legs lay bare. Her blood was everywhere, thick and tacky.

She was shaking uncontrollably. He had no idea what to do for the best, so he ripped the coat off his back. Scooping up her frail body, he wrapped it tightly around her. He carried her closer to the flames for warmth and knelt with her in his arms as the heat washed over them.

She opened her eyes, and at that moment he was inconsolable. Esme's eyes softened as she saw him. Her limp body tightened slightly, and her hands gripped his arm. He scrabbled around in the dirt. There was nothing and nobody to help.

Then he screamed, animalistic, primeval as he realised, he couldn't do anything. She would live or die, but he couldn't influence it. His default strategy of brute force was useless now. He had left his wife alone and now she lay dying in his arms.

Every moment was a torture that ripped through his soul. It tore all the joy he had ever known from his being. He shook his head wildly, but he couldn't cast the pain away. He slumped, for a moment, his muscles giving in.

As Esme choked and spluttered, he was possessed once more. Frantically and with unskilled hands, he tried to stem her bleeding. He begged her to stay awake. His hand cupped her cheek as he looked down at her. Fear had returned to her eyes. She fought and panicked through lack of oxygen. The shaking was shallower and the choking weaker. As her eyes became glazed, he realised she was slipping away.

Nat spat out words intended to calm. He was torn between stroking her hair, losing himself in her eyes and holding her tight. Shallow breaths through blood-filled lungs punctuated those moments. Then her face calmed as the life drained from her body. Nat buried his face into the small of her neck, heaving with grief and wailed apologies.

They had beaten and raped his wife before shooting her in the back as she ran.

As she slipped away, he looked at her face. He ground his teeth, the fury tensing his muscles like an electrical current. He got to his feet with Esme's limp body in his arms. He looked up into the sky and screamed at the night.

Nat Bell had finished with life. But he was just beginning with death, whether it was his own or that of every one of those responsible for this killing.

SEVEN

Nat had staggered a few paces, before the grief had brought him to his knees again. Now, his legs were numb with kneeling. Esme's broken body had been in his arms for a good hour. She was hardly recognisable. He swept her matted hair away from her eyes, which stared back at him. They were cold and distant – not Esme's anymore. Nat wiped his face with a blood-soaked hand. He swallowed in great gulps and growled, shaking his head and tensing his body to fight the need to wail.

His tears waned though, as rage leached into his soul, and the cold began to take hold of him. The rain was coming down again, so he scrambled to his feet. With her slight body in his arms, he grabbed a shovel, and set off up the hill.

He carried her for over two miles, trudging through the dark, one drenching step after another, the rain hitting his face like a thousand pins pitched at point blank range, up the exposed fell, into the woodland and over the brow of the hill. The relative calm of the hill's northern slope encased him. The silence it pressed against his ears as the hillside sheltered him from the wind. It made life easier. Then he looked at Esme and focussed again.

He staggered down the steep bank towards the little burn that had scythed its way through the land and into the deep narrow gorge. A little way down was a point where the water hit an outcrop of bedrock and pooled behind it. The water exploded over the breach to create a waterfall. In the dull moonlight he saw the remnants of the fire they had enjoyed the last time they were in the valley. So many memories; there was nowhere else he was going to let his wife rest.

On the southern bank of the burn, was water meadow and a little further, clear of the flood waterline, stood a glorious oak tree. The bulging, heaving trunk grew at an angle from the hillside and the branches stretched out towards the river and away in search of the sun.

Nat laid Esme's body in the grass. He ran his hand through her hair and across her face. He shook his head.

Turning away, he took the shovel and began to hack the dirt from a solid cake to a thick, muddy mass. He threw it to one side in heavy wads; the toil relieved his tortured mind. Obstinately he shifted soil until he stood thigh deep in the hole. That he managed to dig between the roots of the old oak tree gave him some comfort – Esme would become part of the tree – but no sooner had he thought it, and tears came to his eyes again. He banished the thought; he had no time for weakness now.

He crawled through the dirt to his wife and knelt by her body, stroking her hair one last time. He kissed her swollen lips and swept her gently off the grass. He closed her eyes and kissed her head once more in silence before laying her in the ground.

He climbed out of the shallow grave, looked with sorrow at his wife one last time, then shovelled fresh sodden dirt directly onto her corpse without uttering a word. His body shook and his shoulders shuddered with misery. After returning the soil into the hole, he heaved boulders from the river up to the grave. He covered it with an enduring heap of stones, a marker and monument to her. He thought briefly that she would be happy here. He said no prayers. He had never needed religion, tribalism through a life of perpetual threat and fear. He preferred to rely on his hands. He sat exhausted on the boulders and thought about his immediate future.

It was past six in the morning. The dark night remained heavy, but the cold air was becoming moist with dew. Thoroughly exhausted, he knew he had to rest.

He hauled his weary carcass to its feet and trudged back up the steep slope, through his beloved woodland and down the fell to the house. When he got there, the heat remained ferocious, but the flames had died down from the earlier blaze. Everything from the floors to the walls, from farming paperwork to the Aga was a mass of charred rubble. He shook his head as he thought about his perfect life. There were no tears now. His jaw tightened and his heartbeat in sheer, bitter determination. His head filled with molten lava.

First, he needed guns. He looked for where he had left his rifle, a silenced .308 Winchester. He had dropped it when he'd noticed Esme's hair the night before. As he walked across the farmyard, he also found Amber's twenty-eight-inch stack barrelled shotgun lying in the dirt. He put the guns on the workbench in the barn which was untouched by the fire and piled all the ammunition he could find next to them.

Then he looked around in search of a bag. He knew it was there somewhere, but he hadn't put his hands on it for years. His eyes scanned the heaps of stuff, junk to many but a life to him. He dived into piles of material; blankets, plastic sheeting and old curtains. Then he found it under the curtains: an old military style canvas holdall.

He put the guns and ammunition into the flexible bag then rounded up the other supplies he needed: a hammer, a saw, matches, firelighters, two large plastic sheets, three wax jackets. Quickly he moved to the other side of the barn. Esme would drape the horse blankets over a trailer there. He took two, folding them and stuffed them into the brimming bag. He set off west from the farm.

He was heading to an isolated field shelter that he used for his lambs. It was watertight and gave him a clear lookout over the approach to the farm. The first light of dawn was lighting up the blackness and the eastern skyline glowed a deep dark blue. He took out his knife and hacked two armfuls of heather from the earth. He put them on the floor of the shed as a makeshift mattress to insulate against the bare cold ground. He shaped them with his boot. Then he threw one of the horse blankets over the heather. Looking longingly at the crude bedding, he rubbed his chin with a muddy hand. He didn't stay awake for long, but while he did, he thought of Esme.

EIGHT

Amber had been exhausted when she arrived at Stuart's farmhouse. Waking from a deep sound sleep, she had no memory of getting to bed. Her room was beautiful, not through design but from the accrual of objects over years. She perched on the side of a wooden bed, painted a nautical colour that some would call blue, others green. Her scruffy rucksack rested on an ivory-coloured chest of drawers. The sun sliced threw a crack in the curtains upon an old rocking chair with the richest sheen from decades of varnishing. The curtains draped across the large window matched the throw resting over the bed; both were a bohemian tapestry of vibrant patches sewn together.

Amber stretched before pushing herself off the bed and padded across the room, the creak of loose floorboards breaking the silence.

She opened the curtains and breathed in as she absorbed the view. To the front and left of the house stood an old fir tree, robed like a pontiff in needles. This and the rough stone path leading up to the front door gave perspective to the breath-taking valley beyond. The meandering burn frothed and boiled over huge round boulders. The valley sides were steep, but in many places the land had slipped, giving it the look of a green giant's furrowed brow. Other than the lush grass and the occasional patch of heather, vegetation in the valley was sparse, with rocky outcrops piercing the surface. There was a coniferous forest at its head that looked like an army charging over the hillside consuming everything that stood in its way. In the distance, Stuart laid out hay for his cattle.

Amber stretched, yawned and shook her thick head of hair as if to ready herself for the day ahead. *What did her father want them to sort out and when would they be heading back?* She watched Stuart with his bovine clan.

She ambled through the old house, which stirred her senses with every step, she thought of Claire, her mother's best friend and Stuart's girlfriend, and her obvious influence here. Thick velvety rugs laid over bare floorboards massaged her feet. The walls and furniture, a jumble of colour and design, drew her attention this way and that. The rich smell of wood smoke from the open fires wafted through the rooms, while the random creak of floorboards and the harmonic tick of an old clock that she couldn't see were the only sounds to be heard.

The kitchen was no less enchanting but was clearly where Stuart did most of his living. The huge slab of oak that was the kitchen table had a mug and a plate with bread at one end; there was a motorcycle engine at the other. Every surface was covered with paperwork, tools or foodstuff – for animals or humans. The rest of the motorbike stood upturned and without wheels on the flagstone floor.

After warming herself in front of the Aga, she made herself tea and toast. She found a cordless phone that had to be at least forty years old, lying next to the motorbike engine.

She picked it up and slipped it into the oversized pocket of her thick woollen cardigan and carried her tea and toast over to the big old armchair nestled in the corner. She kicked two coats and some newspapers onto the floor and sank into it, pulling her knees up to her chest and taking the phone from her pocket.

She dialled her home number, and it took no time at all before the monotone shrill of a dead line came back down the receiver. She entered the numbers twice more to make sure she hadn't misdialled. The same bleak tone came back at her every time. Finally, she pressed the worn red button once more and tapped the receiver to her chin. She could feel her stomach tighten with worry as she tried to find a reason for their phone being down. She cursed her parents' stubbornness. They refused to use mobile phones. Her da always said *if I need to speak to somebody, I'll go and see them...* She admired that. Until now.

She dialled Bob and Jean's number then – their elderly neighbours a mile down the road. Her nerves grew as she heard a dial tone. She listened to it for minutes, her mind elsewhere, drawn into the void of dark thoughts about what was happening to her parents. The lack of answer confirmed only one thing: the phones weren't down.

It was unlike her father. She felt sure that he would have been keen to know that they had arrived safely and would worry that she might be anxious.

She put her mug of tea down on the corner of the table and looked around the room as though she might find answers there. There was a pair of mud-encrusted wellies at the back door. She pulled them on and ran out into cold, dew laden air. She struggled in the oversized boots, but she focused solely on reaching Stuart. The beauty of the morning passed her by, as her worry turned to panic. 'Stuart!' She shouted down the hillside to her startled host, 'I can't get hold of me mam and da! Their line's dead!'

The farmer waved her back to the house. 'Get back in the warm, lassie! I'm coming up now.'

'But we need to –'

'Dinnae worry. Ye know your da…'

'Let's get done whatever he sent me up here to help with and then get back down to them.' She kicked the dirt at her feet.

Stuart looked at her blankly. She thought it was strange.

'Make me a brew, an' we'll work out a plan,' he said.

Amber buried her hands deep in her pockets. Her gaze lingered on him. 'What did he want us to do?'

Stuart rubbed his chin and studied his boots. 'He asked me tae keep ye here. Safe. 'Til things settle…'

'No, he asked me to help you with something – weapons or something. I thought…' It began to dawn on her. '…And then we'd both go back…' She felt her eyes welling up.

Stuart shrugged, his face full of sympathy. She shook her head and turned dejectedly back toward the house.

Ten minutes later, Amber heard Stuart kick off his work boots. He pushed aside some of the mess on the kitchen table and sat down.

Amber was making him tea. 'Still two sugars?'

'Aye, strong and sweet...'

'Yeah, yeah. Not now, eh?' She knew how he took his tea; she was just filling the silence. She put his mug of tea in front of him and he swept it up in one of his shovel-like hands. The other coursed through his greasy mop of shoulder length hair, clearing the strands from his face and exposing the greying patches around his temples and ears. His soggy socks and jeans steamed in the warmth of the kitchen. Amber sat back down in the big armchair and broke the silence.

'We've got t' go back. We cannot just wait!'

'Naw. We wait. I made a promise to your da.'

'That's ridiculous. The rebels need everybody!'

'Forget the rebels. Your folks are our only concern.'

Amber picked at the material on the arm of her chair. She tried to hide her frustration, but she could feel the pressure rise. She wasn't going to wait for long whatever Stuart said.

Stuart watched the dust particles dancing in the sunlight and allowed the tick of the clock to pace his mind. He was also unsure how long he could remain without news of his friends. Three days? Two? Still too long. He knew in his heart that he couldn't just sit back and wait.

His thoughts turned to Amber, whom he loved as if she was his own daughter. At eighteen, she was a young woman; he could leave her behind if he had to cross the border, but he knew she was too headstrong, too wily. She would follow him, follow but not be *with* him. No, he would take her with him if he went – at least then he could look out for her. It was hardly a perfect plan, but what else could he do? And he knew that she could look after herself if necessary.

He looked over at Amber as she chewed the tip of her finger. He wouldn't tell her of his decision. He thought it better to sleep on it. If there was no news in the morning, they would leave for Nat's farm. He stood up. 'I've got tae get back tae the beasts. Help yersel to whatever ye need. I'll be in the bottom field if ye feel like working off the worry.'

He watched Amber stare at the floor, a tear trickled down her cheek. She wiped it away and breathed in deeply. With that, he quietly glugged the last of his brew, moved to where his boots lay, tugged them back onto his feet and left the house.

Nat woke with a jolt. His scalp tightened as his mind ground into action. Had it all been a nightmare? Then his guts churned as he remembered every devastating moment.

The world around him remained the same, unaware that his had changed forever. He looked up at the roof of the shelter, the dusty cobwebs spanning every corner were perfectly dry and he was pleased with his building work. He felt a pang of guilt. How could such banal thoughts enter his mind at a time like this?

Slowly, at first, he moved through the stiffness of his muscles and stood outside the shelter. For once there was no wind. The hill fell away towards the farmhouse. Tynedale rolled away to the west, a breath-taking mishmash of organic matter bisected by the churning waters of the river, which from this distance was just a glinting ribbon winding its way around the undulations of the valley floor. He knew the view so well it was captured in his mind's eye. Now however it was simply a swathe of darkness against a diesel blue sky.

The first objective of the day was to fill his stomach. Rolling out in front of him was a hillside hopping with food. He took the Winchester and lay down in the open end of the shelter. Although this was akin to cracking an egg with a sledgehammer, he took aim and fired. The rabbit rolled limp across the ground. He stood, leaned the rifle against the shelter wall and walked down into the field. He found it quickly in the dull light as the chilled, clean air filled his lungs.

He dressed it where it lay; there was no point in bringing the guts closer to the shelter. He snatched it by its hind legs and held the small body upright. He felt softly across its belly with knotted fingers. He squeezed the lower abdomen to empty the rabbit's bladder. Then he took up his blade and made a shallow incision just below the rib cage.

As Nat worked, Esme appeared vividly in his thoughts, and he felt himself convulse. He had to stop what he was doing. He cursed and growled to release the pressure building in his head. *She was gone.*

Through bitter tears he returned to his task. Once he had removed the rabbit's innards, he sliced through the membrane between meat and fur and skinned the animal. Leaving what he didn't want where it landed in the field, he picked it up by its hind legs and carried it back to the shelter. He then collected fallen branches from a nearby beech tree and prepared a fire. He paused for a moment, staring west up the valley. *Who might see the smoke?* He had to eat, so he lit the fire. Soon enough the moisture in the sticks showed in the form of a thick plume of smoke. Nat wafted the smoke and looked down towards the road. It soon died back when the fire broke into flame, but he continually eyed the approach to his land. All remained quiet, for now.

His mind turned back to his breakfast as he fashioned a rough spit out of three sticks and roasted the meat over the open fire. He also opened one of the tins of beans and put it near the fire to warm.

He ate as he gazed west up the Tyne Valley towards the chimneys of the chipboard factory in the distance. For as long as he could remember, those chimneys continuously belched some brew of gases. Today they were dormant. He wondered what the rest of the country was doing. *Was there civil war? Were people resisting?* It didn't look like it to him, the countryside was quiet, but then he didn't imagine bombs would be flying from either direction.

It was seven miles into Hexham. He briefly considered walking but then thought better of it. Time was against him. He'd take his chances in the truck. After gnawing the last of the meat from the rabbit's bones, he put the fire out with loose soil from a nearby molehill. He walked into the shelter and delved into the canvas bag. He pulled out the ball-peen hammer and weighed it in his fist, studying the rounded steel of the hammer's head.

He put the hammer in his inside pocket and the rifle back in the bag. Then he put the canvas bag into a plastic feed sack to keep it all dry. He set off with it towards the house. Halfway up the steady incline he ducked into a small overgrown thicket, inside was an outcrop of rock that concealed a small cave. He pushed the bag inside and moved off towards the house with the hammer in his pocket.

His home was now just a smouldering mess of stone, charred wood and melted man-made materials. He stepped up into his truck. The keys were still in the ignition, and he fired up the engine. As he reversed, the engine grunted, and the truck strained against its suspension; he had embedded the bumper into the blue NSO car when he'd crashed into it the previous night. He grunted in frustration then slammed his foot down on the accelerator. The powerful engine roared. The truck lurched to the extremities of its suspension. The tyres were true, biting into the gravel, before throwing it aside and hitting the earth underneath. There was an almighty hollow crack of plastic passing its breaking point. A squeal of tearing metal filled his ears, as his truck came free from its bumper. He tore off down the driveway, mostly under control.

He entered the centre of Hexham from Priestpopple. The local shops were open for business, but not the chain stores; they were all looted or burned out. He stared in disbelief at the state of the department store, emptied and smashed at the hands of local people. He lowered his head as he saw faces, he recognised milling in the street.

He turned onto Beaumont Street. Grand Victorian buildings flanked one side of the street, a park the other. Hexham Abbey towered above the town at the far end of the road.

He decided to wait there. He pulled his truck off the road and parked across four spaces. He could be seen by anyone who passed. He got out and walked to a bench at the gates to the park. He pulled his collars high and buried his hands deep inside his pockets, looked left, then right, before he sat down and waited.

The junction was unusually quiet. As the time past, he felt the chill of the night creep under the layers of his clothes. He pulled his jacket in tighter, committed to the idea that waiting here would be enough.

He watched as the same cars passed him. They were full of people, but there was no music blaring, no 'fun' being had. This was a patrol. Nat's heart thumped inside his chest. He was ready – in fact, he was eager. Out of the corner of his eye, he saw movement.

He studied the outline of a lone, rotund figure shuffling up the street towards him, but as he watched the figure approach a white car came up the hill. He sat up straight, the buzz of adrenalin making his stomach turn and his muscles tense. The car turned into the street where he sat. He recognised it from the night before.

As the car cruised past him, he stared at the windows. He couldn't see the occupants, but he tried to propel pure hatred from his eyes. He removed his fists from his pockets; they balled into rock hard clubs.

After slowing briefly, the car hastened away. Nat turned back to the man who approached. He recognised the gait and then the face of his old friend, Wes Milburn.

'Nat? I thought it was you. You okay? I heard about your trouble…'

'Esme's dead,' Nat said.

Wes eyed his old friend as if unsure of his state of mind.

'The NSO representative told us about the explosion, saying you caused it yersel…'

'Aye, suppose I killed Esme too… damn lies.' Nat stood up. He could feel the fury inside. Wes looked at him, distraught and speechless – then fearful as he realised why Nat Bell was there. Suddenly aghast, Wes looked up and down the street but before he could say anything else their attention was drawn to the white car approaching up the hill once more, and it had a black car following closely behind it.

'Go. *Now!*' Nat pushed Wes away. He turned on his heels and shuffled off in the direction from which he had come.

Somewhere in the dark behind Nat, the breeze rustled chill through the naked trees. He stood square onto the road, straightened his back and he fought for control. He slipped the ball peen hammer from his pocket and held it behind his thigh.

With a hiss of brakes, the two cars pulled into spaces next to his truck and cut their engines. Nat stood planted to the spot and waited.

As they pulled up to the curb, Roland's hands tightened on the wheel at the sight of Nat Bell.

'It's him!' Roland looked across at Gerry.

'Yeah, don't worry, mate.' Gerry was sheepish. 'We'll leave Bill to deal with this one.'

'That's what worries me,' Roland said.

Davey sank as low into the backseat as he could. 'Last night, man… big mistake,' he murmured to Gerry.

'Would someone just tell me what happened?' Roland had not accompanied the others on their subsequent visits to Carlins Law.

Davey looked at Gerry and Gerry looked at Steve. Steve smirked, '…crazy bitch.'

'It got out of hand but…' Gerry didn't look at Roland; his eyes were fixed on Steve.

'C'mon, he still deserves payback for what his Mrs did.' said Steve urgently as they saw Ludlum get out of the other car.

Roland paused as Gerry climbed from the car. He watched Ludlum's goons as they stood up to face the farmer.

Bayzili and George were the odd couple, George, an ex-security guard who lived to be a mercenary, and Bazyli, an ex-mercenary who wanted nothing more than to go back home to Polish/Ukrainian border, but he wasn't going to take that up with the Kremlin anytime soon, so he was stuck in England, employing skills he'd learnt growing top in a war zone.

Ludlum, and George, with Bazyli on his shoulder approached the farmer with a self-assured swagger.

Nat squared up to the men, committed now. Rage had subdued his nerves. As they lined up in front of him, the three men who had arrived with the boss in the black car looked instantly more capable than the ones he had met before. They lined up in front of him.

The skinny kid with the ugly face, and the one with the scar who had done most of the talking that first time, hung back beside the white car. In front of them stood a thickset man in a black Gore-Tex jacket, black cargo pants and sturdy boots. Next to him and in similar clothes was a giant who looked as though he had fought with every person he had ever met. He wore similar clothes to his accomplice. The two oozed ex-military.

In the middle was the boss, whose demeanour turned Nat's blood to molten lava. Though his hair was styled, and his face wore a designer tan, he wasn't soft. Nat could see the coldness in his eyes. The man Nat most wanted to break was dangerous. His soft tones broke the heavy silence.

'You're in serious trouble, Mr Bell. Your little conflagration killed people last night and your old lady… well, she was crazy – three of mine dead, two in hospital.' He shook his head and blew through his lips, but his eyes didn't leave Nat's. 'We had no choice…' His glare remained but a smirk spread across his face. Nat wanted to make him suffer. 'You did us a favour actually. You've got no home to give up now. But you are under arrest for the murder of three of our NSO colleagues. Also, for the unlawful killing of your wife, Esme Bell. You've committed serious crimes.' He smiled, a broad smile. 'Don't make the situation worse for yourself.'

Nat seethed at how the story had been spun. He could see how the NSO would cover up this atrocity. Feeling like a cornered animal and so full of rage, his grip tightened on the ball-peen hammer. He focussed on the men who stood closest to him. The smaller ex-military type was about three paces away.

The orange glow of the streetlights bathed the faces of the men opposite Nat. Their breath was beginning to plume as the air temperature dropped. The street was dead quiet, and a slight drizzle began to fall. Nat had no plan. He had a hammer. It seemed likely that at least some of them had guns. The boss appeared to be losing patience with the silence. The other men watched intently, unnervingly calm but with hard eyes, imposing and aggressive. Nat understood that this situation was second nature to them.

'Were you at my house last night?' Nat said to the closest military type.

'Maybe,' the man replied, with a grin. As he lifted his chin smugly, Nat saw deep scratch marks on his neck.

'You shouldn't have done that.'

'Done what?' The man straightened his back, with a brief glance at his mates.

'The woman. My wife…'

Roland noticed the farmers eyes through the gloom, a wild azure blue that sparked as he moved. The speed and ferocity with which he moved pinned Roland back in his seat, he was immobilised by the shock.

The farmer lunged forward, his arm swung in a huge arc, it was only after George's face cracked to the side and blood spewed from his broken jaw that Roland registered the hammer. George was on his way down when the hammer met his skull a second time on the farmers backhand swing.

George's body hit the pavement, it was convulsing, his mind unable to process the irreparable damage inflicted, but the farmer had not finished.

He swung the hammer again, this time aiming for Bazyli, who managed to raise his arm to protect his skull. Roland heard the dull thud through the closed window of the car. Bazyli went down on one knee, crying out in pain. Bill pulled his handgun out and the farmer reacted by throwing the hammer at him. Bill ducked and the hammer flew past his head and directly towards the windscreen that Roland was looking through. The glass cracked and Roland shut his eyes, at the same time, shots rang out in the night air, but they came from behind his car.

When he opened his eyes again, the ball peen hammer was imbedded in the glass. George's blood dripped from the rounded head onto the dashboard of the car. He trained his gaze beyond the murder weapon; the farmer had disappeared into the mist.

Ludlum was watching a land rover as it sped away, then his gaze turned towards their car.

'What the fuck are you doing!' Ludlum screamed, 'Roland, Davey get out of that pissing car! Bazyli move! Gerry where the fuck were you?'

'My gun's in the boot!' Screamed Gerry as he ran to the back of the car. Roland heard the boot open and Gerry ready his weapon.

There was a bang on his window, 'I'm not gonna tell you again Roland…'

Nat sprinted into the darkness of the park, changing direction as he went. With every step he began to think he was in the clear, then three shots were fired. The first whistled past his head; the second slammed into a tree trunk to his right; the third ripped through his left shoulder like a freight train smashing through a car left on the tracks. The force of the impact threw him off balance and he rolled through the dirt, but he was back to his feet in the same motion, and he carried on running for his life.

It was only after another ten paces that the agonising burning sensation wracked his body, spreading from the wound in his shoulder. The paralysis of the pain seizure lasted for about ten seconds, in which he staggered on. Then his mind began to clear, the adrenalin kicked in once more and he was running again.

He knew this park. The burn running through it went underground about fifty yards ahead of him. He crouched behind a tree to see what his pursuers were up to. They were still under the streetlights standing over the dead man. One knelt by him. Two, including their leader had guns drawn. The giant rubbed his shoulder and the other two cowered by their car. Nat turned back towards the burn. On the Southern side of the park, he saw Wes's old Land Rover tearing off up the street. He owed the old man his life.

Nat slipped through the shadows holding his shoulder to try to stem the blood that he could feel running freely down his arm. He had to move quickly. He climbed the low wall and skidded down the gully to where the burn disappeared into its underground channel. The pain from his arm was ferocious as he crouched down but there was nothing he could do about it for now.

The tunnel was only chest-high, so he staggered along hunched over, almost crawling. The riverbed was rocky and slippery and there were branches and logs stuck inside. The tunnel roof was hard and rough as it scraped his back, and the darkness made this hell even more challenging. The cold water filled his boots and washed over his lower arms. He gasped to catch his breath.

He had struggled only a short distance into the tunnel when he heard voices behind him. He cursed as bright torchlight lit up the walls and washed over him for a second.

'There!' shouted one of his pursuers.

Helped by the enforcer's torchlight, Nat saw a stout tree trunk left by a previous flood. He flung himself through the small gap between the roof of the tunnel and the top of the trunk and crouched behind it. When the beam zeroed back on the spot where he had been. It rebounded off the log.

'Nah... Just a tree stump innit,' echoed a voice.
Nat breathed a sigh of relief.
'No, I saw something move in there.'
'Well, you get in and have a look then.'

'Ah shit...'

Nat's breathing was shallow and snatched. He was desperate to control his panting from the sprint. He kept his upper torso at an awkward angle to remain behind the log, but also out of the water. It was taxing his stomach muscles, but he knew the small margins were the difference between life and death. He gritted his teeth and took the strain. He picked up a jagged rock from the riverbed, it was the size of his fist, and he waited.

The light from the torch washed over the log and beyond, into the tunnel above Nat's head. He could hear his pursuer cursing as he stumbled along the riverbed.

'There's no room in here, Gerry! I can hardly move... I don't think it could've been him down here!' The man shouted back to his mate.

'Just check it out to that stump! I saw something...'

The watery steps continued to get closer. As Nat peeked through the roots of the tree stump, he could see his pursuers' legs about three feet away. The torch was flashing all around the tunnel.

Nat looked down at his legs. The beam was brightening everything. It was time to make his move. He drew his legs slowly into a crouching position and turned to face the stump. His calves cramped in the cold water.

'I've got to the log and there's nothing here! I'll take a look the other side, then I'm coming back!' The man had turned back the way he came to shout back his report. Nat wasted no time. He crept above the log and out of the shadows like an angel of death. Hunched and ogre-like, Nat was only a couple of feet from his pursuer's face when the man turned back awkwardly towards him.

Nat swung the rock and the enforcer staggered backwards in fright. As he fell, he had the presence of mind to lift his gun. He released a shot in Nat's direction but missed comfortably. Nat caught the end of the man's chin as he went down. Bone shattered under the weight of the stone and the enforcer fell into the water. Nat threw himself over the log, grabbing the big man by the scruff of the neck. Illuminated by the torch lying close by, Nat saw abject fear in the enforcer's eyes but was unmoved. Rage had taken hold of him, and he brought the rock down once more in a devastating blow to the side of the mercenary's head. He dropped the body into the shallow water and grabbed the torch. He quickly found the handgun nearby on the riverbed then he shone the light back down the tunnel. Holding it as a rest underneath the weapon, he searched for the other man. He couldn't see anything clearly, but then heard a voice.

'Bazyli! You okay? What's happening?'

Gerry stood at the mouth of the tunnel, at first there was only the sound of the stream. He considered the darkness and the ominous lack of response from Bazyli. His heartbeat hard in his chest, and then he heard it. He couldn't see the farmer, but he could hear a voice: a dark, low whisper. He strained his eyes and his ears. The growl echoed through the tunnel again and this time he made out the words.

'Come on, boy.'

Gerry turned falling on his backside as two shots rang out. The rounds fizzed past him, slapping into the bank upstream. He scrambled, struggling to find his feet in his panic to get away from the tunnel, his innards knotting with fear. Once out of danger, he fired his gun into the darkness until his magazine was empty. Then he turned and sidled back to the rest of the enforcers.

'Where's the farmer? Who was firing? Where's Bayzili?' Asked Ludlum.

Gerry pointed aimlessly into the darkness. 'We traded shots, don't know if I got him, I lost them both.' He bent over, hands on his knees to catch his breath. He felt Ludlum's stare, but he wasn't going to look at him.

He kept his eyes on the floor for what felt like an eternity.

'Fucking idiots!' said Ludlum.

Only as he heard the boss's footsteps move away towards the cars did Gerry sheepishly raise his head. Steve stood close by. He rolled his eyes and gave Gerry a sympathetic nod. 'C'mon.' He flicked his head towards the cars.

Nat pushed on through the tunnel. The torch made the going much easier than before, but when he climbed out into the open it was a small victory. As the pressure released from his back, and he could stand straight again, he stretched out the stiffness. He looked back at the dark hole he had just left and considered his next move.

He dumped the torch as he passed a bin, preferring to let his eyes get used to the night. He moved through the shadows with ease, north through town towards the River Tyne. He knew the recent rains had swollen the waters, so he headed for the bridge. He left the streets and shops behind him, as he approached the river. Out in the open he was a shadow moving through shadows. The bridge was in front of him but there were at least two cars parked on it. He cursed not knowing who they were. Unwilling to risk another confrontation, especially without the element of surprise and with his wounded arm, he had to avoid another fight if he possibly could.

He reached the riverbank and shuddered as he investigated the darkness. He could sense the water in front of him and knew that the river was higher than normal. He took off his jacket and rested it flat on the grass then emptied his pockets – handgun, knife, everything – and laid them on it. He undressed and piled his clothes and his boots roughly into the open coat. The breeze of the cold night air sliced at his skin but, knowing there was worse to come, he put it out of his mind. He zipped the jacket up around his belongings, clothes, and boots, then folded it collar to midriff and tail past collar. Using the sleeves, he then tied everything together into a tight bundle.

He lifted the bundle with his left hand – the injured arm. The pain was torturous, but he managed to get it up and rested on top of his head. He also hoped this would stem the steady flow of blood he was losing. His good hand was free to help him balance as he stepped into the icy water. Accustomed to the cold as he was, it was a shock to the system. He trudged stoically onwards without pausing, fighting the shallow panicked breaths. His bones ached, his muscles knotted, and his skin stung. His toe crashed into a boulder on the riverbed. Though the cold numbed the pain, his body was so stiff that the effort to keep his feet and preserve his bundle sent him stumbling forward. As his head went under, his good arm flailed in the roiling water like a fish on the end of a hook. His brain ached as he regained his footing and he stood for a second to gather composure before setting off once more.

In the deepest part of the river, the current was carrying him downstream with every step. Since his upper body was already soaked, he turned his back towards the bank to which he was heading, lifted his bundle above the water with both hands and, half swimming, half bouncing like an astronaut on the moon, he moved across and down river with the current.

The bridge loomed in the back of his mind, and ominously above his head. Three-quarters of the way across, he could regain his footing properly, but he persevered with the backwards walking method; it allowed him to crouch down and keep his eyes on the bridge. He was only a short distance from it now and could make out four heads above the wall. They were talking and laughing, though he couldn't make out what they were saying or who they were. The only certainty was that he didn't want them to know he was there.

Once the water was less than a couple of feet deep, he bounded for the bank. He was shivering uncontrollably now, numb and in real danger of hypothermia. Once out of the water and in the shadows of the trees, he untied his parcel, grabbed the t-shirt and dried his body and legs with it as best he could. His skin burned, as the blood vessels tried to reheat his extremities. His fingers felt like they would snap off and the deep ache of chilblains set in.

With the relative heaven of dry clothes, he stomped his deadened feet quickly through the countryside beyond the town limits and his limbs came back to life as he jogged through the dense and relentless night. It darkened even more as he reached the steep bank that led up to Oakwood.

With one dogged step after another up the steep incline, he thought about Amber, about Scotland and Stuart. He should go to them. He and Amber could stay there for a few weeks or months in safety – see how the situation evolved in England. He could help his daughter through the sadness of losing her mother. The thought of Esme turned his stomach. *And what? Let them get away with it?* His pace quickened. *Was he content to let her killers go unpunished?*

After a couple of miles, he reached an overgrown driveway leading to a little cottage. The exercise and his furious thought processes had his blood pumping, and his clothes were steaming in the night air. His shoulder burned with pain, but he was in control again. He felt strong.

The dim light emanating from the cottage was encouraging. He tapped the wobbly Victorian glass of the front door, but there was no answer. Then the light went out. He knocked on the wood much harder and leaned down to the letterbox calling through it. 'Claire, it's me! Nat! Come and let me in!'

Almost immediately the light came back on, and he saw a shape coming towards the door. Claire opened it. 'Nat, are you pissed? What the hell are you doing?' Then she saw the state of him, and his wounded arm. 'Shit, are you okay?

What happened?'

'I'm alright... alright...'

She pulled him with care down the hallway and into the golden hue of her kitchen. A patchouli joss stick smoked in the corner of the room, the butt of a joint lay in the ashtray and Roy Harper cried out from speakers hidden somewhere amongst the books and art that filled the shelves. The fire was roaring, and the curtains were closed.

Nat slumped onto a kitchen chair. 'Please patch me up and I'll explain everything...' He slipped his coat off and grimaced with the pain.

Claire took a sharp intake of breath, and her hand covered her mouth. 'That's a bloody bullet wound!'

'Aye,' he said, solemnly as their eyes met.

Her gaze lingered. He saw the calculation in her eyes, but he looked away. She pulled him up suddenly and hauled him over to the big armchair next to the fire, which churned out the dry heat that his body craved. He realised then that the clothes he thought were dry were far from it. It didn't matter now. When she hurried out of the room, Nat closed his eyes. He let his head rest on the back of the armchair, drifting with the soft music that filled the room and the crackling of the fire.

Claire came back with a bottle of brandy under her arm and a first aid kit with two glasses on top. She put the items onto the small table at the side of the armchair. Then she grabbed an old three-legged stool from the other side of the fireplace and plonked it onto the flagstones.

Claire's familiarity moved Nat, he felt so tired suddenly. She was like a sister to him. She was his wife's best friend and had been a constant in his life, just like Esme.

'What is it Nat? What's happened?' She poured two large measures of brandy into the bulbous tumblers and smiled at him, a soft, gentle smile, 'Here. Get your lips around that. Helps the brain, the pain and the shame.'

When Claire smiled at him, reality tugged him back from the warmth of her company, and he saw in her eyes that she realised the world she had known was no longer the same.

The fire and the brandy touched him, and fatigue overwhelmed him. As he looked at Claire, the tears filled his eyes. He sank down in the chair and his shoulders began to heave.

'She's dead.'

He couldn't look at her.

'What are you talking about? Who?' Claire said. But Nat could tell by the crack in her voice that she knew. He avoided her glare as he allowed silence to convey what he could not put into words.

'No. *No!*' she screamed – and then she slapped him. 'What did you do?' The tears rolled down her cheeks and she grabbed his arms and shook him, wailing now. He gasped in pain and the wound in his shoulder oozed fresh blood. She collapsed in a heap at his knees, shuddering with grief. He pushed himself up. Leaning over her, he hugged her tight.

He held her like that for a long time, until her tears were spent. Claire gathered herself. She raised her head and Nat managed to look her in the eye this time.

'You should've never fought with these people,' she stated solemnly. 'And the changes they're making, they're to make life better. I don't know what you were thinking and now… poor Esme!' She watched the flames dancing in the fire. 'I never even saw her for days… I never said goodbye. I'll never hug her again… Fuck, Nat, you –'

'I *know*. Don't you think I know?'

Claire welled up again, pushing up and away from him. She paced to the other side of the room and stood with her back to him. She was trembling. 'What'll you do now?'

He sat, and she stood, in silence for long moments, she did not turn, until he answered.

'Finish what I started.'

She tutted, 'get *yourself* fucking killed you mean.'

'Aye? We'll see. Now, please…' He turned his shoulder towards her.

'You'll leave that beautiful daughter of yours with no family…'

Her eyes washed over him, taking him in like a mother looks at her child when she hasn't the energy to argue anymore. She shook her head slightly and approached him again. Without another word, she sat back down on the stool and cleaned his wound, then stitched it. Tears trickled down rosy cheeks as she worked. A dark cloud had settled over her.

'Really, what are you going to do, Nat? Carry on killing people until one of them kills you?'

He stared at her with an unflinching resolve, 'aye. Or until I feel like stopping.'

Claire looked puzzled, as if dumbfounded by his fatalism. She shook her head again and poured herself a large glass of brandy. She gulped it straight down. 'You're not thinking straight man.'

'They killed her. They abused their position, and they started a war.'

'What do you sound like, man?' she said, and then twitched as though she had just remembered something.

'Where *is* Amber?'

'She's safe. With Stuart.'

Claire's eyes flickered up when he mentioned Stuart. Their romance had started twenty years before and the roller coaster had been running since. Neither had settled with anyone else because nobody else had measured up. They never managed to commit because they were both stubborn: Claire loved Northumberland and Stuart would never give up his Scottish farm.

She placed a heavy-duty plaster gently over the fresh stitches and smoothed the edges over his unbroken skin, silent for a moment. Finally, she put a hand to his cheek.

'I'm sorry.'

She leaned forward and they hugged – that much needed human contact, safe, reassuring and good for the soul, but once they parted, his mind turned to survival.

'I've got to get away from here,' he said, 'it's not safe for you.'

Claire cooked him food. Nat showered and dressed in dry clothes that Stuart had left over the years. They were slightly bigger than Nat would have liked but they would serve. As he wolfed down the food, he thought about his next step.

'Can I use your car?' he said through a mouthful of pasta.

'No, you can't. That would be great for me, wouldn't it if they nabbed you driving around in my car? And, anyway, I need it.' She thought for a second. 'My brother's scrambler is still in the garage. But I don't even know if it works…' 'That'll do. I've just got to get back to the farm.'

He stepped out into the cold early morning. It was near four, still dark for a good four hours. He had plenty of time to get back to safety and get some sleep in the field shelter. The weather was reassuringly settled.

Claire's driveway was a rustic cobbled affair. Ivy framed the big wooden garage doors; it twisted and tangled its way up the sides and across the roof. He opened one side of the old, rotting double doors. The wood was a mushy pulp where it scraped over the cobbles. He stepped into the dusty garage and turned the light on; it flickered to a dim light.

He shook his head and glanced at Claire, who shrugged unashamed as he turned back to the clutter in front of him. He cast his eye methodically over the jumble. Then he caught the black rubber grip of one side of the handlebars of the bike. He moved in, but it took a while. There was no end of speculatively useful junk that needed shifting before he could get his hands on the bike. Finally, he freed the machine and set about discovering whether it would start.

He checked the fuel tank – half-full – then the spark plugs and the battery – life in both. He opened the throttle, pushed off down the drive and put it into gear. The engine puttered to a start, and he was good to go. He took a small rucksack from the garage and put his supplies in it.

He set off into the darkness, taking the road north out of Oakwood. It was a steep climb up to the military road that ran parallel with Hadrian's Wall.

A few hundred yards before the military road, he passed Rowell's farm. At the end of the drive stood the familiar high beech hedge and grandiose stone gate pillars. But they weren't what caught Nat's attention; the old man had barricaded his gates with the trailer from his articulated lorry. He had welded side panels fashioned from corrugated iron. It was like something from a war zone. Nat realised he was not totally alone. He smiled grimly to himself before settling back on the bike and twisting the throttle.

He turned right onto the long, straight, undulating road that crossed east to west across the country, following the course of the old Roman road that once ran along the southern side of Hadrian's Wall. There was no sign of headlights in either direction, so he revved the engine, put his head down and took the bike to its top speed, heading east towards home. He had no headlight on the bike, but his eyes were used to the dark and there was some moonlight. Within ten minutes, he was skidding into his driveway.

There was nobody on the roads: no early commuters, no night shift workers returning home, no farmers getting a march on the hours in the day. A chilling testament to the reforms; if previous governments had survived by capitalising on the nation's fears, this new regime was creating fear to dictate to the population.

Nat fell into the field shelter. His body was heavy with fatigue, but as he closed his eyes, his heart began pounding in his chest. He replayed the night in his head. He went over what could have happened, how reckless he had been. His mind worked at a thousand miles an hour and sleep was impossible.

As he lay in the darkness, he heard the scream of a fox, he knew what it was, but it still sounded like a human out there in the darkness. Esme flashed into his head as the land fell silent again. Then he heard something else: a rustle in the bushes. The wind, he thought. He knew it, but there it was again. He sat up. His hand reached out for his shotgun, and he rested it across his lap.

The minutes drifted by as he stared into the darkness, his ears felt as though they strained against the side of his head. Every noise made his heartbeat faster. A twig snapped. It was close. He sprung to his feet and crouched at the entrance to the shelter. He strained his eyes, but the darkness was all encompassing.

More minutes slipped by as he listened to the silence. He was about to turn back into the shelter when he heard it. It was the soft drone of a distant engine on the road below. He rose to his feet. There was no doubt now, no ghosts or ghouls creeping in the dark. The vehicle approaching would meet him on his terms. He leant the shotgun against the wall of the shelter, picked up his rifle and filled his pockets with rounds.

He strode into the darkness, up the hill towards the tree line.

NINE

Lucas Dart remained at the side of the room, away from the makeshift stage – a stout workbench that Baines had dragged into place so that he could take questions from the audience.

Dart was attending at Baines's insistence. He maintained conversation with Lee Mannion, the minister for industry, while his security detail created an intimidating ring around him. His eyes flickered around the room but quite intentionally never paused long enough to give anyone the impression he was willing to interact.

He was, however, interested in this business; it was a factory to produce un-manned vehicles, and he wanted it to produce drones.

He watched Baines address the room in his usual style, with no pomp, no ceremony; he was in shirt sleeves – rolled up to the elbow of course. He had been answering questions and speaking to people for some twenty minutes. The room was packed with workers and representatives from the press. Baines was just wrapping up.

'…In the years to come, we will look back and see what we have built. The loaded dice of capitalism will no longer decide our collective destiny. We will build a better future for every one of us. I make no bones about it… the journey has been long and rocky.'

Lucas watched Ben work the room with his gaze, he would draw them one by one with eye contact.

'But it was a journey that we made together. England called on us to pull together. And we answered her! Traditionalists and reformists, rich and poor, white collar and blue collar.' He paused nodding as he looked around the sea of faces. 'Together we are stronger!'

The crowd erupted and the flashing cameras went wild. Dart felt his stomach turn, but as the noise ebbed, he saw hands go up in the crowd and he felt the buzz of anticipation.

'Mr Baines…' It was a female voice. Dart craned his neck but couldn't see who it was. 'What information can you give us about the land reforms? Will you carry on with the current policy in the face of increasing resistance and even violence?'

Baines bought a moment to think by searching for the enquirer in the sea of faces. When he failed to pinpoint her, his face turned solemn. 'Your question concerns something that is giving me many sleepless nights,' he said, earnestly. 'I want no violence.' He stopped pacing and stood up straight.

Dart climbed onto a chair to get a better view and Lee Mannion followed his lead. They watched as the audience became transfixed on Baines. Excitement burned in Dart's belly.

'The old economic system is finished!' Baines boomed. 'We need to accept this. Governments no longer prop up failing banks. Corporations no longer extort our hard-earned cash. We have taken back control!' Baines turned away, head down and thinking on the hoof. Dart caught himself shaking his head; he stopped instantly and gave the room an inane grin, but no one was looking at him.

'Now, I speak to those who gave up or lost businesses or property. Those who surrendered control.' Dart watched Baines's eyes search the crowd and the TV cameras. 'To you I make this promise… that we will never see boom and bust again. There is another kind of wealth, one that does not come at the cost of your peers. You can still achieve. We still need leaders… but the system we work within will no longer warrant inequality. As I stand before you now, reform with us! You will not be disappointed. Let us show the world that England is united!' The room exploded in a cacophonous roar. Even case-hardened journalists rose to their feet, but he hushed them once more. Dart watched with horror. Baines waited patiently until the room fell silent.

'Perhaps that sounded too much like rhetoric. I really don't want to engage in political speak and I want to return to that very pertinent question.' Baines lowered his voice and the room remained silent – stunned. 'I want no violence… none whatsoever. But I also want to change our world. We cannot do that if we allow the one percent to continue dictating to us.' He looked out to the crowd, sincerity etched across his face. 'I tell you now, on record, let us talk to all sections of our society. Let us compromise – reach some common ground to take those people with us on our journey! If only we could do that, I would grasp the opportunity and try my damnedest to make it work! But I cannot and *will* not be bent by violence.'

The gathered media rained questions on the leader as he accepted the applause with smiles and raised hands, but he couldn't hear them – or chose not to.

Dart stood with his back to the wall, at once both fascinated and frustrated by Ben's performance. Lee Mannion leaned towards him. Dart noticed the frantic clapping and joined in.

'He's brilliant, isn't he?' said Mannion.

Dart shot him a tired look, but Mannion was still watching Baines. Dart climbed down from the chair. He barged his way awkwardly through the throng until he broke clear at the side of the bench Baines was standing on. For no conscious reason, Dart looked up at Baines. Baines was looking down at him. Dread shivered through him as Baines raised the microphone to his lips, a twinkle in his eye.

'Lucas, please come up and join me!' he said, with practiced warmth. 'Share a few words with us.'

Dart raised his hand and waved away the invite. He gestured to the crowd and clapped Baines as if to say that this was the Leader's stage.

Baines persisted, turning back to the crowd. 'Nothing that we have accomplished could have been done without this man. He quietly goes about his business with determination and meticulous planning. He is my stalwart, my rock... Mr Lucas Dart!'

Baines whipped around to look down again at his Deputy. Dart felt terror saturate his muscles; he felt breathless, cumbersome. He managed to maintain a grin, but he felt the beads of sweat on his brow. He looked at Baines and he saw the glee in his face. Then he looked at the makeshift platform, then the crowd, and he began to climb.

Dart rested his palms on the platform, his belly almost resting on it, too. After two attempts, he managed to get his leg up. Then he shuffled and rolled until he found himself on all fours. He realised how quiet the crowd had become. He was on his knees when he looked up at Baines again. Ben offered him a hand. Both men blinked as the camera flashes created a strobe effect. Dart slapped his Leader's hand aside and pushed himself to his feet. He smiled and nodded at the crowd. Never the most confident of public speakers he felt the usual awkwardness, exacerbated this time by a deep sense of humiliation. Baines handed him the microphone and patted his back. The smile on his face cut Dart like a knife. 'Knock em' dead, kid!' Baines whispered in his ear, then he jumped off the table with a youthful spring in his step, before he disappeared through the door behind them.

As he raised the microphone slowly to his lips, he racked his brain for the reason Ben was humiliating him this way. He wiped sweat from his brow with his free hand, all too aware of the deafening silence.

'TOGETHER WE ARE STRONGER! That man...'

He pointed after Baines. '...he'll make this country great again!' His stomach churned with embarrassment; there were no cheers now. And then the questions came like a surging tide. Questions the media had never had the opportunity to ask or had dared not ask him before.

'What do you make of reports of violence on the streets?'

'Would you like to see martial law?'

He heard a few that pierced the racket, but as he opened his mouth to answer he was bombarded by more.

'Are you attempting to undermine your leader?'

'Who's in charge of your enforcement squads?'

'The Opposition has been robustly vocal about our schedule of militarisation. Can you comment, sir?' said another.

He caught the last journalist's eye; he tried to maintain a smile, aware that these reporters were baying for a meltdown of nuclear proportions.

'Opposition? What Opposition?' he said loudly into the microphone, ending the deluge of questions. He didn't care anymore that his voice sounded aggressive rather than jocular, he just needed to end this indignity.

'I want to see every person in work and contributing. The army provides employment. Not to mention discipline and security. This is a volatile world. Look at our friends across the pond... a great nation tearing itself apart due to a polarised political system. Conflict created by inequality I might add!' He felt flushed but was gradually starting to feel that he was asserting a measure of control over the belligerent crowd, but then a lone voice came from the crowd.

'Do you believe in Ben Baines's ideology, Mr. Dart?' The question came from a young journalist with a slight northern accent.

Lucas shifted on his feet. Like a thief in the stocks, he was trapped, exposed to whatever they threw at him. Charm was not his go to quality.

'Of course. Do you?'

'Yes, sir. I do.' The young journalist straightened his back.

'Well, then. We're agreed.' He hoped he'd bled the tension from the confrontation.

'But really, you agree with his system one hundred percent?' The journalist's voice had become a little shriller.

Lucas's felt his face redden. He preserved a grin for the crowd, but suspected his eyes were not smiling.

'I've answered your question. You better be more specific if you want more from me.'

He turned away from the journalist and gave an exasperated look to the crowd. He realised he was repeatedly opening and clenching his fist. Checking himself, he buried it deep within his pocket. He gave a barely discernible shake of the head, but the journalist had not finished.

'CIVIL LIBERTIES!' He called out.

Lucas froze, then turned slowly. The crowd parted somewhat, leaving Rory Henderson isolated, and the Deputy faced him across the floor.

'What?' he was aware his voice was barely audible, even though the room was deathly silent.

'Do you believe in personal freedom, that governments cannot negate without due process, sir?' a tremor rippled in Rory's voice.

For a moment Lucas was unsure of himself. It was the kind of challenge that was completely unexpected. He glanced right and then left. The silence was deafening. 'What kind of question is that?' He glanced towards his security detail, and they approached the table, stopping a few paces behind it. As he turned back to face Henderson, he didn't disguise his feelings anymore.

The journalist took a step back. A slight twitch appeared on his face and Lucas noticed that his leg began to tremble. He stared at the young journalist.

'My apologies, sir. It was the wrong way to ask. I was meaning… do you believe that civil liberty and collectivism can thrive side by side?'

'You keep digging that bloody hole,' he growled, maintaining eye contact with Henderson for uncomfortable seconds. Then he tried a smile, and in a louder voice, he addressed the rest of the crowd. 'Nothing is closer to my heart than freedom. Now… if you will excuse me.'

He turned to dismount from the 'platform'. He got to his knees then sat on his backside on the edge of the workbench and finally pushed himself gently to the floor. The silence behind him was intense. He was acutely aware of the awkwardness, and it manifested as sweat dripping from his brow.

As Ben sunk his teeth into a custard cream, the door to the anteroom burst open and Dart bowled through it.

'SNIVELLING LITTLE BASTARD!' Ben noticed Lucas was looking directly at him, but then he appeared to check himself, 'we need to get a grip on those hacks!'

He enjoyed a Dart meltdown. He couldn't help but chuckle.

'The media bomb backfire, did it?'

'I mean it, Ben, they will undermine our authority.'

'The press is free to write their stories. If you don't like what they say about you, you need to work on your appeal.'

'They need to be giving the right message – *our* message.'

'Well, get them on side. Don't rise to the bait.' Ben crossed the room to his colleague and slapped a hand on his massive shoulder. 'You're very thin-skinned for a big old rhino.'

'Anyway, what the hell was all that about?' Ben looked him in the eye and leaned in close to his friend, 'it's important for you to remember that people are watching you. Including me. I'm sick of people telling me you're out of control.'

Lucas dismissed him with a sideways glance and a shrug. Ben grabbed his arm.

'I know you want to take a hard line. I know we have many existential threats. But we are a democracy, with due process. If you continue this draconian path, we'll lose any support we have for our reforms…'

'That's exactly why we must not delay. Dithering will give the one percent a foothold.'

'No, we will lose our mandate.'

Ben was surprised as Lucas turned to him with a look of contempt, 'we'll have to agree to disagree on this one. I know what must be done.'

He snatched the coffee and biscuits offered by an uneasy young server. He tossed a whole custard cream into his mouth and munched away at it. 'All very fucking funny,' he said, spraying crumbs.

Ben was suddenly being ushered away by four aides, 'we haven't finished on this Lucas…' he called over his shoulder as he was introduced to waiting press.

Dart stopped chewing for a moment. Mannion appeared at his shoulder.

'He can be a real bastard when he wants to be, eh?' Mannion muttered under his breath.

'Don't you worry about me,' Dart spat, as he watched Baines leave.

Bill Ludlum marched through the grim corridors of Hexham Police Station; his base and where he spent his time these days. His phone began to vibrate, when he looked at the caller there was no ID, he shook his head, mumbling, 'this is all I need…Ludlum,' he said.

'Hello Bill, we've had some disturbing news from your neck of the woods.'

'Oh yeah, what's that then?'

'I was hoping you would put my mind at ease… if you could tell me that there have been no fatalities that would be a good start.'

'I thought my orders were to rid you of the vermin that is the landed gentry…'

'Your orders are land reform.'

'Well, these idiots you sent me are getting restless, drinking then visiting farms, they're getting heavy handed. Your boss doesn't help matters with his rhetoric…'

'Mr Dart's rhetoric are your orders, Bill. If it takes a heavy hand to speed up the process, then so be it. That is the consensus in London.'

'Well then, why are you calling me about fatalities?'

'Because it's your job to make sure the heavy hand is silent.'

Bill stopped in the corridor; he was outside a heavy steel door.

'Ridiculous,' he said as he looked at the floor.

'I understand that a landowner has attacked your men?'

'Jesus, that didn't take long… yeah so, this farmer is pissed off. His wife set their farm on fire.'

'I'm happy with the story Bill, but if you think I don't know what really happened then you must be in cloud cuckoo land. You should have arrested the husband.'

'I would've, if he hadn't caved one of my men's heads in with a hammer. For Christ's sake!'

There was a long pause on the line. Bill waited in the dark tiled corridor; his stomach knotted with frustration.

'Best make it a priority.' The man finally said.

Bill snorted, 'yeah thanks, I'll do that. If only I were blessed with the detachment, you get sitting down there in that fucking office!'

'It's *our* hands isn't it, Bill?'

He found himself pacing back and forth now, he grabbed the back of his neck and stretched his head upwards, 'anything else?'

'Keep your men in order, tidy up your activities. That's it. We can't have stories of unrest bleeding into the press.'

'Do you want it done or not?'

The line went silent again, as Bill was about to speak the voice returned, calm and assured, 'we're watching Bill.'

The phone clicked and the line went dead, Bill looked at the phone, he snorted again and shook his head, already playing the conversation back in his mind. He hated them, the higher ups, sitting in their offices, gathering information. It either went the way they wanted it to, or it was his fault.

He unlocked the door in front of him and pulled it towards him. The light flooded into the cell and Wes Milburn, slumped against the wall, brought his hands up to shield his eyes.

He stood over the old farmer who had given Nat Bell vital seconds to escape.

'What'll we do with you?' Bill said, more to himself than the farmer.

'He's going to haunt you.' Said Wes out of nowhere.

'What makes you say that?'

The old man smirked, 'history, I seen 'im grow -'

'Yeah.' He looked down at him, sat there spouting.

'He's got the devil in 'im.'

The farmers eyes were piercing. Bill waited for more, but the farmer just stared him in the eye, gently nodding as the faintest grin appeared across his weathered features.

Bill turned to leave, but then the farmer spoke again, 'I seen him do terrible things, he was younger then, didn't have Esme to mellow him out... but those bad things were over a spilled drink or a wrong look...' he smiled now, broad and knowing, 'wouldn't surprise me if he skins *you* alive.'

He couldn't take it, everyone chipping away at him, the pressure, he had to make the old man see that he was in charge. Before he knew what he was doing he had kicked the farmer in the face twice, three times, now he knelt on his abdomen and pummelled his head with his fists. He couldn't control himself; he felt the burden release as the man's head bounced, he watched the blood splatter across the floor as this landowner paid his debt. As he tired, he felt the power of the party, no more mercy for these vermin, if they wanted land reform, they'd get it from his region and the former people would learn to fear his enforcers tenfold. Justice would be served in the name of the NSO and there would be no quarter for the hidebound.

He dropped the farmer, and the old man's head cracked against the hard concrete with a final lifeless loll. As he turned, Bill faced Roland and Gerry at the door to the cell, he could see their expressions, and he'd be lying if he didn't acknowledge the sinking feeling in his stomach, but he steeled his nerve.

'Gerry get him out of here!' he barked, 'Roland, organise to take the golf course in Slaley... we'll hold the 'Formers' there, I want every Former purged from their land and in that forest before this year's end!'

'A concentration camp?'

Bill grabbed Roland by his throat and slammed him against the cell wall. Roland squealed and he felt Gerry's hand on his arm. He lashed out, pointing at the enforcer, 'you'll both shut the fuck up, and follow my orders or I'll put you both in the forest with the rest of them, do you hear me?'

As he let Roland go, Bill noticed the tear in his eye. He shook his head and left the room with absolute confirmation that violence was power.

Lucas was feeling tired as he walked into the office floor that Baines shared with the rest of the staff; it was a cavernous open plan space. Lee Mannion followed behind him. Ben stood at the large meeting table,

Jocelyn Waterman sat to his right and other ministers were also present.

It was odd that Ben didn't acknowledge him as he sat down at the far end of the table. He reclined in his seat and listened, trying to catch up, boredom setting in already.

Ben put his hand up to the person he was talking to, excusing himself. He picked up a newspaper that lay on the table in front of him. He walked calmly towards Lucas, who felt himself sit up straight. Ben threw the paper onto the table in front of him.

'Read that...'

He picked it up nonchalantly and began to read. He noted immediately that it was an article written by Rory Henderson, apparently a local to the area and the very same journalist who had just attacked him in the factory. He looked at Ben and saw him glance back in his direction and he knew then that not only had Ben made him suffer the humiliation on the workbench, but he had also probably been in cahoots with this journo.

The report suggested that government forces had burned a farm to the ground killing a local woman, and three of their own in the resulting explosion. The story carried on, describing retribution by the woman's husband resulting in the murder of two government paramilitaries.

Lucas threw the paper down in front of him, if Ben wanted to betray his trust, then so be it, it would not divert him from his path. He watched Ben as he looked blankly at a sheet full of statistics. Jocelyn was speaking and he smirked as Ben nodded and pretended to study the sheet.

'We are ahead of the curve with all the infrastructure services,' she said. 'Education, healthcare, roads, construction – we are on point with all targets. If anything, labour shortages are the issue; we are struggling to train up the trades to keep up with demand. But overall, it couldn't be working better,' she was brimming with pride, he could see it and it made him irate.

'Surely the Migrant Plan will help with that?' Ben said.

'Oh, for sure, but it's such early days, we've only just begun the migrant passages. The plan will be taking shape in the next year I'd say. Then productivity should rise exponentially.'

'What about money, Steve?' Baines, looking at the wiry man who occupied the seat next to Lucas.

'There is not enough,' said Steve. 'We've frozen the bank accounts of the one percent, but it appears most of their money was abroad anyway, or we gave them too much opportunity to move it.'

Steve looked to Lucas and so he nodded in encouragement.

'Lucas has drawn up a far-reaching treaty with the Southern Bloc that will protect our future,' said Steve. 'We need more of that. Our allies in France and Southern

Europe will give us security and open trade.'

Lucas watched Ben fold his arms, head down, deep in thought. He walked to the head of the table, the opposite end to Steve Jones. At the same time Lucas stood up and paced briefly, stretching his legs. The ministers who remained seated at the table braced and looked to their leader, whichever of the two men that might be.

'No that is not what we need,' said Jocelyn suddenly, 'we become, the stick with which they will prod the Scandinavian Arc thanks to that bloody treaty, which was not sanctioned by anybody else in this government!' She flashed a look at Lucas.

He couldn't help himself, as she said the words, he spun around to face her head on.

'We will not progress like that.' she added, with far less bluster.

'Scotland, the Arc, is too strong,' Steve responded. 'Germany will be given full membership to the

Scandinavian Arc in the coming months, we have the most powerful alliance of countries since the European Union on our northern border and their most pressing concern is with the implications of the New Socialist Order.'

'I'll qualify that,' Lucas interjected. 'The only concern of The Scandinavian Arc is to see that the NSO fails and that our ideology is never seen again in world politics.'

'If we all thought like that, then it would be in our interests to see the end of The Arc,' countered Ben.

Lucas said nothing. He smiled at Ben, giving him time to catch up.

'Is that the plan, is it?' Ben shook his head, 'Is it *our* plan or just yours?'

'Scotland is ours. Always has been.' He replied.

'I am pretty sure the Scots would disagree.' Ben looked around the stunned faces.

'The Arc could roll into England at any time, and you know it,' Lucas said. 'We are completely at their mercy. Having the Southern Bloc as an ally makes us far less vulnerable –'

'Or far more likely to become a theatre of war. I'm sure our comrades in the South would prefer to go to war with The Arc on English soil rather than at home. That's how it works isn't it?' said Jocelyn.

He couldn't help showing his disdain for the woman; ignoring her words entirely he walked around the table and Ben took a couple of paces towards him in return.

'I don't want to hear her voice,' he said, without taking his eyes off Baines, yet pointing at Jocelyn.

Jocelyn rose to her feet. 'You try and ignore me again and I'll wipe that smile off your face.' He looked at her now.

'Shall we discuss the geopolitical impact of your kowtowing to the Southern Bloc? *Can* you discuss that?' Her eyes were fixed upon him. He looked at Ben and rolled his eyes. 'I didn't think so. Maybe that's why he didn't want to hear my voice.' She looked around at her colleagues.

'I don't think Lucas wants another mauling.' Ben said.

Lucas felt the stab of betrayal, he couldn't understand why Ben could not see it his way, in fact the man was veering off the path at a rate of knots.

'We'll chalk it up to you having a bad day, eh?' Ben added.

He stared at Baines and shook his head slowly and burying his hands in his pockets.

'Unbelievable,' he said to Baines.

'So, what about this story?' Baines tapped a finger on the paper still lying on the table.

'Complete rubbish! That hacks got it in for me, it's a witch hunt! There's a rogue farmer who has murdered some of our security detail. But he's just one man. We'll find him today. That bloody journalist is just spinning the story to make trouble for us.' He glared at his leader. 'You seem quite pally with him. You should have a word…'

Ben ignored the dig; he was skimming the report in the paper yet again. 'When did this happen? When was someone going to tell me? I don't want to read these things in the bloody paper!'

The room was silent. Lucas decided to keep quiet now too, he'd received enough attention today. The eyes around the table were lowered. Ben looked, but no one returned his gaze.

Lucas walked back to his seat. The chair creaked loudly as he sat down, and again as he leaned back, coolly tapping his pen against fingers.

'Who is this guy?' asked Ben. 'Is he a murderer, working under the shadow of the system change? Or have we played a part in this? We do not need some folk hero fuelling the resistance.'

'Definitely the first. He's a crazy old hermit.' Lucas saw his opportunity. 'We visited the farm; his wife burned it down and killed one of our men. That was two days ago. He disappeared into the countryside. We caught up with him last night in a local town, but he managed to kill two more of our men. Our people are no good! We need military personnel on the ground.'

'Did he escape?'

'Yes, he is still at large. But he's one man. We'll find him and arrest him.'

'Who's in charge on the ground?'

'A guy named Bill Ludlum. He's ex-military. He's capable.'

'Capable of *what*? We don't want war! We must negotiate with these people. There must be a peaceful resolu –'

'Impossible. Anyway, forget the farmer, there's hundreds, maybe thousands organising over the border. You're betraying the people who brought you to power.'

'The last time I checked, they wanted jobs, equality – not war.'

'Very clever. You know what I mean… I'm not doing deals with the landed gentry.'

'You'll do what I tell you to do, Lucas.'

'Will I?' He gave Ben an insolent smile and walked away from the table.

Ben watched Lucas go, while he wracked his brain for something to say to the gobsmacked ministers sitting in front of him.

'Right, where are the stats on housing?'

Jocelyn stood and leaned across the table to reach a file. She turned to Ben. 'You're okay now, Ben. I've got this. Haven't you got a meeting?'

It took a moment for Ben to wise up. He nodded. 'Er… yes. Thanks Jocelyn.' He smiled apologetically to his ministers and slipped into the meeting room behind him. He picked up the phone and dialled a number from his head. A cold, hard voice picked up after two rings.

'Yes?'

'Hi, you okay?' He asked, hesitantly.

'What do you have for me?'

Ben's head dropped. He thought for a second about avoiding this – just persevering instead. But then he nodded gently to himself and moved straight to business. 'I have a problem in Northumberland. I don't know whether Lucas's people can handle it… Sorry… Really, I just have no idea what's going on up there. Can you go up, find out and let me know?'

'Do you want me to sort it?'

'No, no… just Intel and report back.'

He heard a click at the other end. Baines looked at his desk, looked at the receiver, and then put it back on the main body of the telephone.

TEN

Nat stepped from the tree line as the first hint of sunrise was pushing the horizon. All he could see was the black block of the land against the deep blue of the earliest of morning skies. So thick and bold were the two colours that there was a profound beauty in its simplicity. There were no streetlights, no headlights and no house lights.

The car he had heard in the night was not coming for him, but he had not slept. His muscles were stiff, and it was a cold morning. He sucked it up, forgetting for a moment the chaos that had become his existence.

He considered what Claire had said to him about leaving for Scotland, but that felt like betrayal – a betrayal of Esme, of home and of all those other farmers who might stay and fight the regime. He regretted not calling Amber from Claire's house. He knew she would be worried – and angry that he had sent her to Stuart under false pretences. He couldn't face that conversation. He was honest enough to admit that to himself. There was no way of calling them now.

The sun rose and washed the land with gold that warmed his craggy skin. As he walked, the breeze whipped the straggles of hair around his eyes forcing him to squint. The vast Northumbrian sky opened out in front of him. The clouds hung low between enormous gaps of vivid blue, but as he scanned the distance, the clouds covered the sky.

He returned to the field shelter. In front of him, the rough grazing land fell away down the valley side. The endless bluster blew thick tufts of grass this way and that. Two small trees shaped like battered witches' hats grew in the field about two hundred feet in front of him. His gaze shifted to the sheep grazing further down on the more sheltered part of the hillside, and on again to his arable fields. *How on earth would he manage to turn and seed them in the coming weeks?*

Across the valley to the far side, he saw the patchwork of greens and browns stretching off into the distance. All that land toiled by local people for centuries. Overall, it had worked well. He sat on the grass, picked stones from the dirt, and threw them into the air as he tried to understand.

It was not these country people who had swindled and cheated to generate enormous profits. Perhaps they needed to change the banking system and huge dominating corporations, but not destroy the heartbeat of the country. It was, after all, his country too.

He decided to pay a visit to Rowell's farm that day. There, he could begin to get consensus on a plan for the rest of his life. The breeze changed direction and snapped him out of his thoughts.

With twigs gathered nearby, he made a small fire. His eyes darted constantly from the faint stream of smoke to the road and up the valley. While he dressed another rabbit, he decided that he'd move camp, deeper into his land.

He tore the hot flesh from its bones with his teeth, and the meal vanished in a flash, but it was good to have some sustenance. He was picking at the bones and sipping hot tea when his attention was caught by crows leaving their roosts in the middle distance. There was nothing odd as such about this – crows had to eat too – but the number of birds that had taken to the wing was unusual. Their roost was along the road at the edge of his property. He turned his ears and listened. At first, he heard nothing man made but, within a few moments, there it was: the hum of engines powering along the road towards his gates.

He looked down at the fire. Though it was not smoking much, he grabbed the circle of turf he had cut away to dig the fire pit and threw it over the embers.

Leaping to his feet, he snatched up his rifle and sprinted as fast as he could across the open ground. In the corner of his eye, he could see two cars moving along the lane, not slow but not speeding. It was a race now: he had around two hundred yards to make; the cars had to cover three-quarters of a mile. He had to take the advantage; two cars meant potentially eight or even ten men. He had a full magazine the day before but had spent two rounds on breakfast – so fourteen left in the clip. As he ran, he scolded himself for not picking up another box of ammunition. Simple mistakes lead to misery, he thought.

Running across open land, he saw the cars turn into his driveway. If they hadn't seen him now, they were even more useless than he thought. He was about fifty yards from his destination: the copse that curled over the brow of the hill above their home. If they saw him, they would think he was running, and they would follow – he hoped.

His back was turned to the cars now, running as fast as he could up the hill. His ears filled with the wisp of his boots through the thick grass and rasp of his aging lungs trawling vainly for enough air to power his engine up the hill. He could no longer hear the cars when his tall frame broke the tree line. He skidded onto his belly, turning to face back down the hill and bringing the rifle sights to his right eye in one fluid movement.

He fought to regain his composure, lungs and muscles burning. As he looked through the sights, his panting made the gun rise and fall, obscuring his view, so he looked at his pursuers without the aid of magnification. The sweat began to bead on his forehead as he watched the men step out of the two cars. They were the same cars as those he had seen the night before. He put his head down for a few seconds as his breath began to regulate. The rich damp peat filled his nostrils with a sweet smell and the adrenalin began to subside. He looked back at the cars.

Roland drove the first car, with Steve to his left. Davey was in the back seat with a new guy, Dylan. Dylan had arrived in Northumberland a few days before, fresh out of the police and he made Conor look like a saint. Roland wasn't even surprised anymore. Ludlum and Gerry followed behind.

'I don't know why we're doing this. We never signed up to become bounty hunters...,' said Roland.

'We just gotta do what we're told, mate,' replied Steve. Roland noticed a resignation in Steve's voice and when he glanced over, Steve was staring out of the window.

'You okay?' Roland asked, quietly. 'Thought this was right up your alley.'

Steve shook his head softly but didn't look around. 'This isn't fighting for something... feels like sport. Only that fucking psycho in the car behind knows what we're up to now.'

'Tell me what happened up here the other night,' Roland asked for the umpteenth time. 'What's this all about?'

Dylan's head appeared between the front seats. 'Don't worry about it Roland, leave it to the big boys.'

Roland glanced in the rear-view mirror. Dylan caught his eye, the smirk on his face turned threatening in a flash. As Steve turned to look at him, Dylan gave him a whack on the arm and the pair shared a conspiratorial giggle. Roland noticed that Steve's mirth faded fast as Dylan reclined again.

'Fuck you guys,' Roland said. 'Not so funny now...'

'Tssst, what's he gonna do really? We'll have him now...,' said Steve.

Dylan grinned. 'That's why Bill brought me this time.'

'Yeah, well, *you* should be stopping him, not me,' said Roland.

'I'll have a word with Ludlum if you want, mate?' said Steve.

Roland softened. 'Ha ha, I'm sure that wanker would be very understanding.'

'We know what we're doing. Don't worry about this farmer. Last night he took everyone by surprise. Now we know what we're up against, we can get our game face on, and give him as much respect as he deserves.' Said Steve.

'I've got no idea what that means,' Roland said, 'but I'll take your word for it.'

As the car pulled up the drive, Davey exclaimed, 'Look up there in the field above the house! That's someone running into the trees!'

Roland craned his neck to look but couldn't see anything. Neither apparently had Steve or Dylan.

'You better be sure about that, Davey,' Steve said, 'cos if I have to walk all the way up there and we don't find him, you won't be coming back with us.'

'Whey I'm not absolutely a hundred percent, like.' Davey now seemed circumspect and wary. 'I just saw *something* move.'

In the mirror, Roland saw Davey shrivel in his seat. He looked briefly at his fingernails before he began gnawing on them. Roland reverted to the road ahead but was distracted again by sudden movement in the back of the car. Dylan had punched Davey on the top of his arm. Davey curled up as his 'dead arm' throbbed.

'Idiot!' Dylan chortled. He sucked his teeth and shook his head at Davey.

'Don't be such a dick, Dylan!' shouted Roland. 'Shit, this is just a *nightmare!*'

The car pulled to a stop in front of the burned down house. All four men opened their respective doors and climbed out into the mild morning air.

Ludlum pulled his car in alongside theirs and barked through the open window. 'Find the bastard lads. Let's put a lid on this.'

Gerry remained in the car with Ludlum.

The four of them got to it. Moving around to the back of the car, Steve leaned deep into the boot and pulled out two shotguns, one of which he handed to Roland with a grin. 'Here you go, mate! Just squeeze here to shoot.'

Dylan pulled out an SA80, which he described to Roland as 'an oldy but a goody'. He then threw a handgun to Davey, who dropped it – much to the copper's delight.

'Don't bother taking the safety off that, Davey – you'll shoot yourself,' Steve joked, glancing at Ludlum with an exasperated look.

Ludlum stared back coldly, and Steve's eyes fell to the floor. He appeared to shrink, and Roland couldn't help thinking that the big marine's need for acceptance would, sooner or later, lead to trouble.

Roland turned to Davey and whispered, 'who knows when these were last fired.' He looked down at the gun he held, 'and I really don't want to start shooting people.'

'Hey Roland,' Ludlum called over, 'you come and sit with me. We need to talk. And, anyway, I don't think you're really the type for this.'

He turned to Gerry who was on the other side of the car.

'You were part of that calamity the other night... you go and get him.'

Roland looked at Davey as he processed Ludlum's order. He struggled to catch his breath and he felt tears in his eyes. Davey couldn't hold his gaze. Roland offered a faint smile before both looked at the floor – anywhere but in the boss's direction. Davey kicked at a stone on the ground. Roland felt for him as he watched him turn and jog in the other direction. It seemed that, whatever government held power, some people never got the breaks.

Gerry ran to catch up with the marines. As he past Roland, he reached out for the weapon. Roland's disgust at what his friend had done failed to register immediately in the face of his reprieve. Now, he held on tightly to the shotgun so that Gerry had to stop and look at him.

'What became of you?' asked Roland.

Gerry looked away but his hands remained on the weapon. 'C'mon, not now,' he said. But Roland didn't let go. 'It all happened so fast… It was chaos… *I dunno*… I'm sorry!'

Roland stepped in closer to his old friend. 'Never *mate*,' he spat. 'Never. I will *never* accept an explanation.' He tugged the gun slightly. 'If there is a God, you had better pray for mercy. You're a monster.' He pushed the gun into Gerry's arms and turned away from him.

Gerry stood for a moment before jogging feebly after the others. When they reached the barn, Steve directed Gerry to push open the big heavy door. The marine pointed his gun into the shadows and entered. Davey hung around by the barn door, but when he noticed he was under Ludlum's gaze, he stiffened, before creeping into the barn after the others.

Roland settled into the passenger's seat of Ludlum's car. He felt sick and repulsed at being any part of this atrocity. He saw Ludlum through the windscreen. He was surveying the surrounding countryside as if sniffing the air for the scent of his prey.

Roland was beginning to realise that these people were not what he had imagined. This vicious edge, this murderous thuggery… it had no part in the NSO that he had idealised. It was never supposed to be about rape and murder – of terrorising people, whatever their political persuasion. It was a far cry from the joy of empowerment and equality that had appeared to be Baines's ideology. In the years before the NSO came to power, everything had been so exciting and invigorating. Those years were full of romance.

He had loved the struggle of the underground movement. He thought about Parliament Square, where he stood arm-in-arm with fellow protestors, the atmosphere heavy with tension, a wall of riot police standing before them, the water cannons in reserve. He remembered the girl next to him: '*Checkmate!*' she had screamed at the police. '*Attack us, you lose… leave us alone, we win!*' He remembered looking at the police, the whites of their eyes through their helmets, visors and riot shields - the feeling of strength and unity the protesters shared within the ranks, the honour and dignity of their cause. He remembered the euphoria as the police backed down, and the party they had in occupation. He followed that girl around for hours afterwards – too chicken to speak to her, though.

Life now, as a government enforcer, was mostly about pain and anger. He felt the misery of the lives they were destroying. Also, whereas before, he was one among thousands, in the small group he found himself now, contact with enemies was far more likely and far less watered down. He was on the frontline. He didn't want to be there, but he was in the eye of the storm. And the only thing more terrifying than the farmer they were looking for was Bill Ludlum.

As Nat watched from his vantage point, the four men disappeared into the farmyard while the other climbed into the second car. He looked down his sights and focused on the man still in view. It was the leader from the previous night. Dressed all in black, he stood behind the open driver's side door with one foot remaining in the foot well. He showed no emotion as he scanned the countryside.

Nat could read his thoughts. They were alike in some ways; Nat could see the wolf, the hunter in him.

Conversely, Nat sensed the man trying to climb inside his own head, pondering Nat's options and attempting to predict his next move. The leader of the enforcers knew he was there and that this fight was going to continue.

Bill felt his stomach knot as his men reappeared from the barn, Gerry and Davey were laden with items they had stolen.

'What are you doing, you fucking idiots!' Bill moved away from the car and slammed the door shut in anger. 'Do you think we're here to steal junk? You drop that shit now or I'll shoot you myself. There are plenty of people out there who would jump at the chance to have your privileges!' He stood square to all four men who stood forlornly and dropped their booty at their feet.

He saw Gerry turn red. Davey's shoulders sagged and he scratched at the back of his neck. Steve and Dylan had turned their backs to them, and they were searching the distant countryside, but Bill knew they would have been the instigators.

Gerry pulled his shotgun across his front in what he hoped was a gesture of resolve and determination. Bill kept his eyes fixed on him.

'Get into those fields and don't come back here until you have him.' he said.

'Davey,' Steve chirped up, 'where was it that you saw something?'

'What did you say?' asked Bill with as much exasperation as he could muster.

Gerry glared at Steve, and Dylan unleashed a growl of frustration as he looked to the heavens. The raid on the barn was embarrassing; the fact they had ignored movement in the fields was indefensible.

Bill watched dumbfounded as Steve pointed at Davey. 'He said he saw something move up there when we pulled into the drive, but then he said it was nothing.'

Bill turned his scrutiny to Davey and the young man recoiled.

'What did you see, Davey?' He asked, calm and reassuring.

'Em... Was a gadgy. Running...'

'A what?'

'A bloke, a man.' said Gerry.

'...need a fucking translator now,' mumbled Bill. 'Where was he?'

Davey pointed. 'Way off into them trees.'

'Why didn't you tell me before?'

Davey hesitated, glancing at Dylan and Steve. Then at Roland, who gave him a reassuring nod from where he remained in the car.

''Cos, he told us, if we got sent all the way up there for nothin' then I wouldn't be comin' back down again...'

Bill moved towards Steve. Steve was grinning, but the smile failed to soften his approaching boss and soon fell from his face. As he approached the marine, he drew his handgun like lightening and pistol-whipped Steve across the face.

Steve gasped in pain and brought a hand up to his eye. Blood trickled through his fingers from the gash that had been opened beneath it. He glared back at Bill with a face like thunder. Then Dylan took a step forward, Bill turned to face him down.

'Please try it,' he said, with a smile. 'You'll end up being a lesson for the rest of these clowns.' He gave them a derogatory nod of his head. 'So come on... you could have me.' He stared at Dylan, head nodding, he allowed the smile to peel across his face as the confrontation made his blood pump. 'Come on, you fucker...' Dylan stopped in his tracks, he glanced at Steve, who was holding a blood-soaked rag to his cheek. 'No? Not so confident. Come on, you're bigger than me, younger than me...'

Nobody moved at first and nobody spoke. Bill noticed Davey look at the gun in his hands. Gerry reached out to help Steve up, but Steve slapped his hand away with a grunt. All the while, Bill held Dylan in the challenge, but when his glare returned towards him, the enforcer looked at the ground. He was backing down.

'Right then,' said Bill finally, 'now we are back to normality, you get into your hollow heads that *I* give the orders here. And this is grown up stuff… you don't do what I say there will be very serious consequences. You do as I say, and you'll have a nice, trouble-free life.' His eyes pierced each of the men, breaking their will that little bit more. 'Now you arseholes, get up that hill.' He turned to Steve and Dylan, 'you come back down that hill without the farmer and I'll kill *you*.'

The four of them set off. Gerry trudged alongside Davey a few paces behind Steve and Dylan. Davey's weapon was hanging in his hand, limp, by his side. Gerry could hear mumbling from the other two over the rustle of grass under their feet. He couldn't make out the words, but he guessed the bravado was back now that they were away from Ludlum.

Steve's pistol whipping had heightened Gerry's sense that he had become a captive in his own life and of the choices he had made. He couldn't shake off a deep sense of shame over his involvement in what had happened to the farmer's wife. He felt both trapped and contaminated by the company he was keeping, and his own life had never felt cheaper.

'C'mon lads,' he said. 'Let's get a grip, find this wanker and get Ludlum off our backs. We're the law after all. Let's sort this then get a beer eh?' What came out of his mouth was strong and sincere, but he had already decided to disappear in the forest up the hill and make a break for the Scottish Border.

Gerry breathed hard now on the steady incline. They had come about two-thirds of the way to the tree line, about two hundred yards out from the blackened farmstead. The woodland was no longer the wash of a landscape painting: the individual trees were coming into focus as the breeze fluttered through the branches; the individual stones of the dry-stone wall showed their moss-covered faces.

A tall and familiar figure appeared. He was rangy with shoulders broad enough to hang saddles on. His white locks drifted around his face in the breeze and his teeth were clenched in a grimace. A hunting rifle rested casually on his hip; the barrel pointed into the sky, but his right hand gripped near the trigger. He stood as motionless as he had done when they approached the house the first time. They stopped in their tracks. Nervous looks flashed between them, but none of the enforcers took their eyes off Bell for long.

'You're a wanted man!' Dylan shouted up the hill.

'That right?'

'We gotta take you down the hill now. Upright or on your back – it's up to you.'

'You better come and get me, then.'

'Come on, there's four of us. You can't keep this up.'

A lamb was calling for its mother in the field, and the crows cawed in the high tops of the trees. The fresh country air filled their nostrils as Bell raised his rifle. The action was smooth, casual, fluid and fast.

Steve managed to drop to one knee and raise his weapon, but that was as far as he got. Gerry heard the shot, then felt blood bone and brains splatter his face. Steve dropped to his knees, his mouth agape. His expression unchanged. But there was a fist-sized hole torn in the back of his head. He toppled forward and flat onto his cratered face. Before his head met with the earth, Dylan, in the middle of taking aim, fell backwards. Everything happened in split seconds - Gerry realised he was rooted to the spot. It was as though someone had hit Dylan in the forehead with a baseball bat. Again, the breeze carried away atomised blood and gore across the beautiful landscape. Then Gerry felt his heart jolt, and he took off back down towards the farmhouse. Davey was already running ahead of him.

Bill watched the situation unfold from the bottom of the hill. To his credit, Roland started forward to go to their aid, but he gestured for him to stay where he was. He saw the muzzle flashes from Nat's weapon and the two men go down. Now, he watched Gerry and Davey running in a straight line back down the hill. *Fuck!* He needed capable men, not these headless chickens. He watched and waited for the farmer to pick them off.

When Gerry overtook Davey in their headlong dash down the hillside, Davey's sense of panic increased so much that he thought his heart would burst. If he'd had enough breath in his lungs he'd have probably screamed. Now that he was closer to the mad farmer on the hill, he was sure that he would feel a bullet between his shoulder blades at any moment. When he heard the crack of the rifle he whimpered pitifully, but it was Gerry who tumbled through the air as if he had been hit by a train. He rolled down the hill and stopped in a motionless heap.

Time began to move slowly for Davey, the sensation of warm wetness that made its way down his legs, tears flooded his cheeks as he came level with Gerry and saw him lying face down blood everywhere. Davey almost lost his footing but managed to keep running until something hit the back of his calf. He tumbled through the soft grass coming to rest a few metres further down the hill than where Gerry lay. For a moment, he just lay in the grass. He had a strange sensation of security. It seemed quiet and sheltered. But then his leg felt as though someone was holding a blowtorch to the bare flesh. It burned with paralysing ferocity, and he wailed and sobbed like a child.

Nat stood just outside the tree line for a short while, resting the butt of his gun on his hip, the barrel pointed skywards once more, his finger on the trigger. He began a slow jaunt down to his prey. As he walked, he felt part of the environment, as though he were untouchable out here, against such enemies. They just didn't understand the land, the nature of open spaces.

His eyes remained on the blond man who was standing about four hundred yards away. Nat thought about shooting at him, but he was resolved to take more time with the leader.

He approached his four victims calmly. Strapping his rifle across his back, he bent down without stopping, grabbed the first two carcasses by the scruff of the neck and dragged them down to where the other two men lay. Both men were easily fifteen stones, but Nat could haul deadweight all day and he shifted them with ease, slumping them downhill from the third man that he'd taken in the chest. Then he turned to the timid young punk.

'Please,' he cried, 'I didn't do nothin'! Please! I'm beggin'...' Tears and snot were all over his face and Nat could smell that he had already pissed himself. Nat leaned over the youth and could now see how frail, and how young he was. As he looked down into his fearful eyes, he had to remind himself of what the animal had done before he carried on. He punched his fist into the top of the punk's chest, seized a fistful of clothing and lifted him man like a bale of hay. He moved him like this at waist height and threw him on top of the two corpses. Davey cried out, writhing on top of the two dead men, evidently repulsed by the idea of lying on lifeless bodies.

'I-I din't touch her! I din't! I-I swear…' The protests were choked off as he vomited.

Nat raised his head to make sure that the men by the car had not moved, then he stepped over to where his third victim lay. It was the man with the scars and the cockney accent. He was whimpering and gurgling, his lungs filling with blood.

'Not so full o' yersel now…' Nat muttered.

Pain and fear racked the man's face; it was so different from the first time they met when he was brimming. Now he was broken and lost in a hell he could never have imagined. He didn't manage any words, but the tears rolled down his cheeks and his eyes, pleading for mercy.

Nat had no time for compassion now. The war had begun and all he could think about was Esme. He dragged the gasping and spluttering man towards the young wimp and kicked him onto his front. He glanced down the hill again and then scragged a handful of hair and pulled Scarface's head up high, stretching out his neck. Blood spluttered from his mouth. Nat raised his head and looked downhill, at the leader, but the man by the car remained still, just watching.

Davey could hardly bear to watch as the grizzled figure pitched Gerry to the ground in front of him. Then, to Davey's horror, he pulled Gerry's head sharply upwards. One huge handheld Gerry's head up fast, the other unsheathed a gleaming hunting knife.

The farmer's face was gaunt, his eyes shrouded in a heavy scowl, teeth gritted and lips snarling, all framed by dirty white hair that whipped around his face. Face to face with the devil himself, Davey felt as though a car was parked on his chest.

Suddenly, he realised that he still had the handgun in his pocket. He had put it there when he had started running. He slowly inched his hand towards it as the farmer looked down the hill towards the farmhouse. The next thing he knew, his nemesis had dropped Gerry to the ground and was looming above him. A huge boot landed in his guts. Davey heaved and bent double, gasping, unable to catch his breath.

He didn't resist as the farmer rifled through his pockets and took the weapon. Roughly, the old man hauled him back upright and repeatedly slapped him hard across the face as if to say, *I'm in charge.* He picked the knife up from where he had thrown it into the ground and rested the glinting blade on the nape of Davey's neck.

'Behave boy, and you'll live,' he hissed. Their eyes met, Bell's were cobalt flames like diamonds under a spotlight, demonic and wild. 'Try anything else an' I'll gut ye. Understand?'

Davey mustered a frantic nod, weeping openly. He was lying back against the two dead men, their bodies still warm. He put his head in his hands and wept. He looked at his wound through his fingers and could see that the round had exited through his shin. He could see the bright white of bone and couldn't stop himself from vomiting through his hands and down his front. It was all too much to take in, much less contend with. It was as though he were having a nightmare and couldn't wake himself up.

'Look at me,' growled Bell. 'LOOK AT ME!'

Davey dragged himself into reality and looked up through his tears.

Nat stood up tall and looked down the hill towards the leader of these government men, watching from below. He raised his knife and pointed it at him, holding the gesture for a long moment. Then put his palm on the top of Scarface's head, hooking his fingers into the top of his eye sockets. He looked down at the men beside the cars. He looked at the punk. He pulled Scarface's head back, hard, arching his back to full stretch. His victim coughed and spluttered, his panic was evident, but he lacked the strength to fight.

Nat steeled himself against what he was about to do. He swamped his mind with thoughts of his wife's final moments. With all his strength, he drew the sharp steel across his victim's neck in one steady, powerful arc.

He would never forget the sound of the cold blade slicing through muscle, gristle, and blood vessels. Shrill but smothered, dampened by gore. He was staring the youth in the eye when the blade carved through Gerry's jugular. The youth dug the heel of his good leg into the dirt, pushing his back against the two dead men. He squealed as his friend's blood sprayed a dark crimson all over him.

Bill watched the scene unfold. He knew that it took a certain despair to slice through another man's throat, especially in front of an audience. He also knew of the strength involved in the act and the knowledge of the weapon needed to carry it out in a single movement.

Aware that he was watching, Bell pushed Gerry's head violently to the floor and stood up tall on the hill. It was like the final flourish of some bloody gladiatorial combat.

The two men stared at each other from a distance: Bill, with his foot resting on the sill of the car, resolved to appear calm and casual despite the mayhem; Bell, with dripping knife in hand, arms hanging by his side, feet apart, Gerry's inert corpse lying at his feet.

At last Bill nodded at the hyperventilating Roland and the two men ducked into the car. Both were speechless, numbed by the carnage they had witnessed. He turned the key, revved the engine, and drove away without saying a word.

Nat watched them as they left, eyes squinting in the breeze, his heart returning to its regular beat and the primal blood lust waning to be replaced by a feeling of guilt and disgust.

He banished those thoughts to the back of his mind as he took three long strides over to where the boy lay whimpering. Crazed by fear, he had his hands up, shielding himself as though a car was about to hit him. Nat smacked his arms with his palm, knocking them away from his face. He looked up at Nat, still petrified.

'What did you expect? That I'd run away? That you'd hunt me down and kill me?' He reached down and took the youth by the scruff of the neck. He stood on the ankle of his wounded leg, and the boy screamed in pain. He then put his arm around his throat and tightened his grip. Nat's knife, still in his hand, sank into the youth's cheek, slicing a deep gash. 'Stay here, or I'll pick ye off with the rifle before y' get fifty yards. Understand?'

With that, Nat let the choking man slump back down on top of his mates' bodies, and he strode down the hill towards the ruined farmhouse. The bleak grey clouds boiled above him as he went, and a cold wind whipped through the grass.

Davey shivered. His throat was raw, the pain in his leg was excruciating and there was a tacky, crimson mask of blood on his face – his own as well as Gerry's. He looked around. It seemed a long way to the trees, and it would be almost impossible to reach them with a broken shin. He didn't want this psycho hunting him down. All he could do was to stare up at the clouds rushing across the enormous sky. He heard an engine. He turned painfully to see the farmer coming back up the hill. He was on a quad bike with trailer in tow.

Nat accelerated up the hill like he always did. He pulled to a stop next to the dead bodies and the skinny kid. He jumped off the machine and faced to the breeze for a moment, checking the perimeters of his land, smelling, watching, listening for anything out of the ordinary. Nothing disturbed him, so he turned to the carnage that lay behind him and heaved the bodies onto the trailer. Finally, he lifted the boy and threw him on top of the whole bloody mess.

As he drove the quad back down the hill. Davey's crying was beginning to affect him. He wanted to help the boy but knew he had to do this – he had to finish his statement. He pulled up next to Gerry's car. He lifted Gerry's body off the trailer and rifled roughly through the dead man's pockets. Finding the keys at last, he went to open the boot – it was already unlocked. He compared the space in the boot with the bulk of the four men and shook his head at the challenge.

After he ripped the boot shelf from the car, he took the bodies, one by one, up onto his shoulder and laid them like sacks of spuds across the boot, curling their legs up to get them in. Finally, he grabbed the skinny kid and, ignoring his protestations, threw him on top of the others. He was right up against the rear window of the car as Nat slammed it shut in his face.

He went back to the trailer and picked up the items he had thrown in it from the barn: a piece of sheet metal, a pot of black metal paint, a brush and a bundle of pull ties. They all went in the car and then he swung his rifle off his back and put it in the passenger foot well. He drove the quad bike back to the barns with the latest additions to his arsenal: two handguns, two shotguns and an SA80. He put one handgun into his waistband, pumped the shotgun and put it over his shoulder before returning to the car. The back of the car had gone eerily quiet, but the skinny kid was still there.

Nat drove fast into the centre of Hexham. He stopped in the marketplace next to the monument in the middle of the square where a crowd was milling around. Nat knew many of them – either by name or sight. Some of those he knew had affiliations in some way with the NSO. Nobody approached as he began to daub on the sheet metal. The gathering crowd could see the youth in the back of the steamed-up car, where his face and hands pressed against the rear window. No doubt they saw the state Nat was in, covered in dirt and blood, wild and unkempt. Some would notice the rifle and shotgun in the passenger side foot well through the open driver's side door. Mobile phones appeared from pockets; some made calls, others made videos. Most local people had heard by now that Nat had gone mad or gone rogue, depending on their loyalties. Most had not witnessed any real opposition to the NSO – until now.

Once he finished with the paint, he left the metal sheet on the roof and moved around to the boot. He opened it, and skinny kid started immediately to scream for help. Nat beat him in the face with his fist until he stopped. Then he turned to the crowd and looked for trouble. When nobody stepped forward, he dragged the kid out of the car by the scruff of his neck. His legs fell limp to the ground. Nat hauled him up to the monument, dropped him and went back to the vehicle. From the corner of his eye, Nat saw two men approaching – he knew them. He walked back to the open door and leaned in. He pulled out the shotgun and turned to them. They slowed their pace when they saw the weapon in his hands.

'This is not your business, Brendan,' Nat said to the taller of the two men. They were brothers, policemen from Hexham and now NSO enforcers in the town.

'You know it *is*, Nat. We can't let you carry on like this.'

'Aye, but you can,' Nat growled, 'or I'll be laying you out next to these animals. You do what y' have to do, but nobody'll think any the less if you go back to your office and report this. Come back when there's more of you."

The two men looked at each other. They both knew Nat by reputation, and maybe they'd heard a few stories in the last day or so.

'We'll be back soon, right enough,' Brendan said. 'You have t'be stopped.'

They turned, jogged back to their car and screeched off. Nat presumed they were headed back to base to do exactly as he had suggested. So, he stepped the momentum up a gear, hauled the three bodies out of the boot and dumped them roughly on the cold concrete next to the pulp that was the skinny lad.

He attached the bodies, arms to ankles, with the pull ties and then used a couple more to hang the sign around skinny's neck. He stood back and made a three-sixty, slowly looking at all the faces staring at him in the square. Then, after a moment and within four strides, he was back in the car.

He fired up the engine and hammered down Hallstyle Bank and out of town. He knew that the haunted eyes and recording phones of the crowd focused on the roughly daubed words that underlined the bloody misery of skinny's face…

NOW YOU'VE GOT YOUR WAR

ELEVEN

Nat sat enveloped by the tide of dusk next to Esme's grave. He was aware that by now the graphic evidence of his actions captured by bystanders in Hexham market would have gone viral, stormed every facet of the media and become frontpage headlines in the press. What kind of spin they put on it was out of his control. Quiet moments of remorse smarted in his mind, but the killings were like a release; vengeance numbed his pain, but not for long enough.

He chewed raw beans to assuage the pangs of hunger as he listened to the rotor blades of a light chopper circling his ruined farmhouse.

His backside rested hard on the cold ground and his clothes were constantly damp, but it didn't bother him; he was warm enough and at home here where he felt somehow close to Esme beneath the still sky. Apart from the babbling of the burn and the distant beat of the rotor blades, the wood was quiet. Maybe too quiet.

He had the sudden sensation that somebody else was present. He reached for the cold but comforting steel of his handgun, put it on a rock next to him and pulled his shotgun up over his lap. He turned his attention to the increasingly blue-black mantle that engulfed him. His ears pricked and his eyes narrowed but there was nothing to see, so he dug back into his beans and shovelled in the nourishment. There was no point savouring cold beans anyway. As he scraped the spoon around the bottom of the tin, he heard it: a barely audible pop like the opening of a plastic container for pills or camera film. He knew exactly what it might have been: the sound of a night-sight lens cover being removed. He froze, heart pounding, and stared into the darkness, marshalling every one of his senses. *Was the hunter becoming prey?*

The man in dark fatigues and with the fully blacked-out face nestled in the undergrowth high up above the ravine. His eye focussed through his night-sight on the green and black figure sitting next to the makeshift grave. The image cleared in his mind; he registered the legs planted firm in the dirt. He held a tin of food in his hand and nursed a shotgun across his lap. He had a grim face that the night-sight made grimmer, giving him two black dots for eyes. Those black dots were staring straight back down his lens.

In shock, the man in the dark fatigues jerked his eye away from the sights and stared into the darkness, but there was nothing, no outline, no shadow, no sound, just a swathe of black. Holding his breath in check, he put his eye back to the night-sight and the ghostly chill washed over him again. The ghoulish figure sitting in the coal black night was staring intently and unwaveringly back at him.

The deck of the fishing trawler rose perilously before the stomach-churning drop on the other side of the wave. Was this the Channel or the North Sea? Ben had no idea. He staggered across to Pierre who was pinned to the side of the boat, his head and shoulders hung over the side as he retched into the churning emerald green waters. Baines leaned on the gunwale next to him and patted his friend on the back. 'I forgot you had such strong sea legs.'

'Ha Ha,' Pierre managed. 'You are keen to go swimming, yes?'

'We're supposed to be helping with the fishing.'

'Just shut up. You go. Tell them I am looking for the fish...' Pierre succeeded in glancing at Ben with a puckish grin before the roll of the boat made him retch again.

Ben slapped his friend on the back, chuckling as he looked over at the crew and, of course, the two journalists who had accompanied them on this little trip.

'You look right at home on the high seas Mr Baines!' shouted one of the hacks.

'Don't you start!' Ben grinned at her and then turned to the crew. 'What do you want me to do? When do we get fishing?'

''Nother two hours to the fish!' said a bedraggled trawlerman in yellow slickers.

Ben struggled to maintain his happy face but reminded himself of the political importance of his willingness to put himself in the workers' shoes – whatever their work.

By the time he had lurched across the deck to where the journalists were sitting, Pierre was sitting inside the boat again. He had his back to the starboard quarter and his satellite phone to his ear. Ben's interest was piqued when Pierre looked at him intently. It was obvious that this was serious when Pierre pushed himself to his feet, held his gut for a moment and pushed across the deck.

'Turn this boat around!' he commanded the crew. Then he turned to Ben. 'We must return to London immediately. Something has happened – details are sketchy, but...' he stopped, distracted by the skipper who stormed out of the wheelhouse.

'What's all this about?' he barked.

'Just turn the boat around,' Pierre stood up straight, sickness forgotten, fists beginning to ball and eyes locked upon the skipper.

There was the faintest hesitation before the skipper turned back into the wheelhouse and the fishing boat began to turn back towards port. Pierre turned to Ben and shook his head solemnly. The two journalists on board lifted their mobile phones frantically into the air, but without a satellite phone there was no service out there.

It took two hours for the fishing boat to reach port. Ben patrolled the deck like a caged lion as it crawled towards land. He couldn't reach Lucas Dart, or any of his team for that matter, and this made his blood boil. It was half past nine at night when Ben's car pulled up outside Dart's London residence.

By this time, he had flicked angrily through the various news channels. He imagined with horror the millions of families across the country reacting to the barbaric images that they were witnessing.

Overall, the reports toed a government line on the story; Dart had obviously seen to that. The regime summed up the farmer's actions as those *of a violent and dangerous criminal using the revolution as an excuse for murder*. Language such as *atrocious crimes* and *acts of terror* littered the newsreel.

However, as he sat in the passenger seat of Pierre's car, Ben knew how critical sections of the population would interpret this story. This farmer personified the anti-reform movement - a fire that was already burning brightly, especially in the border counties.

On an amateur video, he watched Bell's massive figure, hauling and dragging bodies from a car as though they were simply bags of coal. The thick white hair and beard hanging around his tanned face as he went about his gruesome business. He hoped the feral appeal that he recognised in the man was not universal.

Before leaving the car, Pierre dialled the number of Rory Henderson. Baines knew the journalist was local to the area and he knew that he would get the truth. The call was answered, and the journalist's voice sounded over the car's hands-free.

'Rory, its Ben Baines…'
'Hello…hello sir?'
'Sorry.'
'Okay, please wait…'

Ben and Pierre shared a dumbfounded look as they waited for the journalist to collect himself. They heard rustling and murmurings and imagined Rory telling whomever he was with what was happening and then running from the room.

'Yes, hello, what can I do for you, sir?' Rory said, finally.

'Can you tell me what's really happening in Northumberland?'

After a brief pause, Rory clicked into his professional mode. 'Well, there is violence increasing on both sides. The conflict in Hexham... well, each side is becoming more polarised.'

'Conflict?'

'I'd call it that. We have NSO militia forcibly removing landowners and we have landowners fighting back. The landowners are getting organised though. So, you may well see the tide turn.'

'What about this Bell guy?'

'He's well known in the area. He has a fearsome reputation if you get on the wrong side of him, but he was... er, *is* influential in the Tynedale farming community and his wife even more so...' There was a pause on the line. '... before you arrested her,' Rory added sheepishly.

'Not *me*. I had nothing to do with it. Was it NSO definitely?'

'Yes, looks that way... although nothing has been publicly acknowledged, she's just disappeared!' Ben heard.

Rory took a deep breath. 'If I can speak freely?'

'Yes, go ahead...'

'No matter what your nationality or politics, observers across the globe agree on two things...'

'Go on!'

'Lucas Dart is working to his own agenda, and you are either complicit or blinded by an unwavering trust and loyalty to him.'

Ben gritted his teeth and wiped his palms down his trousers. He was seething with anger.

'Thank you, Rory. Try and find some middle ground in your reporting. I will sort this…' Ben nodded to Pierre, who ended the call.

When they climbed out of the car, the street was quiet. Ben looked all around then he crossed the road. They walked side by side to the concrete barriers that stopped cars speeding into Lucas Dart's mews address. They didn't meet security until they reach the front door, but the fact it was opened before they got there indicated that they had been watched all the way.

Ben stormed past the guard and into the hall.

'Sir!' the guard reached out and put his hand on Ben's shoulder.

No sooner had Ben felt the contact and begun to turn his head, the guard cried out in pain. Ben looked down to find the man on one knee, his face contorted in agony and his arm high above his head. The security guard's hand was white and misshapen like a discarded leather glove. Pierre held it in a vice like grip.

'You do not touch Mr Baines,' Pierre said calmly.

Ben continued into the house, but doors opened, and men appeared with weapons in hand. He stopped abruptly – dumbstruck. Pierre reached for his own gun with his free hand.

'What the hell?' shouted Ben, his hands stretched out from his hips, 'have you gone mad?'

No one replied. The hallway fell silent. The seconds past and Ben felt his legs shaking. He glanced around at Pierre. One hand pointed his revolver at the armed minders, the other gripped the wincing and gasping security guard's hand.

Footfalls sounded from along the corridor, metal studded heals on the tiled floor – the rhythm conveyed a certain swagger. Dart's head of security appeared with a self-satisfied smile on his face.

'He'll see you now.'

'You're damn right he will!' exclaimed Ben. 'This is a bloody joke.'

'But *he'll* have to wait for you outside.' The minders all looked at Pierre.

'Non!' Pierre's response was instinctive and immediate. Then he spoke directly to the security chief. 'I will not leave in this situation.'

'Then I'm afraid Mr Dart is not available.'

'Okay, okay.' Ben turned to Pierre. 'Wait for me, Pierre, it's okay. What's he going to do, bump me off?' Pierre raised his eyebrows and shrugged.

'I'll take my chances.' Ben walked towards the security detail. 'Bloody ridiculous!' he added, as he passed the head of security. He heard a very satisfying yelp from the security guard by the door and imagined his friend giving his hand a final twist before letting him go.

Ben followed the security agents down the corridor. He peered down the hall to see if he could get a clue as to where he was being taken. 'Do you always greet visitors like that?' he asked the head of security.

'We adhere to a zero-tolerance policy for uninvited guests...'

'You know damn well who I am!' He couldn't help himself, but as soon as the words left his lips, he had that sinking feeling. The security head stopped so abruptly Ben almost walked into him. When he turned, their eyes met.

'Sir, you could have been Jesus Christ himself, but we'd still put a bullet in your head if you threatened our leader.'

Ben took a step backwards. 'The last I heard; I *was* your leader.'

The man's gaze didn't waver. He glared at Baines but offered no explanation.

Baines looked at the men surrounding him; they were all squashed together in the tight corridor. He tried to decipher whether these nutjobs had some security code loyalty thing going on or whether this was a directive from above. Finally, his gaze returned to the man in charge. 'Whatever.' He waved his hand for them to get moving again. 'Where is he?' He was directed to the sitting room and buried his hands in his pockets as he took a few steps inside. 'Well today has been a strange one,' he said with a shake of the head, 'but you three look cosy and relaxed.'

In front of him, Lucas Dart filled a huge armchair, his pot belly rested on his lap. Steve Jones and Lee Mannion occupied the sofa opposite. Each man had a drink in hand, and they were watching television. 'Did you two get attacked by The Republican Guard too?' Ben asked the other guests.

Jones and Mannion didn't answer. Dart had raised his hand.

'What the hell was all that about?' Ben demanded.

'Sssssht,' Dart hissed, 'your mate's on the telly.'

Baines looked at the television to see Rory Henderson's baby face. He was standing outside in a soggy mac looking bullied by the rain. Dart turned the sound up higher.

'...Questions fall at the new government's door concerning its enforcement units. Rumours abound in this rural idyll that the enforcement squads' brutality sparked the farmer's bloody rampage – that the NSO's actions led to these killings..."

Mrs Bell's striking face appeared on the screen. Dart chortled at the image as Ben slumped onto the arm of the sofa.

'...Esme Bell has not been seen since their farm burnt to the ground following a visit from NSO enforcers. There has been no official statement of her whereabouts, but witnesses say that she died at the scene. Locally NSO aggression is resulting in a response from those in the rural community and many see Nat Bell's deeds as an act of war rather than of murder. Insurgency is rife in this volatile region. There are those who think the administration must face its failings, rather than resorting to violence and that diplomacy

should be the order of the day. Perhaps what may be an increasingly marginalised population are less likely to see things the Government's way, when a man like Nat Bell is fighting back. This is Rory Henderson reporting from Hexham, Northumberland for News Today.'

The reporter's image disappeared to be replaced by a still of Nat Bell from that day in the market square. His sapphire blue eyes stared straight down the lens and his teeth were gritted. White hair was streaked with what looked like blood from his victims. His clenched fists were like clubs and his legs were set wide like two tree trunks.

Baines felt a prickling over every part of his skin. Light-headed, he tried to gather his composure and face his colleagues without showing the degree of panic that he felt. The leader knew about Revolution. As he digested the image of this wild man fighting back, he knew it would strike a chord in the psyche of the very people who had brought him to power. He was sure of this because he felt it himself. As he watched Bell, Ben admired his strength, and his guts. But most of all, he recognised this barbarian's ability to make a statement – consciously or not. Bell might be playing at politics but his methods, more visceral though they were, echoed those of his own and of the NSO.

He turned his attention to Dart, anger overwhelming shock. 'What happened to the wife? What happened at his farm?'

Dart shifted in his armchair. He leaned forward, perched on the edge of the seat. His eyes were trained on the floor, and he clasped his hands in front of him. His head shook, softly at first. Ben read the body language as contrition, but then Dart raised his head.

Claire had called Stuart after Nat left. As she watched him putter away on the small motorbike, she had known that his friend needed to know everything.

Shortly after speaking to Claire, Stuart told Amber about her home, her father and her mother. Amber had broken down in his arms and sobbed on his shoulder. But her father's genes enabled her to pull herself together and she pushed the sadness deep down. That steely look appeared in her eye, and she had demanded they return to fight alongside her father. Stuart had refused.

It was mid-afternoon when they watched the news, and his friend dumping the bodies in the marketplace. Amber looked across at Stuart, her cheeks flushed with colour, her movements twitching with nerves and anger. 'I don't care whether you come with me or not. I'm going.'

'Aye. I'll be coming wi' ye,' he said.

The blue light of the television washed over Amber's face. He knew this young woman would go whether he liked it or not. She would follow him if he tried to go alone. She would vanish overnight if he tried to stop her leaving. He had known her from birth. She was as decisive and determined – as pig-headed – as her father, and in some ways more capable.

She had spent years roaming the border country alone. Those who knew of it marvelled at her ability to disappear into its wild hills and forests. She had a gift for nature. She loved it, was part of it and Carlins Law was her home.

'I'm going to pack my bag,' she said quietly.

'How d' we get ower the border?'

'There is no way that they've finished that wall in the last three days. We just need to find a gap.'

'Okay.' He raised his hands in resignation. 'But we go on one condition: we try to persuade your father to leave wi' us. He cannae win this war he's started. Not one man agin' the Regime.'

'Well, he isn't one man now, is he? There's three of us, and he'll want to fight with the rebels as much as I do, now – I know it. You get me there safe and then y' can leave – come back up here to safety.' She smiled a caustic smile then left the room and ran upstairs.

Stuart slammed his palms down on the arms of his chair and looked to the ceiling for answers. He growled his frustration as the emotions ebbed and flowed inside: fear, anger, sadness – but then something inside that drew him towards the conflict. He was knotted to Nat's struggle as though it was his own. He knew that he should be choosing his peaceful life in Scotland over walking into his friend's struggles but that was something he simply could not do. He pushed himself up, found himself a holdall and went straight to the gun cabinet.

Lucas Dart looked at the floor for a long time while Ben waited expectantly for a sign of contrition. Jones and Mannion shifted uncomfortably on the sofa. As Ben looked at Lucas, he couldn't help but feel warmth towards his old comrade and he gave him time to find the words.

When Lucas finally raised his head, it was with the expression that Ben had become increasingly familiar: menace. His eyebrows were raised, and he was grinning. Dart looked at Jones and Mannion, nodding faintly. They met his gaze with encouraging and provocative nods. When Ben turned back to his deputy, he had no words. He suddenly felt alone.

Dart clapped his hands and rubbed them together, drew breath and turned to him. For the first time since Ben had walked into the room, Dart's eyes focused on him.

'You've lost sight of the big picture. We are losing the border, and the Scots are licking their lips. If we don't regain control of the North, we will be finished. Forget this farmer, he is a nonsense, but there are thousands more like him and we need to stop them. We need troops in Northumberland to defend the Scottish Border and deter the Arc from aggression.'

As Ben stared at Lucas, he realised that he had made a terrible mistake, and he registered the immediacy of his isolation.

'We must use our military to counter the threat from the North.' Dart added.

Ben's chest was tight, 'so, what are you saying?'

There was a long pause, Ben could see Lucas calculating, but he couldn't help himself, 'I have prepared a force to send North.'

'A force?'

'Yes, Beaston and Harris will lead them, we'll shut down any rebellion in the border country and then we will militarise the border, any incursion from the Scots will receive an appropriate response.'

'An appropriate response! Lucas, you'll lead us into war…'

Dart smiled, 'my friend, your fanciful approach has offered us up to our international competitors like a fat duck. I am protecting you, and your ideology, but I will not wait for you to see I'm right - if I did that, we'd be part of the Arc before you finally see that sometimes strength is the answer.'

Ben felt shaken to the core, he had to escape, he was unprepared for this, and the embarrassment of this betrayal cut him to the quick, if he opened his mouth, the words that fell out would worsen this situation.

'I want detail tomorrow, all of it…' he said, turning quickly before an answer was given.

Ben paused outside the room absorbing his new reality, but the security detail soon returned to show him out. They marched him to the front door and left him on the steps and slammed the door behind him. He began the short walk to the street where Pierre would be waiting. The silence of the mews became eerie. Shivers crawled across his skin. He looked behind him – nothing. Ahead was just the glimmering orange of streetlights reflecting off wet tarmac. He was aware that his steps were stuttering, his heart pounding. *Where was Pierre?*

In the street at the end of the Mews, he looked both ways, but there was no one there. The cars lining the road were unfamiliar, the pavements empty. He felt sick.

There was the snarl of an engine, and he glanced back up the road to see the headlights of a vehicle. It was coming fast. He had no idea what was going on, but he knew it wasn't good. Then he saw Pierre, running at full speed towards him.

'Run! RUN!' Pierre threw his arm to gesture in the opposite direction. 'Don't wait!'

Ben turned and flew off up the street, he felt as though he was gliding over the pavement at a sprinters speed, adrenalin and fear driving him on. As he reached the corner, he looked back to see Pierre crouching down. He aimed his gun at the van as it sped past him. Ben didn't stop to see the result, but he heard the volley of gunshots then the crack and scream of crumpling metal.

He turned the corner and ran on until he was sure the van was no longer behind him. Then he rested his hands on his knees and looked around, panting hard, his eyes darting from shadow to shadow, thoughts rushing through his head as he gathered himself. *Who was that? Dart's people? Surely not – he'd just been in there. On the other hand, some things would certainly be neater if performed outside...* He turned up the collar of his jacket and shoved his hands deep into his pockets. Keeping his eyes on the pavement, he started walking. Pierre had always taught him that in such situations he had to keep moving towards the agreed rendezvous.

Rain fell in thick lumps of water – a typical London drenching. It didn't bother him. His head was spinning. Like a chess player, he tried to anticipate the outcomes of the moves available to him.

He was leaving the quiet residential streets of foreign dignitaries and politicians and was tramping along Park Street towards the corner of Oxford Street. He stopped at the sight of crowds milling around. The shops were closing and people on their way home.

He turned back and almost bumped into a pair of women walking behind him. He saw the wave of recognition drift across their faces. As one of them began to fumble in her handbag, he spun around and walked quickly away into the melee on Oxford Street. With his shoulders hunched and his head down, he seemed to barge every other person he passed. His heart raced. Every time he looked up, he was sure that the passers-by were looking directly at him. His stomach knotted as he imagined the crowd behind staring and pointing, videoing his hunched figure as it bustled away.

He stopped abruptly. Standing in front of him, clipboard in hand, was a woman in her fifties, her mac buttoned up so tightly that he wondered how she could breathe. 'Good evening, sir. Can you spare –' Her look of recognition gave way to excitement. His stomach turned, but he gave her a stern glare and shook his head. Her mouth fell open. Ben side stepped her and continued.

He only managed a few more steps when he met a wall of teenagers blocking the pavement. He looked up in sheer dread of picking his way through the gang. He glanced behind and the woman was talking to someone and pointing in his direction. As he looked forward again, he came face to face with one of the teens – hoodie, smooth skin, hard face. He grinned as he recognised Ben, and he tapped a mate to his right. They pushed towards their country's leader with mischief glinting in their eyes.

Ben breathed deeply and took a step towards the inevitable confrontation, but it wasn't necessary: at the sound of metal sliding against metal, the gang backed off. There was a white van at the side of the road and a door had slid open. Four men in Kevlar vests and armed with automatic weapons jumped out.

'Best come with us, Mr Baines…' said one of them.

Ben took a step backwards, but one of the detail grabbed his arm. Although the action may have looked protective to bystanders, the man's firm grip indicated that Ben had no choice in the matter. He was bundled into the back of the vehicle, and as the door closed behind the last of the paramilitaries, Ben fought the panic that was setting in.

'Who *are* you? What is this?' He looked around their faces, but nobody returned eye contact. He narrowed down the possibilities.

'Are you criminals?' No response. 'The Arc?' Nothing.

'You work for Lucas Dart?'

There was a smirk from one of them but still no eye contact.

As the van raced through the streets, Ben noticed they were keeping off the main thoroughfares. He craned his neck to see where they were going. He was not restrained, and the men made no effort to hide their route from him. He had no idea which direction they had taken until the vehicle screeched onto Piccadilly and around Hyde Park Corner. He clung to his seat as the van lurched into the park.

'Where are you taking me? My security will be- '

The man closest to Ben looked at him with a simper, a blend of sympathy and ridicule. His captors were in complete control. They displayed no stress and gave nothing away.

The van took the road along the south edge of the park but veered sharply right onto the pedestrian walkway towards the Serpentine. They skidded to a halt next to the boating lake and the door was opened with a loud whoosh. Ben found himself clinging to the fabric of the seat as one of the detail ordered him to get out.

'Go on – we're not coming with you…' He nodded at the door.

Ben froze. He couldn't make sense of the situation. He felt no immediate threat but couldn't see how this could possibly end well.

'I don't want to have to throw you out,' the man added.

Ben gulped. His grip slowly eased off the seat and he began to move towards the door. The man closest to it helped him through with a firm nudge. No sooner had his feet touched the tarmac, the door slammed shut and the van sped away. He watched it disappear as he tried to catch his breath.

Left in silence he looked around. The pedalos and rowing boats were moored and all but forgotten, dirty and unloved, bobbing gently in the rippling water. There was nobody around. But when he turned away from the water, his heart skipped a beat once more as he noticed the man sitting on the bench behind him.

'How long have you been there?' Ben asked with as much tedium in his voice as he could muster.

'Long enough to see you squirm.'

'Very elaborate… dramatic…'

'I think, on reflection, you'll realise we got you out of a fairly sticky spot back there…'

'Whatever.' Ben ventured over to take a seat. 'What the hell are you doing in London, let alone England?'

The man was in a tailored suit beneath an unbuttoned overcoat. He didn't look across at Ben. He was sagging in the jowls but immaculately presented: shirt cuffs standing proud no more than an inch from his jacket; shoes polished, worn but well-kept; a Windsor knot in his tie nestled in a perfect stiff collar. Ben had never met him, but he recognised Trevor Eastman – a ghost – the King's personal head of security. He was still one of the cogs that made the world go around.

'We have things to discuss,' he said.

'I can't imagine we have anything to discuss.' Ben replied.

'Ha! You think?'

Ben studied the agent's profile as he gazed across the water, then Eastman turned his head and their eyes met for the first time.

'The King is impotent, holed up in Balmoral. You've seen to that. But remember the Arc has gained a strong ally in him and whatever the polls say, he is just one of a huge number of people who want to see their wealth returned.'

'And?'

'As the real foundation of this great country, we will not allow civil war.'

Ben shook his head incredulously. 'The Establishment is finished. You have no influence here anymore...'

'Aren't you supposed to be the Establishment?' Eastman chortled. 'The Great Leader... the superstar. You really have no fucking clue, do you.' Eastman's eyes were harsh now and Ben felt the sting of ridicule. 'Politics is cyclical. Even when you suppress the opposition, you've only got about three and a half years.'

'Our policies are very successful...'

'Most government policies are. It's the ones that fail that bring you down. And you've failed with Dart.'

Ben put his hands on his knees and stood up. 'I don't have time for this...' He turned away to face the Serpentine; he didn't want Eastman to see humiliation and anger battling for control of his face. 'It has ramifications for all of us,' Ben offered with a conciliatory tone.

'Chaos under the NSO can't be bad for me, or the King.'

Eastman patted the bench next to him; inviting Ben to sit back down. He pulled his overcoat tightly around his stomach as he looked out across the lake again.

'Civil war would be the end of your 'new socialism.'' Eastman smiled. 'Maybe I should be talking to Dart.'

Ben stared at him. 'Are you serious?'

Eastman shrugged and then nodded down at the space next to him again. Ben's mind raced. Could Eastman already be interfering with government? He stayed on his feet and stared at the King's man.

'Sit down, Baines!' barked Eastman abruptly – with a cursory look around after. 'We want to make you an offer…'

'*What?*'

'You'll get out of this mess, unscathed and beyond indictment.'

'You're mad…'

'We want rid of all of you...' The 'ghost' pushed himself up off the bench to stand face to face with Ben. 'We can take him out of the equation by specific force or by public discontent. The latter, however, will be long and bloody. Specific force is the line we are exploring. You cannot overlook the likelihood of civil war. Your military is growing, but what is it? Say two hundred thousand strong.'

Eastman looked at Ben, he was nodding faintly to underline his words, and Ben felt the cogs working, and the situation slipping from his grip.

Eastman continued, 'two million English escaped your reforms to Arc countries. Should Dart be allowed to continue, if a small percentage of those decide to return then civil war would be inevitable!'

Eastman buried his hands in his pockets. He seemed deep in thought, distracted for a moment. Ben found himself hanging on the agent's words.

'It is palatable, but should our country go to war with itself then there will certainly be some messy outcomes… Welsh independence … Scotland annexing Northumberland and Cumbria. That would be unconscionable, an outcome that we cannot allow – cannot even consider.'

'I don't want war,' said Ben. 'I never wanted any of this.'

Eastman took a deep breath. His jowls wobbled as he shook his head. 'Even contentment in the cities is waning because crime is so prevalent. The principal antagonists are your militias. It's as though a criminal gang is governing the country.'

'And if we do choose to address matters with specific force?'

'That's where you could be most useful. The security around Dart is so tight. He doesn't venture out of his inner circle. He rarely appears in public – except when you stitch him up.' Eastman looked at him with a conspiratorial smile.

Ben returned the gesture and nodded remembering the public dressing down at the factory.

'So, having you on the inside obviously has its benefits.' Eastman looked at the tarmac at his feet and kicked a stone. 'But maybe that bird flew when they ousted you.' He pulled his hands from his pockets and stamped his feet restlessly as his gaze returned to Ben.

'No. I'm not done yet.' Ben suddenly felt the breeze up his spine. He shivered and looked around, too.

They fell silent, deep in thought. It was becoming clear that neither had a plan at this stage, and they had spent enough time in the open. Eastman pulled a mobile phone from his pocket and handed it over to Ben.

'There's one number in there, and it's secure. Use it to contact me. You call me. I'll never call you, so never answer it. If it rings, it's compromised. If I need to get a message to you, I'll do it another way.'

Eastman looked around again. 'Little risky you out here all alone, isn't it?' he said with a little spite.

'Don't you worry about me. I'm never alone…'

Pierre stepped out from the shadows twenty yards away. Eastman nodded to the Frenchman. Ben could see Pierre's shoulders rise and fall, still breathing heavy from the foot race to catch them up.

Eastman began to walk away, but then turned back. 'You may have caused this mess, but now you have a chance to help put it right before the country is torn apart.'

The two men stood and looked at each other, their eyes darted towards each other's right hand. Ben's arm moved almost imperceptibly as he felt compelled to offer his hand – but he resisted.

Eastman smiled. 'The situation with these land reforms is more far reaching than you think, you know? Your vision of self-sufficiency needs a co-operative countryside. They're the ones that put the food on our tables and dispose of our rubbish and produce our energy. So, now they've stopped playing ball, all your workers in the cities are beginning to go hungry. You can't take people's farms and put workers on them who don't know what they're doing. You need the landowners to manage it.'

Ben knew all this. He couldn't argue. He simply responded, 'It wasn't meant to be like this…'

'I'm sure you were party to the pact he has signed with the Southern Bloc. England is now, to all intents and purposes, a French colony. They are arming, funding and training Dart's rapidly growing army. Were you any good at history?'

Ben, humiliated by the freedom he had given Dart, made no comment.

'Well… *were* you?'

'Don't fuck around, Eastman.'

'The Vietnam War and the arms race, social justice were the catalysts for the flower power movement. You know… everyone dancing around on acid, screwing each other the nice way. Well, your era will go down as the antithesis of that. Your lovey-dovey, super-righteous ideology has spawned a tyrant who has the potential to unleash bloodshed and tyranny over an innocent population the like of which has not been seen since Netanyahu rolled into Gaza. We all know what happened there…'

'I can see what's happening. Don't underestimate me. I'll find a way to put this right.'

Eastman looked unconvinced, 'most of the people who would react are on the payroll. His first rule is the mixed squads. So, your educated followers are now serving in military units next to violent thugs and criminals who are benefiting from the brutality of the regime. Fear keeps the peace better than any other form of control. He uses the lawlessness to preserve the terror within the rank and file of the NSO, as well as the general population; too many variables in society for idealism.'

'You just stick to creeping around in the shadows. I'll handle him. Just remember one thing… It was me who brought about this revolution. It was me they followed. Not you. Not Dart. No one else.'

'Maybe. But the last twenty years was nothing in comparison to the mess you're in now.'

He turned to walk away and called back over his shoulder, 'You make sure you call me. Do the right thing.'

Ben watched him go. As he reached the road, a black Jaguar pulled up fast and he hopped into the rear seat. It sped off with a low growl as it left the curb. Ben looked around quickly, remembering that he was entirely exposed. He looked at the phone in his hand, slipped it into his coat pocket and began the walk back to his office. Pierre appeared at his shoulder.

'You know that bastard Eastman will kill you.'

'I don't know anything anymore.'

'I think this is not true. I think Lucas will be very interested to hear you have been meeting with the Establishment.'

'You know how it is…' Ben gave his friend a wicked smile.

'*Keep them guessing!*' they said in unison.

Rain lashed their faces as Amber and Stuart roared down the country roads on his powerful quad bike. Amber sat behind, their packs providing a backrest. She was sheltered by his bulk, but her mind raced like the wind that rushed past his shoulders. The gear consisted merely of a full jerry can, a holdall containing two shotguns and a hunting rifle, some dry clothes and some food. Both wore ponchos as shelter from the driving rain, which flapped behind them like the capes of Victorian horsemen.

As night fell, they reached the giant concrete structure of the border wall. The crossing point that Amber and Matty had used days earlier was now an enormous grey barrier. They followed along the foot of the wall westward, where the construction workers had cleared the land. After a mile, the evidence of building became more obvious; they were getting close to the end of the wall as it stood so far.

Stuart slowed to a stop and turned off the engine. They listened to the woodland but heard construction over the wind, a human sound of engines and whistles, and of metal meeting concrete.

'We walk from here,' Stuart said.

'Aye, go around.' Amber pointed into the forest and gestured a wide arc.

He nodded. They grabbed their gear and slipped silently into the darkness of the thick forest. Rain began to fall and the trees above them rocked wildly in the wind that had begun to pick up swiftly. The sound of creaking and cracking wood filled their ears. Amber tugged on Stuart's sleeve.

'Widow makers.' She pointed upwards.

He looked up. An ear-splitting crack of wood sounded through the trees, and he pulled Amber in close to a tree trunk. He grinned.

'Sod's law we get killed by a falling branch.'

Suddenly, Amber tugged him down and they dropped to their haunches. She put a finger to her lips and pointed through the trees. Stuart peered into the gloom and then gave her a blank, enquiring look. She nodded at him to stay down and be quiet.

The NSO guard was almost upon them as she crept low through the undergrowth. She was armed. She must have sensed them, a few feet away but hadn't seen them yet. Stuart edged forward but Amber held him back. The guard stood up straight suddenly and shook her head. She took a couple of steps into the scrub and proceeded to answer the call of nature. Amber and Stuart crouched in the undergrowth behind her. The only thing that might have given them away was the glint of Amber's blade in the sunlight that occasionally pierced the wildly waving trees.

They emerged from the forest on Deadwater Fell, northwest of Kielder and looked out across the wilderness of the border moors. It was bleak, the storm raged from the east, throwing water horizontally across the landscape. Livestock lay behind tumbledown stone walls and the trees that littered the view were bouncing on their roots.

'It's a day's walk!' shouted Amber above the gale.

'We can't stay here!' The gusts tore through the trees and rain spill sloshed through every gully. 'Find a car?'

'Aye,' replied Amber, 'a few miles to Kielder you reckon?'

'Aye, at least. The Pheasant Inn, on the other side of the reservoir?'

'It'll be warm and dry – and it'll be open…'

With a nod, Amber pulled her hood over her head and ducked into the tempest.

The land was austere, with desolate rolling hills cut by small run-off valleys. The occasional tumbledown ruin of a byre was the only evidence that man had trod this place. The black curtains of rain gave it a dark hue under the churning grey sky.

'Should ye not be at work, Billy?' the bearded landlord of the Pheasant Inn said to the regular across the bar.

'Ah dae enough to keep us in beer money… the missus'll sort the rest.'

'It's people like ye they're complainin' aboot, man. Ye have t' pull your weight now you're on the payroll.'

'Give us another Blonde and let me worry about that. I'm paying your wages, aren't I?' He pushed his glass across the bar. 'I never asked for this shit, I was happy signin' on...'

'Don't worry, Billy. I'm not complaining!' said the Landlord.

'Ha, they never planned for the lazy fuckers, did they?' Chirped the other man at the bar.

'Aye, well they wanna pay us then fine,' said Billy. 'Doesn't mean I'm gonna do fuck all!'

'Not likely in this weather,' said the other customer.

The heavy door creaked open a little before the wind caught it and swung it hard against the stone wall of the old pub. The razor cold of the storm instantly overwhelmed the dry heat from the fire and the men at the bar turned towards the door, as the big man pushed hard to shut it against the wind. They stared at the newcomers as they pulled down their hoods. They all knew the girl whose auburn curls tumbled over her shoulders; she stood as tall as the men. They watched in silence, unsure of what was about to happen. Amber Bell's hair seemed to burn in the glimmering firelight. Her face was hard, with a slight grimace, and her eyes were green and wild.

The men at the bar glanced from the landlord to the visitors and back again. Everyone knew the Bells of Carlins Law. Even before the recent trouble started, they were not to be crossed. The regulars moved to the edges of their stools and the landlord's hand drifted under the counter. 'You're not welcome here Amber,' he said.

'Oh aye? Since when's that Matt? Me money was always good enough for you before.'

'Yer father's gonna get us all killed. This pub's NSO...'

'Since when?' she said.

'Since everybody got jobs and these idiots have money to spend in my pub.' The landlord gulped; his eyes flickered between them. He felt sweat gathering on his brow. 'There's nae Formers welcome in this place,' he said.

Stuart raised his hand. 'We dinnae want trouble – just t' be able tae dry off an hour or so, eh?'

'And when the NSO turn up?' Matt shook his head. 'You lot need t' just disappear. There's nae place for you here.' He snatched up the heavy shotgun and pointed it in their direction. The men at the bar pushed back off their stools and backed away to the other side of the room. They all took their drinks.

Stuart was ready. He had been holding his own shotgun inside the bag he was carrying. He allowed the bag to fall with a thud as he trained the gun on the landlord in a flash. The publican took a step back, Amber raised her hands out to the side of her body. Then she slowly raised them out in front of her. 'We don't want this. Whatever you say, we're the same,' she said calmly.

'Not nae more.' The landlord shook his head, panic etched across his face. 'Not since yer father went to war. Go. *Please.*'

Amber glanced across at the regulars then walked slowly towards the bar. She laid her palms down on its surface. The landlord kept the gun aimed at her. The long barrel was almost touching her head. 'You being watched by the NSO?' she asked.

The landlord glanced at the locals. 'Everybody's watchin,' he said softly. '*Now go!*' he shouted for the sake of prying ears.

He pulled the shotgun tight into his shoulder, but Stuart mirrored the act behind Amber.

'Naw,' said Stuart.

The landlord remained stiff, his eyes on Amber. The wind whistled through the door frame. Amber held his gaze.

'What happened to our community?' she asked.

'Politics…' he said, without shifting his aim.

Amber shook her head and raised her hands off the bar.

'We're going,' she said.

The barman held the gun on them as they turned to leave. When they approached the door, he lowered it. 'Get north o' the border. Get yersels safe. There's nae fight left in England!' he called after them, as they ducked back into the storm.

Amber grimaced as they left the warmth and the cold, wet wind lashed her face. Stuart pointed to farm buildings across the road. They tumbled into a byre and hoped the rain might ease. He looked around, inside and out of the old building. Amber watched him go about his business like a ferret on the scent of a rat. Finally, he appeared in the doorway and stopped. Rain dripped from his beard and his hair was flat and heavy against his head. He smiled.

'Nothing?' asked Amber.

'Nothing.'

She turned to the opening that looked out across the road and back towards the pub. She saw one of the locals leave by the same door they had used ten minutes before. He shielded his face from the driving rain with his arm.

'I'm gonna have a wee look at the farm,' said Stuart.

Amber nodded, still watching the man struggle away from the Pheasant Inn. Something important must have called him away from the warmth and the beer. She imagined his wife or his boss calling the pub and him having to leave after a scolding.

She sat in the dry, watching the rain. Stuart had been gone for twenty minutes or so when two cars pulled up outside the pub. A chill washed up her spine and she ducked down to her knees. Seven men got out, pulled guns from the boots of the cars and went into the pub.

Shortly after, they dragged four men from the building, their faces already bloodied. Matt, the

Landlord was one of them. Amber watched with horror as the NSO beat them relentlessly in the street.

Stuart crept back alongside her. 'There's a quad bike in the yard.' he said, as they watched the brutal kicking unfold. As though he could read her mind, his hand came to rest upon her shoulder just as she began to get to her feet.

Across the road, Matt lay in the street as the boots of the enforcers piled into him.

'Naw, lass. We need tae think about your da.'

'What've we come to?' she muttered as they backed away from their vantage point. She climbed onto the back of the quad as she remembered the man leaving the pub – clearly an informer. Everything she had witnessed was etched in her mind – and all brought about by the NSO.

Stuart twisted the throttle. The bike chewed up the sludgy dirt until the deep treads found traction and they pulled out of the farmyard and sped over open countryside.

A short while later they slipped from mud onto tarmac next to an old stone bridge. The rain was easing off, but the cloud cover was thick and dark as a theatre drape. The road was smooth and fast compared to the fields and woodland trails. Amber hunkered down in the cold, breathless from the speeding bike. Stuart made the perfect windbreak. His solid frame was unmoved by the chill, the ups and downs or the shifting camber of the road.

An hour later, they skidded to a stop outside Amber's ruined home. The muscle memory of the vibrations from the bike left her numb. She pulled her stiff legs off it, and stretched out, looking at the charred black lump that was once her home. Stuart put his arm around her as if preparing for tears, but she brushed it away. Taking a few paces towards the charred ruin, she took it all in. The wind blew her auburn curls across her face, and she swept them aside with a decisive hand. 'Let's take the bike up the hill. I know where he'll be.' The quad climbed the steep incline with ease. Unable to compete with the snarl of the engine, Amber directed Stuart with gestures and taps on his shoulders. As they approached the gate into the wood, she jumped off the bike and ran over to it. Her hand came to rest on the sodden moss-covered gatepost, and she felt for the latch. The smell of the cold dusk and damp foliage filled her nostrils. A voice came, almost a whisper on the wind.

'What're y' doin' back here, lass?'

Amber squinted into the gloom. Only five paces in front of her, a shadowy figure appeared in the middle of the path. She pulled the latch over the post, flung back the gate and ran into her father's embrace.

He hugged her tight and long. He couldn't speak and he couldn't let go of her.

Stuart, standing close, rested his hand on his friend's back. Nat finally released his daughter and turned to his old friend. The two men embraced briefly and then Nat stood back, his hands still on his friend's arms.

'I thought y' were going to keep her in Scotland?'

'She's your daughter, pal. Ye ken she'd have come by hersel.'

'Aye.' Nat managed a rare smile and slapped Stuart on the shoulder. 'It's good to see you both.'

Nat looked down at his daughter, for a moment so young again. Then his heart began to pound as he thought about Esme and death and killing whilst looking into Amber's eyes.

'Well, I need a brew and somewhere to get my beauty sleep eh?' said Stuart.

Nat looked at his friend and saw Stuart smile. 'Aye, howay then.' He shook his head and glanced apologetically at his daughter.

They spoke little as their feet whispered through the dewy ferns and mosses of the woodland floor. The early hours brought the cold, cold air. It was on their nostrils like pure oxygen, fresh and invigorating. The night was unmoving and silent. Nat led them to the little valley where he had made his rough camp.

As they ventured down the steep side of the ravine, the moonlight lit the waters of the burn and the smooth round boulders. The grass and trees absorbed the silvery light and appeared as thick black shadows. Amber went to sit by her mother's grave and put a tentative hand on the cold stones.

'Tell me what happened…' she said, without raising her head or looking at Nat; her voice simply drifted across the night.

Nat felt his throat constrict. He began picking up kindling to make a fire as he cleared his throat.

'When I got back to the house, it was a blaze, and she was gone. She wouldn't have known anything love…'

He knew that his tone was not the most convincing. Fortunately, there was no eye contact with her as he busied himself with the fire. *What did it matter anyway?* Nothing would bring her mother back; the details wouldn't change that.

Amber pulled her knees up to her chin and her jumper down over her legs. She sat quietly, resting her arms on her knees. Stuart joined Nat at the fire.

'So, what are things like here?' Stuart said. 'Much fighting?'

'I reckon it's getting worse but, to be honest, other than my bit of daftness, I haven't risked getting out and about much. They're a mixture of thugs and kids. There's some that know what they're doing. I think there's a lot of resistance. I hear gunshots – mostly at night. So, I cannot be the only one fighting.'

Nat flattened the burning sticks with his boot. His friend picked up the pan of water and put it next to the fire. Nat unzipped his jacket and closed his eyes for a moment as the flames warmed his face.

'At least yer dress sense has improved,' said Stuart.

Nat opened his eyes, looked at Stuart and then down at the shirt he was wearing. 'Oh, aye… Was at Claire's a couple of days ago…'

Stuart stared at him intensely. 'She alright? She safe?'

Nat leaned his shoulder across and nudged him. 'They shot me, and she patched me up. She's fine – don't worry. Keeping her head down.'

'We've got to get her with us, make sure she stays safe.' Stuart's eyes were embroiled in the flames of the catching fire whose orange glow washed over his rugged features.

'We'll get her. After I finish with the bastards that killed Esme. Then we make a break for Scotland until all this sorts itself out.'

'It might not be sae easy for ye now after what ye did. When all's said and done, it was murder.'

'Aye well… I never wanted to be famous. I'll drift back into obscurity long before this misery is over.'

'Ye can never tell how these things pan out. There's resistance to the regime in Cornwall, Wales and all ower the

North.'

'Is that what the news said?'

Stuart flashed him a look, before turning back to the fire. 'Aye, that's what it said…'

Both men chuckled into the fire, as Amber crept over and nestled herself between the two hulking figures. Nat added a pot of water to the flames. They watched the orange wisps lick the pan and the water began to steam.

Nat put his arm around his daughter as the grey-blue light of dusk was overwhelmed by the dark of night. 'It's good to see ye, my lamb.'

Half a mile from the little valley where Nat, Amber and Stuart sat sipping hot coffee in the fresh air a ghostly figure floated silently across the farmyard and into one of the barns. The place smelled of dust and diesel oil. He felt his way across the dark interior looking for a safe vantage point and soon discovered the ladder leading up to the hay loft. The rickety wooden staircase creaked wildly with every step as he climbed. Once at the top, he found a place where the joists were much thicker – he couldn't risk an injury from crashing through rotten floorboards – and he crouched over to where the dawn light would filter through the gaps in the shuttered window.

He took the lightweight sniper's rifle from across his back and the silenced revolver from the holster under his arm. He laid out the weapons, so their barrels were parallel with his thighs. After two decades living the horrors of other people's wars, he had developed an obsession with detail. It kept him alive.

He bore the scars of a life spent in solitude, mostly behind enemy lines. He stretched and rubbed his leg and back where the damp and cold of the Northumbrian climate made his bones ache in the places where steel plates held him together.

He did not consider himself a bad man – merely a professional, committed to the dispassionate and unswerving execution of his clients' instructions. He pulled the phone from its case on his chest and dialled the only number he ever called these days. It was answered immediately.

'Things have changed, Tom,' Baines spoke urgently; he had not used the agent's first name in years.

'Tell me,' whispered the spectre in the darkness of Bell's barn.

'The farmer, you need to extract him, get him north of the border…or quietly gone.'

'Won't be straight forward.'

'Doesn't matter, it's imperative. Dart is inciting violence, courting it to create instability.'

'That'll make the Scot's nervous.'

'Exactly.' There was a pause on the line, then Ben added, 'I met with Trevor Eastman – or should I say he snatched me.'

'And?'

'Offered me a deal.'

'Let me guess… They want rid of Dart?'

'About sums it up.'

'Ha! Well, he'll support you while you're useful.'

'It'll never happen. After Dart, I'll be easily defeated.'

'I'll do my best with the farmer; I'll head over there in the morning.'

'Okay, Tom. And look… I'll see you when this sorts out, yes?'

Tom hung up without answering. The barn was silent but for a few boards rattling in the cool breeze that softened the smell of the farmyard to a sweet aroma. He ripped open a packet of oat biscuits, peeled back the lid on a small tin of pate, and he ate.

Lucas Dart reclined in a large leather armchair by the ornate Victorian fireplace in his office. He took a huge bite from a fat pastrami and gherkin sandwich. He wiped the mustard and pickle that seeped from the corners of his mouth as he listened to an animated Bill Ludlum through the mobile phone.

'I need heavier weapons and some people who can handle them – and themselves! I mean, this is ridiculous. It's like the Wild West up here. I've got insurgents picking us off at every step. They've infiltrated my teams – they seem to know what we're up to all the time. Then I've got that psycho up on the hill. I can't even get close to him because my teams don't have the first idea! This is making a mockery of your security machine, Mr Dart, and I'm losing men to the rebels while listening to stories of this living fucking legend in the hills!'

Bill took a breath before adding, 'we need to step up the reforms, I need manpower and weapons.'

Dart swallowed his sandwich and licked his lips. 'No more negotiating with landowners... if they haven't come across yet, they're not going to. Burn them out, all of them.'

Dart wiped his fingers on a napkin and sat back in his chair as he listened to the silence from Ludlum.

'I have a small job for you also...' he said, 'Find that fucking hack who did that report on our farmer and nullify his future output.'

'Nullify his output?'

'Use your imagination son, I don't want to see him on the telly again.'

'I'm not a damned assassin! That's a journalist, do you understand what you're asking?'

'I'm not asking...' he paused to let it sink in, '... anything. You do whatever you feel is necessary, but if I see him on the television again, I'll know where your loyalties lie.'

Dart hung up, sat up again and grabbed his sandwich.

He stuffed another mouthful to capacity.

TWELVE

Rory Henderson took off his damp mac in the cramped hallway of his rather decrepit cottage. As he caught himself in the mirror, a broad grin spread across his face and the pride oozed out. He made guns with his fingers and pretended to shoot with a 'pow, pow'. He chuckled to himself and shook his chubby head. He no longer cared about how pokey the cottage was, with its dusty furniture, broken gas fire and ancient radiators. His career was on the up, and it was all due to that fortuitous meeting with Baines. The moment the leader joined him on the street in London was the moment his bosses began to take notice of him. Now he was the lead reporter on all things NSO and being local to the Nat Bell story gave him further leverage – his stars were aligning, and he was only just beginning to believe it.

He stepped through the small galley kitchen and into the garage, where he kept a tall fridge. Successful or not, he still had to eat. As he opened the fridge door and reached out for the ham, he heard the click of the lock on the front door.

Faint footsteps padded into the sitting room. He had given his girlfriend keys only a couple of days before and now she was surprising him at lunchtime. He suddenly felt like one of those guys he wished he had been when he was younger: successful, popular, paired off with a gorgeous girl. Dare he say it? *Cool.*

Instead of calling out, he would savour the experience. She knew he was coming home; he had only spoken to her half an hour or so earlier. Maybe, just maybe, she was heading to the bedroom, and he wasn't going to spoil her surprise. He crept back to the kitchen and peeked around the door. He glimpsed the figure creeping slowly and quietly into the sitting room.

He jerked his head back into the garage, his brain locking into an alternative reality. His heart had stopped momentarily, then started again at an alarming rate; he was shaking and couldn't control his breathing. The surprise visitor was not his girlfriend; it was a man dressed in black and carrying a gun.

He searched the garage for an escape route. Shelving blocked the garage door – he had only ever used the space for storage. There was a manhole cover, no windows, and the big fridge – he wasn't going to hide in there. His thoughts were muddled – too many for his brain to digest. He couldn't move. He was closer to the front door than the man moving further into the house, but his muscles wouldn't react to the synapses his brain was releasing. It was as though his feet were set in concrete. The man looking for him had a gun anyway; he couldn't outrun a bullet. He began to cry, silently. The tears rolled down his cheeks as he stood with his back to the wall, ears pricked to hear every creak and squeak from the old cottage.

He picked up the heaviest thing that he could find within arm's reach. So, he stood to the right of the door waiting to club the intruder over the head with a pitchfork when he came in from the kitchen. His feet were apart, and the fork was in both hands and pointed at the open doorway. He was like a soldier in the trenches waiting to run an enemy through with his bayonet.

The seconds felt like minutes, minutes like hours. He could hear hushed creeks and faint bumps as the stranger worked his way systematically through the house. Every so often it fell silent for what seemed too long, and he thought the man had left. But then, the ghostly tremors would reverberate through the building once again and his throat would constrict. His eyes were wide, and his ears strained as his senses reacted to the paralysing fear.

In his mind's eye, Rory followed the intruder through the rooms in his house. He pictured the intruder moving up the stairs and along the landing to Rory's bedroom at the far end of the house. He watched the dust drift across the open doorway, as he tried to block out the tick of the grandfather clock in the hall.

Then, with a barely audible click-crimph, the cupboard door opened in the second bedroom. The next sound was the loose board in the third bedroom followed quickly by the cabinet doors. The intruder was no longer being so careful. The footfalls above his head in the bathroom were no longer soft but regular. Dust fell from the ceiling of the garage after every step. He tried to swallow but his throat was dry. His stomach churned and he began to worry that he would be sick.

As the last footfall left the bathroom, the house fell silent. Rory waited for the next sound. He could feel the sweat beading on his forehead as his eyes and ears strained. But there was nothing, just the tick of the clock and the birdsong outside. He waited… five minutes… ten minutes and still the torture continued. He twisted the pitchfork in his grip to relieve the ache in his arms.

He began to think the man had left. His heart began to settle slightly, and his muscles relaxed. The pitchfork dipped from the horizontal. Then came the scuff of the intruder's boot on the stone steps leading to the garage. Rory fought to catch his breath.

The barrel of a handgun with a silencer attached appeared at the doorframe, followed by the hand and arm that gripped it. Rory's survival instinct kicked in. He lunged forward with the pitchfork at his would-be assailant's gun. The prongs of the fork thrust either side of the intruder's fist, but the force was enough to push the man's gun and arm hard to the left, pinning it against the door frame for a split second before the wrist bones gave way to the pressure, and snapped with a horrific crack. The man yelled in pain as his weapon clattered to the stone floor. Rory swung back the pitchfork and then brought the edge of the prongs down on the back of the man's head. The intruder fell prone to the floor. Rory jumped over his assailant and ran through the kitchen and out of the front door.

The cul-de-sac outside seemed empty as he ran down the hill towards the centre of town, still hefting the pitchfork. The narrow, enclosed road made the ordeal more terrifying. Small, terraced cottages stood to his right and a high stone wall to his left; his only escape route was to push on ahead, praying that the man in his garage would make a slow recovery and didn't have a car close by.

He was gasping for breath, by the time he reached the junction with the main road through Hexham. The Fox and Hounds pub was in front of him and four hundred yards to the left was the police station, which had now become the NSO command centre for the area. To the right was the centre of town and the market square from where he had made his report the day before. There were few cars around and even fewer people.

He stumbled right, running aimlessly towards the town centre. A muddy black pickup truck with a huge bull bar and six lamps mounted above the cab swerved alongside the curb. Rory fell back against the rough stone wall and levelled the pitchfork as the passenger door swung open to reveal a friendly face. Matty Rowell was leaning across the cab from the driver's seat.

'What's up, Rory? You chasing a giant out of town?'

Rory looked fearfully at Matty, his chest heaving, his limbs aching. Then he dropped the pitchfork onto the pavement and hauled himself up into the pickup. 'Go, go, go!' He screamed.

The big truck growled as it hastened away from the curb and Rory slumped into the passenger seat, ducking down as they passed the police station. They left Hexham on the Haydon Bridge Road.

'What's going on?' said Matty.

'They came for me – *they came for me!* A journalist!

How the fuck is that? He was going to kill me! I saw his gun!'

Rory tried to settle his breathing as best he could and wiped away the tears from his face.

'Who was it?' Matty asked, calmly, as if he knew full well what the answer was.

'They came to my house...' Rory panted.

'Look, I'll get you safe. Ye'll have t' come with the rebels now. Ye'll not be safe in Hexham anymore. They obviously don't want anybody t'hear what ye have to say. They're killing people in the countryside. Ye could be our voice...'

'All I want to do is bloody survive. I don't want any of this!'

'Tough shit. This is life now. Ye think any of us saw this coming?'

A short while later the pickup pulled into a driveway.

'The woman who lives here is called Claire,' Matty said. 'She's a friend. She's had to make the same journey as you. Tried to stay out of things for as long as she could – tried to give the NSO the benefit of the doubt. Now she's one of us and helps us any way she can. Bide here with Claire. Tell her I brought you and tell her your story. Ye'll be safe here. Somebody'll come for you in the afternoon to take you north. I'll be seein' you soon!'

Rory climbed down from the truck. Matty pulled away and headed back towards Hexham. Rory walked nervously to the front door, looking behind him with every other step. He feared the wind in the trees and the gravel under his feet, convinced that someone would attack him from the shadows at any moment. He rapped on the delicate stained-glass panel.

The urgency of the knocking worried Claire. She kept to the shadows, squinting to see who was behind the wobbly antique glass. Then she recognised the sweaty red face looking anxiously through the window.

She knew Rory a little; they spoke if they met in the pub, said hello if they passed in the street, but they were acquainted rather than friends and she was a good twenty years his senior. Rory was terrified, that much was clear. She rushed to the door and pulled it open. He almost fell into the house, blurting out a string of words that Claire had to decipher.

'Somebody's trying to kill me... so scared!' she made out.

'Calm down Rory. You need to breathe. You're in shock.' She glanced outside before shutting the front door gently.

With rapid, shallow breaths, Rory leaned against the wall and then slid slowly down it until he sat on the floor, twitching nervously.

'Come into the kitchen, eh? I'll get the kettle on.'

She put her hand gently under his arm and helped him up before guiding him into the kitchen where he slumped down on the worn old sofa that nestled in the corner next to the fire. He appeared to be distracted by the dancing flames.

'Tell me what happened,' Claire said.

'Simple... I went home for my lunch. I thought it was Jenny! I went to have a bloody look and there he was... some damn NSO psycho with a gun.'

'It could have been a burglar...'

'Like hell! He was in the house for a good twenty minutes. Didn't touch my stuff and you tell me how many burglars creep around with silencers on their guns.'

'Ok, so you got away –'

'I think I might have killed him.'

'What? ...Rory?'

'I hit him so hard on the side of the head with a pitchfork... I was scared.'

'Who do you think it could be?'

'NSO definitely – because of my piece on Nat Bell? But I don't get it… I mean I had a call from Ben Baines direct to my phone for God's sake! Why would he –'

'What about Nat?'

'You haven't been watching the news, have you? He's waging a one-man war on the regime. He's slaughtered about ten of them already. And by *slaughtered*, I mean testing the limits of barbarity!' For a moment, Claire was listening to a journalist again. It was almost as if Rory had forgotten his own problems. Then his face dropped again. 'I asked some questions about why a man like Nat would start killing people. It aired this morning and then, two minutes after I get home, this happens.'

Claire almost told Rory about Nat's visit but decided to keep quiet. She was beginning to grasp the gravity of developments and the less Rory knew, the less he could say, which might keep him safe and would protect her and Nat.

'Matty said he was going to send someone back for me, to take me north. The Rowell brothers are up in Wooler with hundreds of rebels. The NSO has no presence up there – it's safe. I know what's happening here and it's become dangerous for all of us. Hexham is becoming a crucial piece of land for the regime. There's word the Scots are arming the rebels and the NSO are sending troops north. War is coming, and Hexham is going to be the front line.'

'How d'you know all this?' In truth, there was little she hadn't heard from Matty once she had decided to cross her own personal Rubicon and join the rebels.

'It's my job…'

There was a knock at the front door. She looked at Rory. She wasn't expecting anyone, and it was surely too soon for Rory's pick-up. He began to gasp for breath again. Claire pointed to the stairs without a word. Rory stole across the room and tiptoed up the stairs, taking two at a time. Claire heard the familiar clicks of the landing cupboard opening and shutting again. She turned back to the front door, shaking and struggling to collect her thoughts. There was a more impatient knock. She shook herself down and tried to clear her mind of fear.

'Hang on! I'm coming!'

She opened the front door to four, grim-looking men, each one carrying a gun. The closest, a thickset, unshaven brute, stepped forward into her personal space. He put one foot inside the door. She tried to slam it closed, but it was too late.

He spoke in a quiet Liverpudlian accent. 'We know all about you, bitch.' With that, he smashed the butt of his gun into Claire's face, knocking her to the floor. The taste of her own blood was the last thing she remembered.

Lucas hunched over the telephone. He had an elastic band between thumb and forefinger, and he twisted it, watching the elastic curl at the ends like a worm as it wound tight. 'Tell me, you've dealt with him.'

'Who? We have the journalist, not the farmer.'

'Well, it's a start. What's wrong with you, Bill? You sound off – tired or something.'

'Had an accident. Broke my arm. It's nothing.'

'Hmm, you tell me if it's getting too much for you. We need to step up the land reform. No time for you to slow down, remember, no more negotiation. We need to secure Northumberland now.'

'I need more men. There are more rebels daily. We took four today who had accents from Birmingham or somewhere. This isn't a local thing anym –'

'What are you doing with the prisoners?'

'We are moving them to a holding facility in Slaley.'

'I'll have more men with you soon. You contain the rebels and get those damn farms cleared of their occupiers.' He put the phone down and turned to the men who sat on the other side of his desk.

The first was a man in his mid-forties with dark, cropped hair, pale skin and a severe expression. Brigadier Quentin Harris was the army's principal instrument of attrition. No one else could reduce enemy numbers like the soldiers under his command. No matter what the odds, Harris's forces ground enemies to dust like a glacier over bedrock. The second man was Harris's boss, Major General Anthony Beaston, a cold and merciless man. Beaston was wiry, not an ounce of fat on his ageing body or his bony face. He appeared in a constant state of alert, his sharp eyes skimming his surroundings like a bird of prey in search of its next meal. He knew the art of war and he understood both the advantages and the means of stealing another man's hope.

'You two will leave tonight. Join your troops at Aldershot Garrison and get up to The Borders. Station yourselves at Albemarle. The mission is simple... secure Northumberland and Cumbria under NSO control. Then, create a militarised zone along the border to stop the Arc medalling in our country.'

'We know the mission, Mr Dart,' General Beaston said, in distinctive nasal tones, 'and have no doubts about the result. We need answers, however, to two questions.' His eyes remained unnervingly trained on Dart.

'I'm listening...,' said Dart.

'What are your views with regards to the local population? And should the instance arise that we are facing Scottish troops, do we open fire on them?'

Dart appraised the men in front of him and they gazed back at him without emotion. He smiled. 'Do whatever you must to win.'

When Claire came to, there was blood caked around her lips and a metallic taste in her mouth. The swelling felt heavy on the side of her face. Disorientated and in pain, she had little strength to face the coming hours. With eyes open wide she could see nothing but blackness. Her mind raced: was she blind or simply in a darkened room? She opened her mouth to speak, but the dull ache exploded into unbearable shards of agony from her jaw. The pain travelled through her skull and down her spine and made her whimper. The enforcers had broken her jaw. There was a shuffling in the darkness.

'I'm sorry Claire... I – I...' Rory's hollow murmur petered out; there was nothing to say.

She didn't answer. She lay slumped in the chair, her head lolling, her backside numbed by the hard plastic. She was paralysed by fear. One thought weighed heavily in her mind: she'd sooner be dead than face the door to that room opening again.

THIRTEEN

The fire crackled as the sun rose and its rays began to find their way into the little valley. The heat from both sun and fire bathed Nat's face. He'd felt the cold the night before and the warmth was a welcome luxury. A blackbird had joined their party and danced around the camp in search of an easy meal. The burn's constant babble seemed louder, more overpowering, this morning. He had woken in a low mood.

He gazed over at his daughter. She was nestled into the grassy bank, at ease in the rough camp. She concentrated on sharpening her hunting knife. In the early grey light of the day, they had been cleaning all the weapons they had amassed.

The crack of Stuart's rifle sent the message that they would be eating meat. Father and daughter did not speak while they worked; neither were good communicators. He knew from her eyes that she had questions; and if he was honest with himself, he knew what they were.

As her vivid green eyes connected with his, the best response he could muster was a thoughtful, reassuring smile before his attention shifted back to what he was doing. The emotion was all too raw for him, but it was all the communication Amber needed. Tears rolled silently down her cheeks as she nodded to him. She wiped them away with the sleeve of her waxed jacket, swept her tight ringlets away from her face and resumed sharpening her knife, with renewed ferocity.

He watched the pot bubbling on the fire, tossing the tea bags around as it boiled. Then it seemed as if the earth hiccupped. The pan of water went over, dousing the fire and sending grey smoke and steam billowing upwards. He looked up into the trees. Roosting crows flew from their perches and the warbled clucks of pheasants filled the air as a seismic wave jolted the forest to life. Then came the rumble of a distant explosion. Nat looked at Amber and without a word they leapt to their feet and started running to the nearest vantage point at the edge of the forest.

They moved quickly through the thick dewy undergrowth; the smell of the fresh morning woodland was rich in peat and leaves. Stuart came bounding out of the trees with four rabbits over his shoulder. 'What the hell was that?' he shouted. They ran together with ease and fluidity through the barrage of foliage and hazards the forest threw at them.

They reached the edge of the wood and looked west onto the wide, open expanse of the valley. In the distance, where the ugly chimneys of the chipboard factory stained the skyline, they saw the source of the blast. A huge black mushroom cloud billowed above the factory. Flames engulfed the buildings and chimneys. The huge piles of wood chip were burning, too. An irrepressible inferno overwhelmed the site.

Nat's eyes surveyed the valley he was so used to admiring. He had never been bored or unmoved by its beauty and ever-changing detail. The drama was no longer natural. Man had placed his boot on the heart of his valley and the scene before him was like Armageddon. To the east, black smoke continued to drift upwards from the ashes of the paper factory, which had been burning for days. In front of them stood the ruin of his home. Burnt to the ground with a collection of vehicles littering the drive – and now this latest devastation.

He looked across at Stuart. 'That's no accident.'
'Looks like war is here, my friend.'
'Rebels, you reckon?'

'I hope so.' Stuart smiled and nodded towards the huge factory burning in the distance. 'If the government think that's a farm, we're all fucked.' He looked out over the rugged country, absorbing the inferno in the distance. 'Clever, though. The NSO'll soon lose support, if they cannae provide people with work. Let's go intae town, make contact with the rebels. Maybe we can help one another.'

'Agreed!' said Amber enthusiastically, setting off down the hill without waiting for a response.

Nat watched his daughter walk away, and then he looked at his old friend. 'Why's she always bolshy when you're about?'

'Aye, right! Just like her father - a right pain in the arse!' Stuart nudged Nat with a big shoulder. 'C'mon.'

The ghost had enjoyed the relative luxury the barn had offered. He had even felt comfortable enough to make himself a brew and eat his beloved flapjack right where he had slept. As his teeth had plunged into the rich oats, the barn had shaken under the seismic waves of the explosion, then the boom had struck. He jumped up knocking his tea over in the process. He cursed himself; he should have left the barn before eating.

Through the cracks in the timber cladding, he could see the inferno that was the chipboard factory. He knew the disturbance would stir the farmer, so he eked his view around through a small slit he had found, his cheek pressed hard against the dusty wood, and he waited.

Sure enough, his subjects appeared at the edge of the wood. As they strode down the hill, his mind found its gear and he turned to his predetermined plan.

The two farmers caught up with Amber as they walked down the hill. Each a few yards apart and in a line, half force of habit, half to spread themselves as a target – just in case.

By the burned-out house was an ever-increasing choice of cars. Since they now moved silently, Stuart gestured to Nat that there were keys in one of the cars. Nat nodded and held up the rabbits that Stuart had passed to him earlier. He turned towards the barn.

He froze as soon as he entered it. A shiver ran down his spine and he looked around briefly. Then he put his head down and moved along the cluttered gangway between his farm equipment, the route he knew so well. His heart beat fast, and his mind raced, but he stuck to the task. As he hung the rabbits on the meat hooks that protruded from the rafters of the mezzanine, a drop of moisture dotted his hand. He managed to control the urge to look upwards. Instead, he wiped the drop across his nose and recognised the familiar aroma of tea.

He knew the feeling of being watched, and it wasn't Esme from beyond the grave. The plastic pop in the trees he'd heard the other night… tea dripping from the rafters of his barn. Ghosts didn't need night sights, and they didn't drink tea.

Tom had cursed his carelessness as the farmer approached the barn. The tea was spilled, so he stood his cup on the floor and looked up at the metal frames hanging from the roof on which the farmer had stored planks of wood. He reached up and grabbed the end of the wooden planks. He kicked his legs up and over his head and onto the planks. He shuffled forward on his front to find that he had a clear view of the wooden stairs and most of the ground floor of the barn. He quietly drew his handgun, screwed on the silencer and pressed the barrel to the plank next to his head. He lined up the shot so that should someone discover his cup and walk over to pick it up, the bullet would find his target.

He controlled his breathing and waited, *watching*, as he always did.

Bell paused as he entered the barn. The spectre wasn't surprised. He ran through the plan in his head and felt his muscles tense as Bell approached. The farmer weaved his way through the machinery and hung some rabbits from a beam – then he was gone.

The ghost slumped and the silenced pistol relaxed in his hand. He leaned his forehead down on the planks. At first, he was baffled. Then he let out a brief chuckle before raising his head again. He had been giving this farmer too much respect.

Amber, squeezed into the back seat of the car Stuart had chosen to drive them into Hexham. Then she watched her father scrunch into the cramped passenger side of the fifteen-year-old Japanese sports car. His knees pulled up tight to his chest, he looked across at Stuart as if to say *great choice!* Stuart caught her eyes in the rear-view mirror; he had that look of mischief and she couldn't help but laugh.

He turned the key, gunned the accelerator and they raced down the long drive. As they descended the hill, she surveyed the livestock grazing either side of the driveway. Then they came to the end of their land, the little car vibrated violently over the cattle grid, and they sped out into the country road.

The thick black smoke rose in plumes up into the vast sky and drifted high along the valley creating a menacing darkness to the day. Stuart drove fast. The little car responded well, flying over the rises of the military road with Hadrian's Wall snaking along the wild country to their right. Every drop and dip in the road sent Amber's stomach through her mouth. She felt sick but knew better than to mention it; a suggestion to Stuart that he might slow down would probably have the opposite effect. She sucked it up and concentrated on the horizon.

It was no time before they all lurched to the right to take a sharp turn onto the narrow road leading into Oakwood. Her dad's hand grabbed the dashboard. Amber knew the driving was making him nervous too, but he'd never give Stuart the pleasure of asking him to slow down.

They were about two hundred yards from Rowell's driveway, where her dad had told them he'd seen the articulated truck barricading the entrance. Now, there was a bus in the familiar blue livery of the local bus company parked at the end of the drive. It had rudimentary grills attached to the windows and metal skirts over the wheel arches. It had to be NSO. Stuart slowed the car rapidly. While her dad's arm took the strain against the dashboard, Amber pressed tight against her taut seat belt as they coasted past the end of the drive at walking speed to assess the scene.

A big JCB had rammed Rowell's trailer out of the way. Both vehicles stood dormant on the grass to the side of the drive. In the distance, they could see men swarming around the farmhouse, itself on fire and smoke billowed from the first-floor windows. The men around the house were merely watching the blaze unfold with their guns at ease. As the NSO bus eclipsed their view of the house, Amber saw three men standing in front of it. Their stares were long and hard, their three heads following the car in unison as it slowly passed them by. Weapons hung across their chests. The beaten-up black-market hardware had gone; they carried shiny new semi-automatic assault rifles. The NSO were getting organised.

Stuart glanced at her dad. 'Do we need tae go and see the factory?'

'No. Turn around down here.' He turned to Amber, his eyes intense. 'You stay put.'

Stuart headed into the side of the road and then spun the wheel to full lock and the car turned easily. Heading back towards Rowell's farm, they drifted slowly into the entrance.

'Make sure the car's side-on to them,' her dad growled.

He lowered his window as they pulled into the driveway and leaned his head out as if to ask what was going on. Two of the guards began to approach. They were waving them on. Her dad cupped a hand to his ear.

'Move along!' one of the guards shouted.

Her dad held his handgun in his lap, gripping it tightly as the men approached – all three of them now. Every step they took made them bigger targets. Amber's heart beat fast as she realised her dad's intentions – he was watching and waiting for the right moment.

The little car was still rolling slightly, and Amber heard the purr of the engine and the crunch of gravel under the tyres. Then there was a slight squeak of brakes as it pulled to a stop. The guard leading the approach raised his gun. He was ten feet away at this point. There was a flash of recognition in the guard's face as he grasped the fact, he was about to face the 'killer from the hills.' But rather than pointing his gun at the car and firing, he lurched toward his comrade, grabbing his arm to warn him of the danger.

Amber's father whipped his handgun up to the open window and fired two rounds into the chest of the lead guard. His legs crumpled beneath him, while he stared at her dad, stunned by the brutal reality of it all.

The third man came directly into Nat's angle of fire, and he fired twice more. He clearly missed with the first shot but hit the man in the cheekbone with the second, the small round ripping through his skull. He was dead before his head bounced on the gravel with a dull crunch.

The guard on the right was alone now, paralysed with fear trying to click the safety off his weapon, but his thumb couldn't flick the switch. She watched Nat train his gun on the nameless man and shoot him in the chest. He fell on his backside, slumped on the drive, and stared blankly at the car.

'Howay, let's move!' Nat growled. 'Quickly, now!' As the three of them scrambled out of the car, the life drifted from the hunched enforcer, and the last ragged breath passed his blood-soaked lips.

Amber's dad stepped over to the body and kicked it to the ground with a fleeting glance over to her; a dead body lying down was somehow more palatable than one sitting. He bent down and picked up an assault rifle and handed it to Amber. He grabbed one for himself and Stuart took the third.

'Stay by the car, lass,' her dad ordered. 'You shoot anybody who comes behind us, now. Okay?'

'Aye' she said, looking at the assault rifle in her hand.

He put his hand on her shoulder. 'If I could go back in time lamb… I didn't want this...'

Amber raised her head, and her eyes met his. 'What they did to us…' She nodded towards the house. 'Go.'

Nat moved towards the farm as smoke billowed across the scene. He opened fire on the bus, peppering the wheels and engine compartment with bullets. Stuart had positioned himself at the gates to the house. Nat joined his friend at the other side of the gate, and he started taking single shots at the NSO men at the house. They began falling to the ground – one, two, three down even before the confusion set in.

At first, the NSO started setting up positions to direct fire at the house, thinking that was where the shots were coming from. Nat felled another four before the NSO fighters realised the shots were coming from behind them. There must have been about twenty men to begin with, now it was closer to ten. The ostentatious stone gateposts that Rowell had built protected the farmers. Nat had laughed when he had seen them for the first time, now he rejoiced in their presence as the NSO rounds whizzed, cracked and ricocheted off the gaudy stone. Only a few of the enemy dug into positions, the rest ran aimlessly for cover or straight at Nat and Stuart in panic. It was a massacre. Nat counted five NSO still breathing by the time Stuart managed to attract his attention.

'What're we up tae? We need to get out of here!'

'I want them dead,' Nat responded, wild eyed. 'What if Rowell is in that house?'

'Well, we cannae just sit here. There could be others comin'! Amber's back there. Think, Nat, *think!*' Stuart shouted over the sporadic fizzing rounds. It was chaos, even in such a relatively small firefight.

The clang of shots hitting the bus behind them rang in their ears. Nat knew his friend was right; it was only a matter of time before one of the stray bullets fired true. He took the lead, bursting from cover as best he could, and leaping behind the trailer that the NSO had barged away from the gates.

He lay on his belly between the rear wheels of the trailer and the corrugated iron sheeting that skirted along it. He had a good open view over the gardens in front of the house. He could see only the lower back of an NSO soldier lying flat behind a raised flower bed. He lined up the shot and squeezed the trigger twice. The red mist of a hit rose from the target.

He raised his eye from the sights and scanned the gardens once again. He saw the muzzle flash of a weapon in the darkness of a small shed. It was to the far left of the garden. Nat's gun swung the small arc with the accuracy of a machine. He pumped four rounds into the dark space without hesitation. He watched patiently for a few minutes – no response. Then he saw a flash of movement: two men ran towards the burning house in a desperate effort to escape the hell. He dropped both bodies with three shots that cracked across the farmyard. Stuart caught Nat's eye, but the Scotsman's despondent expression, did nothing to assuage Nat's hunger for blood.

The gunfire stopped and the principal sound was once more the burning farmstead as it creaked and snapped. The breeze pulled the thick black smoke low over the little theatre of war. At least fourteen bodies lay in the dirt.

Stuart whistled at Nat, a short shrill bleat. He had joined him at the trailer and now he pointed over to the right where a soldier had tied a white rag around the end of his weapon. He waved it from behind the stone wall that separated the drive and front gardens from the field to the north. Stuart looked at his friend and then watched as Nat rested his chin on his rifle for a spell and pondered the situation.

After a few moments, Nat raised his head. 'What're you doin', son?' He pulled the weapon in tight and focussed his eye down the sights on the rag. Stuart scanned the rest of the gardens for a double cross.

'We want to surrender. There's three of us. Nobody wants to fight – please.'

'Should've thought about that before burning down that farm!' Nat's grip stiffened on his assault rifle, and he continued to ponder his next target. 'Was there anybody in there?'

'Dinnae, you shoot that laddie,' whispered Stuart, with as much strength behind the words as he could muster.

'No! Nobody, I swear,' came the desperate answer to Nat's question.

'How old are ye, son?' called Stuart.

'We're all seventeen.'

'C'mon Nat, ye're no' a fuckin' monster...' Stuart implored.

Nat turned towards him with a look of thunder. Stuart, fearful of his friend, instinctively pulled his weapon ready. Nat glared at him, but the steel gradually left his eyes.

He spun back to the white rag.

'What are you doing out here?' he called out.

'Conscripts. Just finished two months' training… They brought us up here… We don't want to fight you!' The voice cracked with fear.

Stuart watched Nat's face. it was impossible to read his thoughts. He was determined to restrain his friend from taking the retribution any further.

'Okay!' Nat called out. Leave your weapons. Hands in the air, then walk slowly towards us.'

Stuart tensed as the three youths appeared from behind the wall.

'We have two of you lined up,' Nat growled, 'so no gambling. Two of you would die in less than a second.'

Stuart could hear the tuc-tuc-tuc of a chopper's rotor blades. It was not the dull thudding of a military helicopter. He guessed it was a news crew. 'We've got tae get goin', afore ye're face ends up on the news again!' he said.

'Get a move on!' Nat shouted.

The fearful lads hurried their steps, trying to walk faster without making any sudden movements. Stuart watched them approach with one nervous eye on his friend, unsure whether he would lose it and open fire at any moment. The three drew closer, stepping timidly towards them.

Nat kept his weapon trained on the three youths. 'Keep walking back to town and on home from there. If we see you again, I'll kill ye – no questions, no second chance.'

They didn't need to be told twice. They walked quickly past the mangled bus and past Amber, their speed increasing if anything. They started out in single file down the narrow country road. It fell away lazily to the left and there were grass ditches to either side, thick with brambles. Dense coniferous woodland flanked the eastern side of the road. To the west was a thick hawthorn hedge raised above the ditch on an overgrown grass bank. In the distance, the spire of St John Lee church rose above the beautiful ancient trees that gave Oakwood its name. The sun was streaming through the cracks in the clouds and brightened all before them with a golden glow.

The three NSO conscripts were a hundred yards away when the loud cracks echoed across the fell. The farmers hit the floor, but whoever fired the weapon was not aiming at them. As they looked, the boys were falling into the bramble covered ditch to their right.

Nat scoured the trees from where the shots must have come. Amber sat in the small car between him and the trees – between him and the sniper. She looked back at him nervously. 'Get out this side and keep low!' he called to her. Amber shuffled quickly across the front seats of the idling car and fell out of the passenger side door onto the dirt.

The helicopter was overhead now. The rapid repetitive thud of the rotors pulsed sonic waves that washed through them from head to toe. The downdraft whipped up dust and debris around them. The smoke from the house curled in great arcs up into the sky.

The situation was getting worse. They had no idea who, or how many people were in the trees beyond their car. The sniper had them pinned down, linking them inextricably to the carnage that lay behind them – something the news crew above them could easily paint as a massacre.

Amber covered her eyes from the swirling dust. Stuart looked at Nat, who pointed to the car and got to his feet. Staying low, he took a curving run towards it. As his back slapped against the cold metal of the vehicle, next to his daughter, Stuart pushed himself to his feet and followed suit, taking a meandering sprint to the car.

All three now sat with their backs against car, looking up at the circling helicopter. Nat brought his weapon slowly up to his eye and aimed at the chopper.

'Ye cannae Nat!' screamed Stuart over the din. 'They did nowt to you, and they'll be recording this!'

Nat didn't flinch from his aim. Stuart lunged towards him, reaching for the assault rifle when the chopper banked suddenly to the right and set off back towards Hexham. As the ruckus died down and the dust began to settle, Nat looked at the Scotsman.

'I'd never have pulled the trigger...'

'Aye, I'll take your word for it.' Stuart slumped back against the car.

Their attention turned once again to the trees. Both men turned slowly and looked through the vehicle into the thick wall of foliage.

'I cannae see anything in there,' whispered Stuart.

'Listen.' Said Nat.

As the rotors of the helicopter faded to a distant throbbing, the loudest sound became the rustle of the trees. The breeze ebbed, and the two men listened intently for a man-made sound. The standoff lasted some time before they heard sticks snapping and the rustle of foliage. Nat looked at his friend in surprise at the commotion.

'It's King Kong...,' said Stuart.

Nat allowed himself a chuckle as he nudged Amber and gestured for her to get back into the car. He had a mind to get away before whoever it was appeared.

'Divvent shoot, Nat!' bellowed a thick Northumbrian accent from the trees, as Amber began to move.

The cracking and swishing in the bushes got louder and louder and Stuart looked at Nat in wonder. Nat shrugged. Then, as the final leaves parted, two muddy figures emerged: Old Man Rowell and his wife, shaken and weary but smiling at their old acquaintances.

The eighty-year-old farmer had a hunting rifle strapped across his back and his wife carried a stick. They lumbered across the road with a curious gait that in someone thirty years younger would have been a jog. Nat, Amber and Stuart got to their feet but didn't move around the car. Instead, the Rowells shuffled over to them.

The old man stood five feet six with boots on. His face was round and ruddy, and his thin grey hair floated in the breeze. His corpulent stomach sat on broad hips, but it was the two fingers missing from his left hand that drew the eye. His wife was a clear four inches taller than he, elegant in comparison.

'Looks like they dealt us similar cards, Nat.' She put her hand on his shoulder and kissed his cheek. 'Aye, Susan it's all changed now.'

She smiled at him with vivacious narrowing eyes. She looked down at the dirt and then back to her husband.

'We'll not lie doon!' grunted Old Man Rowell. 'D'ye knaa why they came here…did this?'

'They want rid of the landowners... control the land.'

'Aye, thors that as well… But it was wor lads that organised the attack on the chipboard factory. They've got an army growin' by the day. We're gan t'fight – an' ye should join us.' He pointed a thick finger at Nat's chest.

'Where are they… Are they safe?' Amber butted in. They all knew her concern was for Matty.

'Aye, lass. Thor up Wooler way. The Scots have been trainin' them and givin' them weapons.' 'How many?' Nat asked.

'Nae idea, man. Hundreds, mebbe thousands. Ah divvent keep track, but mair and mair join ivery day. They come up ower the Pennines through Haltwhistle… Carlisle. Farmers… hinds… country folk from Cumbria, Durham… Yorkshire – even forther I think. Thor all joinin' up with wor lads.'

'Alright then…' Nat looked around, remembering where they were. 'Come with us now. We've got a car ye can take. Get yersels up with your lads and bide safe up north. Divvent come back – you're old for all this.'

As Rowell's gaze drifted past the three of them towards his burning home, his eyes appeared to glaze over. The fire raged on, wood cracked and snapped as it reached breaking point. The whoosh and roar of gas canisters and petrol cans excited the fire sporadically. The bodies of the NSO fighters littered the land in front of the inferno. Susan Rowell, sturdy and dignified, took the hand of her forlorn husband, and led him to the little car. Stuart and Amber busied themselves with collecting the weapons from the dead soldiers and filling the cramped boot of the vehicle.

As they wound down the lanes back to Carlins Law, Susan talked of the violent purge by the NSO, of the camps in Slaley Forest holding those who had shown some degree of resistance to the changes. She went on to mention the latest NSO arrest: the woman and the journalist dragged from her home in Oakwood by NSO thugs.

Nat flashed a concerned look across at Stuart as the big Scot turned in his seat and the mood in the car chilled.

'Who was the woman?'

'It was the nurse, Claire…'

Dart watched Ben enter the room. Jocelyn followed behind him, *always close,* he thought. He looked down at his papers and then put two sugars in his coffee as Ben settled himself at the middle of the table. They locked at each other, but Ben beat him to it.

'Good morning, Lucas.' He said as he arranged some papers.

'Morning,' he replied, although his stomach knotted in frustration and expectation.

'So…,' said Ben.

'Look, I'm sorry about last night, maybe I was too forthright, but you must see that I am right. We rolled out the land reforms and it has met with resistance all over the country, but in the border region we cannot allow it to fester because the Scots, the Arc are stoking the fire of revolt, and they are arming and training the rebels!'

He paused, expecting Baines to speak, but he didn't. Instead, Jocelyn chimed in.

'Should we have explored diplomacy first?'

He looked at her, she was loving this, 'I don't think this is a time for division, do you Jocelyn?'

'Better late than never I reckon,' she answered, 'we should never have used a heavy hand...'

'The world is burning. Borders are falling under the weight of humanity moving from the tropics. The Arc detests our politics, and they particularly hate our plans for open borders with the South! We had no way of knowing that things would escalate as they have,' he sighed and looked to Ben, 'all I've done has been for the NSO, for this country. Hindsight is a wonderful thing, but she wasn't there planning any of this,' he pointed a finger at Jocelyn, 'she never put it all into action. As of this moment we have successfully brought over seventy five percent of land under NSO control. My reforms are working, but it was never going to be pretty!' Jocelyn sighed loudly, but Lucas ignored her, the stats spoke for themselves, and he could see Ben had heard it. 'Is that true, seventy five percent?' Ben asked an aide. 'Yes sir, its actually seventy-seven, the resistance only concerns three areas, Cornwall, Wales, but mainly Northumberland. However, the Northumbrian uprising is the only one that is escalating dramatically and of course has the added complication of lying on the border of The Arc.' The aide replied.

Lucas watched as Ben digested the information, he could see the calculation going on behind the leader's eyes.

'If we are going to make an open border policy work, we must be in control of the land - all of it - we can only succeed if, over time, we can manage our sustainability and the distribution of wealth equitably across the whole population. That requires a hard stance now…'

'And the level of threat from over the border?' Ben was looking at the security advisors.

'On a scale of one to five, we're at five, Scottish involvement is real, and intelligence suggests that they are waiting for a reason to take military action.'

'A reason?'

'Some perceived crime by our government or human rights violation…'

The advisor was interrupted as an aide, burst into the room, she whispered in Ben's ear.

'What now?' Lucas asked.

Ben turned the television on, and Lucas watched as the news bulletin flashed up on the wall-mounted monitor to Ben's right. The sound was low as he saw an aerial view of beautiful, rugged landscape. The dark oranges and purples of the heather highlighted the lush greens, and the basalt outcrops accented the scene with ancient greys.

It was not the wild countryside that demanded attention, however, but the flaming carcass of the burning house, the thick black smoke drifting off to the bottom right and the three gunmen hunkered down behind the small blue car that stood a few yards from the wreckage of an articulated trailer. As the helicopter circled it whipped up the smoke into a wispy valley. As the smoke cleared momentarily, it left a clear view of the scattered corpses littering the land in front of the house. The scrolling banner at the bottom of the screen read: REBEL ATROCITY: ARMED CONFLICT CONTINUES IN RURAL NORTHUMBERLAND

'Turn that damn thing up!' Lucas demanded.

'…the scene, one and a half miles north of Hexham, the town in Northumberland that is becoming the frontline in the fight for power in England. As history repeats itself, this idyllic part of the country has once again become the fault line of war. The battle continues less than one hundred yards from Hadrian's Wall, the

great barrier created by the Roman Emperor to keep the northern tribes at bay.

'Later, the region was well trod by the warring clans of Scots and English raiders known as the Border Reivers. But all that historical strife may soon pale in comparison to the fighting that rages today between rebel forces and the Government's militia.

'Sources suggest three local brothers named Rowell are organising the rebels. Then there is the ruthless insurgent Nathaniel Bell, the known murderer of four government men and the suspected killer of many more. It is believed that he is acting under the rebel's banner and considered part of the same organisation as the Rowell brothers…'

A hushed silence descended over the boardroom. Government office was new to all of them. The country was in chaos. No one in the room felt any measure of control over this – but Lucas couldn't help but enjoy the excitement he felt in his belly.

'… the burning buildings, in fact, constitute the Rowell family farm and reportedly the headquarters of the insurgents' cell. It is unknown whether any rebels were killed or wounded, but it is evident from our pictures there were several NSO fatalities…'

Lucas searched the faces in the room.

Ben was looking directly at him, 'we can't let this happen, where will this end?'

Lucas shrugged, 'it'll end in an invasion and the destruction of all that we have built, everything we have worked for!'

'It should never have got to this!' Exclaimed Jocelyn.

Lucas turned to her, he tried to control his emotions, 'we can't turn the clock back now, can we?'

She turned to Ben, 'I told you, we all warned you, but you left him to…'

'Jocelyn!' Ben held up his hand to silence her and Lucas felt the thrill of winning, Jocelyn folded her arms and sat back in her chair and Ben turned to Lucas, 'so what do you suggest?'

'We must stop the rebellion and sure up our defences in the North, make the Arc think twice. They cannot afford a war, especially with their troubles in the East, and they won't risk it without sufficient division in England.'

Ben paced back and forth, Lucas couldn't see another option, they had to continue with his plan.

'There is another way,' said Jocelyn, Lucas couldn't help himself stare at her, he slammed his hand on the table, but it did nothing to deter her. 'We reach out to the rebels, we talk and negotiate...' she turned to Lucas, 'who knows, we might reach a settlement for peace and in turn show the Arc we are united. They would not attack then.'

'Tsst, how will we reason with the Hidebound, already aligned with the Arc? We must show strength.'

Lucas watched Ben struggle with the decision, the room paused in silence for long moments before Ben turned to face them again.

'Lucas, continue with your plans. We must secure the North.'

'Yes, that is the right course!'

'But we must limit aggression towards our own people, we cannot fight our own, there has to be another way.'

'Yes, I understand, we will do our utmost to suppress the rebellion in a peaceful manner.'

'And Jocelyn, I will reach out to the rebels...'

'How will you do that?' Lucas said, although as soon as he opened his mouth, he wished he hadn't been so quick.

Ben stared at him with that look of suspicion, '*you* don't have to worry about that, leave it to me.'

Jocelyn smirked, 'that's got him nervous,' she mumbled.

Ben sent them all on their way. As he left the room Lucas pulled two aides and the security advisor into an office nearby.

'You did well in there' he said, 'it is now more important than ever that Mr Baines knows only what we want him to know; to protect him he must have deniability.' He looked at each one, searching for weakness.

'We continue as we were but step up the reforms and there must be no quarter for the rebels. Our army will go north, and we will take control of this situation.'

FOURTEEN

Their tightly packed car raced around the country bends, while Stuart bubbled and churned like a volcano ready to blow. Nat drove; the muscles in his jaw tensed and released, tensed and released.

'What'll we do then?' said Stuart.

'No idea, try the police station I reckon, that's where they're based. They'll be waiting for us. And if she's in a cell…'

Silence fell over the car, but only for a second or two.

'I'll tell ye what ye can dae…' rumbled Old Man Rowell from the back seat. 'Ye can torn aroond an' join wor lads at Waters Meet.'

'What the hell are they planning now?'

'An attack on Hexham. They'll tek back what's wors… re-take the toon.'

'What? Armed with shotguns?'

'No, you daft bugger. The Scots have armed them and there are hundreds of them, mebbe thousands. So, turn the bloody car roond.'

'Mind your mouth, Sam!' Rowell's wife blasted across the car. 'Sorry, lass,' she mouthed at Amber, with a swift shake of the head. Amber returned a smile and turned to look out of the window.

Nat nodded thoughtfully. 'We'll take the weapons from my farm. Maybe we'll join your lads, Sam.' Rowell beamed at his wife.

They drove the rest of the way in silence, living in that moment so different from life before. As he drove, Nat thought about his livestock. The hours he had put in caring for beasts, the planning he had carried out, the blood and the sweat he had given in building his farm. He remembered what his father used to tell him, *'Look after you and yours because nothin else is certain.'* Everything he had known had changed. Everything was different. His stomach turned; he hadn't looked after his family. His foot pressed harder on the accelerator as the anger bubbled in his gut and the car sped into his driveway. When they pulled to a stop, they jumped from the car. The Rowells followed, wearily. 'We might see you at Waters Meet.' Nat threw Old Man Rowell the keys.

'Tell your lads.'

Stuart grabbed a tarpaulin and unloaded the captured NSO weapons onto it. Rowell and his wife climbed into the car, the old man labouring to get his round belly into the driver's seat. Stuart slammed the boot; the engine sprang to life and the little car zipped away.

As they watched it streak down the rough gravel, Nat saw Amber gaze up at the woods, *their* woods – the woods she knew better than the route from bedroom to bathroom.

She wore an expression that he had seen many times.

'I know, lass,' Nat whispered softly. 'He was in the barn earlier. Don't let him know – look away now. Go with Stuart. Store the weapons and flank around the wood from the east. We'll flush him out.'

'Who is it?'

'Dunno. But we'll find out now.' He gestured up to the top field with his shotgun, then he trudged off up the hill, breaking the gun and resting it over his forearm. He set off across the open grass.

As he approached the wood, he became one with his surroundings. He took in and used all that he could see, hear or smell. The red squirrel gnawing on an acorn and the birds busy to his left betrayed the lack of potential predators lurking in the undergrowth there. The frenetic calls from the songbirds to his right were like a neon sign advertising the presence of an alien. Nat knew that visibility in the wood reduced to little more than twenty yards. Whoever had eyes on him was close. He respected his visitor; he was clearly good enough to ensure that he was unseen. Nat moved forward along one of a small network of well-trodden paths they used to walk and hunt.

Baines's spy had lowered himself down and out of the barn's shadows, when the two men and the girl had driven off. He had picked up his cup and walking unguarded out into the open, where he made another brew. This time he had enjoyed it, sitting on the stone steps of the burned-out farmhouse. He had sipped his tea and watched the black smoke billow up from the raging inferno at the woodchip factory. Later, he'd listened to the tat-tat-tat and the pup-pup of distant gunfire. He had been sure that the fighting involved the farmer and his companions – the timing all stacked up.

When he'd heard the car returning, he'd cleaned his space quickly and broken for the woodland, where he now watched the giant white-haired farmer come towards him. The big man was conserving energy by trudging methodically with that wide gait. He seemed lost in thought, nonchalant even with that shotgun broken casually over his forearm. Again, it surprised Tom, that someone with Bell's ability to survive was so unaware that he was being watched. The other two had vanished around the hillside to the east carrying a load of weapons in a tarp. There had to be a weapons cache somewhere over there. Perhaps he would explore that later, but Bell was his concern right now. The farmer was a few hundred yards away when the watcher slipped his mobile phone from his pocket, pulled up the only number logged in it and hit dial. Baines picked up immediately.

'Tom, what's new? It's getting out of hand up there now. Dart is sending –'

'Not now,' Tom whispered. 'Quickly – has anything changed with the farmer? I can take him out. He's alone. Do I have a green light?'

'No!' Baines shouted, then collected himself. 'No… all this killing…' Tom listened to a long sigh and a longer pause before Baines seemed to snap out of his distraction. 'Please try and speak to him, we need to make a truce with the rebels, to build a peace. Tell him we are open to talking, to compromise on our land reform.'

The phone clicked off without another word and Tom slipped it back into its pocket.

Bell still meandered through the thick, wet undergrowth, oblivious to his surroundings, head down with his mind in another place and time. He would have to wise up fast - some NSO sharpshooter would put a bullet in his head if he didn't sharpen up. He passed Tom about twenty-five yards to the west, foliage whooshing, sticks cracking and brambles scraping across his clothes as their barbs tried to cling on like fingernails. Tom followed in relative silence, and they approached the northern edge of the trees, the farmer slightly ahead and to the west of Tom but in clear view. Bell was about to break the tree line when he slumped his big frame down on a tree stump and sat still, staring northwards across the open country.

Tom lowered himself to his haunches, looking and listening. Rainwater from a previous shower dripped and splashed as the breeze caught the leaves high in the trees. A wood pigeon called out somewhere to the south. The earthy smell of peat and decaying foliage filled his nostrils as, ahead of him, the grizzled farmer parked himself like a gorilla in the jungle.

The log on which the farmer sat was the bow of an old oak, broken and quickly becoming part of the land, ferns had grown up, around and on it. The rich green of the moss carpeted the rotting wood. The sun broke through the clouds and stabbed shards of hazy gold down onto the rolling acres beyond. The farmer's hunched figure in that most beautiful of settings would have given Constable a worthwhile subject. As Tom's mind drifted it dawned on him: the man had to be carrying an injury. Bell had taken a round and he was bleeding out. It explained his lack of care, his clumsiness.

Tom watched more closely. He saw those broad shoulders move up and down with every laboured breath. He was sure the respirations were becoming shallower, more torturous. That was the moment he felt the chill of cold steel on his Adam's Apple.

'Don't you fucking move.'

It was a woman's voice, soft in pitch, but like razor wire in tone. Tom's blood turned to cement rendering his body rigid, not with fear, but calculation. This is where his training and experience came to the fore. His thoughts were lucid. His body simply awaited instruction from his grey matter. It wasn't easy to cut someone's throat. It was both physically and mentally demanding, involving a great deal of pressure and pints of blood. He had never met a young woman who could stomach such horrors. He raised his arms in surrender.

The first synapses began to order his hand to grab his attacker's arm, but before he moved, the undergrowth in front of him exploded in a thunderous roar. Standing before him and the girl was a giant with a semi-automatic weapon pointed at his forehead.

'Please try that. Then she winnae have to dae the killin'.'

He dropped his arms again. He knew when he was taken, and he knew how to get through it. The big Scot's unkempt hair was wet and stuck to a face filled with threat and promise. The man was not playing at tough. Tom knew what to do: submit and say nothing.

Nat leapt from his perch. As he ripped through the wet foliage, he pulled his handgun from his pocket. Amber drew her knife away from their captive's neck and stepped back from him. Nat burned afresh with the hunger for vengeance now that another opportunity had arisen. Even his old friend must have sensed it as he backed off in surprise.

'Control yersel, Nat! He's alone. We need to ken whae he is!'

Their captive did not flinch as Nat approached and pistol whipped him across the face. The blow gashed the skin on his cheekbone, sending him tumbling into the dirt. Nat stood over him, breathing heavily, his mind roiling as he considered what to do next. The man returned the look calmly and reached slowly into his pocket. Nat's knee came down hard on his forearm, pinning it across his chest.

'My phone… I'm getting my phone! You call the number on there…'

Nat leaned close enough to smell the man's sweat and stuck the barrel of his handgun into his prisoner's eye socket then lifted his weight from his chest. His big hand delved into the man's pocket and retrieved a mobile phone. As it powered up, he looked down at his prisoner and pressed the barrel harder into his eye, pinning his head to the ground.

'There's one number,' the man gasped. 'Call it… tell the guy who answers who you are.'

Nat pressed the green button and put the phone to his ear. It was answered immediately.

'Tom, I haven't heard from you twice in one day since we were kids…' The voice at the other end was cheerful and informal. It seemed vaguely familiar.

Confused, Nat looked at the man at his feet. He was clearly a professional – something to do with the security services – but he seemed far too slick for the NSO.

'This isn't Tom,' Nat growled.

There was gulp down the line and Nat sensed a shuffle of panic. Whether standing or sitting, whoever was on the other end was struggling with something, buying time to get their thoughts in order.

'This is Ben Baines. Where's the man you got the phone from?'

Stunned by the revelation it was Nat's turn to try and wrest control of his thoughts and emotions. Pain, anger and hatred welled up inside him as he looked down at his captive. Since Esme's murder and since exacting a partial revenge on most of those he knew were responsible, hatred wore two faces for Nat: one was that of the enforcer, the other was that of Baines. After hearing the voice on the phone, somehow it was as if it was Baines he had beneath the barrel of his pistol.

'No…' the man whispered, as if he'd read Nat's thoughts.

'I've got a gun pointed in his face,' Nat snarled into the phone.

There was silence for long seconds, before the voice came back. 'You think that I'm the enemy but I'm not. Quite the –'

'Shut it, animal! You're the cause of *all* this. You're the reason my –' He looked across at Amber and flicked his head in a gesture for her to disappear. 'Who's on the phone, Da?' 'Get *away*!' he spat at her.

She flinched but didn't move. 'I'll not. I'm staying right here.'

'Listen to me… *please*!' came Baines's voice down the phone line. 'We *must* talk… I *will* explain…'

Nat spared a glance at Stuart, who looked back at him without any understanding. But Nat was embroiled by his own mental maelstrom. What did this mean? Perhaps there was a God after all – a vengeful, wrathful God, like the one in the Old Testament: *The Lord thy God is a man of war*. Or maybe this was just some dark twist of fate – whatever fate meant. Whatever the source, here was a gift. A chance for revenge that would strike right at the heart of the murderous regime. He pressed the gun barrel into the man's eye with renewed venom as he brought the phone to his mouth once more. 'The lives you have destroyed...'

'Not me! Let me –'

'Fuck you, Baines!'

'I never ordered any of this! I want to make it right!'

'You are the NSO and the NSO is you! It's all *you!*'

'Hang on, Nat!' shouted Stuart. 'Wait! He could help us – he could get Claire back for us!'

Amber grabbed Nat's arm, but he brushed her away violently. He was dimly aware that she seemed to recoil from him as he stared her down.

He shifted his glare to the man at his feet and the gun pushed into his eye. He snarled into the phone. 'You became my enemy...'

'Don't do it! Please don't...'

'...when your people...'

Stuart took a step towards him. 'Don't you fucking do it, Nat!'

Nat fixed him with a psychotic glare.

'Let me speak to him!' Baines cried. 'Tom! Please, he's my brother...'

Tom squirmed under the farmer's weight, but Nat had him pinned with his knee firmly in the centre of Tom's chest. He pointed at Stuart with the hand that held the phone. 'Don't you take another fuckin' step...' he hissed. As he put the phone back to his ear, he heard three words from Baines. 'I'm begging you.' And he replied with two.

'My wife.' As he uttered the words, Nat pulled the trigger. The dampened metallic snap ended the chorus of *No!* ringing out from Stuart, Tom, Baines and Amber.

The wood fell silent, the phone line fell silent, and Nat's heart also fell silent. He felt an immediate release of his pain – and an instant self-loathing. He had no time to contemplate his actions before the Scotsman was upon him, a giant fist knocking him off his feet. Stuart grabbed the phone and hung up. Nat felt a warm trickle run into his left eye. He raised a had to find a lump and a split on his forehead.

205

'What've ye done!' Stuart yelled. 'We could've used him to get Claire back, you stupid bastard! Esme is *fucking dead*, ye idiot! Are ye a *murderer* now?' He paced back and forth. 'Ye're no better than those fuckers... Ye've got a daughter! Ye need tae start thinking! What have you done? Jesus!' He raked his hands through his hair and turned a tight circle as though he were looking for an answer.

Nat got to his knees, spat in the dirt and wiped his brow. He looked at his daughter. A tear rolled down her cheek. When their eyes met, she couldn't hold his gaze and turned away from him.

'Ye probably just killed us all,' Stuart said.

Nat knew his friend was right. He sat in the undergrowth, stunned. He was so tired. He stared at the forlorn body of the man he had just murdered. Stuart stepped over to him, grabbed his collar and lifted him roughly to his feet. He looked him in the eye, drawing the farmer's attention away from the body.

'What did he say... on the phone?'

'It was Ben Baines,' he said in a whisper.

'I know that! What the fuck did he say?'

Nat stood, dazed looking at the space where his daughter had been standing. After a long pause, he looked at the ground, he rubbed his forehead and finally his gaze settled on the corpse. What had been an eye was now a bloody crater.

'He said he was his brother.'

'Ye must be fucking kidding me! You just killed the brother of the leader of the NSO. We are screwed! This place is going to be crawling wi' army – just looking for us.' He ran his hands through his hair and paced again.

'Now he knows how it feels...' Nat said the words without conviction.

'Shut up, Nat! Just shut the fuck up! Ye've lost it, man. I want nae part of this...'

He advanced on Nat with fists clenched but at the last moment turned away and roared up into the trees.

Then he seemed to regain some composure. He looked down at the dirt and kicked at it.

Nat remained where he was, staring at the dead man. Inside his guts churned and his mind tormented him.

'This changes things for me, Nat. We go into Hexham tonight, get Claire and then I leave with her and Amber. I'll take them back ower the border and ye can come or stay – up to you. But I'll no' be staying here.'

'I'm not going back to Scotland without him,' Amber said. There was an acerbic tone to her voice that stole all the warmth from her devotion.

Stuart looked at them both and their faces must have convinced him that they were not going to be persuaded. He looked to the heavens and walked away. 'Ye'll make a bloody murderer of your daughter now, will ye?' he said over his shoulder.

'We have to make them see that we'll not flinch, that we can hurt them too…' Nat called after him. But his words drifted; he was all too aware that his justification was unconvincing. However, much he tried, though he could not escape this madness. It was like swimming away from a whirlpool; his own bloodlust sucked him back towards the carnage.

Amber walked over to the man's discarded mobile phone. She switched it off and put it in her pocket.

Ben stared at his phone with no tangible emotions. His brain still worked on overdrive simply to grasp what had happened. He had heard the farmer's voice – had spoken with him. He had discovered how brutal the man could be. He knew his brother was dead.

He looked around the shallow grandeur of Dart's office. He felt so far from the militant street politician he had been, so far from the people he had set out to benefit. Resigned to the cul de sac down which power had sent him, he was making deals with the old regime as well as being in thrall to the extreme elements of his own party. The worst of it was that he had no control at all over serving the population he had always wanted to lead into a better future.

As the fact of Tom's death swamped his mind, he realised that Lucas was right, the rebels were not people to reason with, and the North must be tamed.

Lucas Dart bowled into the office, the two men looked at each other and Dart smiled. 'I haven't seen that look since our days in Parliament Square, Ben.'

'That farmer just killed my brother.'

Lucas paused for a moment and his eyes narrowed.

'I'm sorry for your loss.'

'I want him to pay for what he's done.'

Dart seemed to study him for a moment. Then he stepped across the room to the sideboard, poured himself a coffee and raised his cup to his old comrade. Ben shook his head. Dart slurped his coffee. 'I won't rest until it's done,' he said.

Ben turned away.

'You must put your principles aside – just for a short time.' Dart crossed the room and put a hand on Ben's shoulder. 'You've seen now what we have to deal with.'

Ben's emotions were in turmoil. The revulsion he had so recently developed for Dart churned around with the pain of Tom's death and a desperate yearning for things past – for a brother that was alive and for a time of both innocence and glory when he and his NSO carried all before them.

'We must crush the insurgents,' Dart said, 'then we can get back to the mission… your ideology.'

Ben held out his hand to him. The two men stood for a time, eye to eye.

'We will succeed,' said Dart after a long silence.

FIFTEEN

No sooner had the morning begun to glow, than the weather turned. A deep blanket of cloud bubbled to the west and a wet wind blustered. Rain was in the air. The three of them sat around a small fire eating a gamey pheasant. The woodland was quiet around them, feeding off their dark moods. Nobody spoke until Nat threw the last of his bones into the fire.

'Better get set in the field shelter. Looks like rain coming.'

'Aye…' Stuart didn't look at him as he got to his feet. He just grabbed his things and left the ravine.

Nat and Amber walked to the field shelter in silence. He spent every step of the journey searching for something to say, but with every step, his stomach knotted further, and his head pounded. As they approached the shelter, they found Stuart sharpening his knife meticulously. He looked up at them briefly before returning to his task.

Amber touched Nat's arm and stopped walking. He turned to face her. She had all three machine guns hanging from her shoulders and a shotgun in her hands. The wind blew her hair across her face, so she turned into it and her eyes narrowed as the breeze swept her curls away. He saw Esme in her: she also had loved to let the weather wash over her face. The vision almost knocked him down with grief, but then his daughter's intense eyes met his.

'You don't have to explain anything to me,' she said softly, then nodded discreetly toward Stuart. 'Or him. I'll never leave you alone again.'

She walked away, and Nat watched her sit down next to his friend. He wandered away from them and found a rocky outcrop where he perched and absorbed the landscape stretching out in front of him. He slipped slowly down the stone until he lay slumped against it on the muddy earth and closed his eyes.

The first spots of rain woke him as the light was beginning to fade. He jumped to his feet, disoriented at first from his deep sleep. The air was brisk and enlivening. Once he came to his senses, he returned to the shelter.

Stuart sat in the opening to it. The rain fell steadily now. Nat nodded at him as he approached, and the Scotsman offered a reassuring smile in return. Nat lowered himself to his haunches next to him and they looked at the evening sky together. The chipboard factory continued to burn but there was no electricity running; not a single light shone across the whole landscape. No cars were on the road. The Tyne Valley was now a war zone, and its people were hunkered down.

'Ye mind on when we met?' Stuart said suddenly.

'The Carts Bog I think it was...'

'Aye, that was a pub, eh? Rough, mind...'

Stuart raised an eyebrow. 'Aye, I seem tae recall ye punching me!'

'You deserved it.' Nat smiled as he looked down at the river, a glinting moonlit ribbon winding across the valley floor.

'Only 'cause that lovely Haltwhistle lassie liked *me*...'

'Not likely man... it was just because you were the biggest bloke in there!' He found himself laughing now. It felt good.

'I couldnae bide ye then.'

'Aye, well... Why'd you come and help me when Cuth died, then?'

'Ye'd changed, man. Esme's father changed ye when he took ye in... When he died ye needed help.'

Nat scowled at him. 'Why ye bringing all this up now?'

'Because the man I saw back there and at Rowell's was the Nat Bell I met that night in the Carts Bog. I didnae like him.'

They said nothing more to each other, and that didn't change when Amber struggled up the hill with the heavy holdall. She put it on the dry ground inside the shelter, reached inside and took out one of the new NSO guns plus six full magazines. She moved over to the far corner of the shelter and taped the magazines, two together head to toe.

'What films've ye been watching lass?' Said Stuart.

She snorted, 'ye might be thanking me later.'

Nat drank tea and stared out across the valley. The rain was coming down in thick grey waves drifting across the landscape.

'Claire's got to be in the police station,' he said suddenly.

Stuart looked at Amber, eyebrows raised, then back at Nat. 'How the hell will we get her out? Or more to the point, how will we get in?'

'Aye, that's the question,' Nat pondered.

'There's no way we'll get in and survive,' said Amber. 'It's full of NSO – guaranteed! Waters Meet… join the others. It's the only way.'

Nat's ears pricked to the sound of engines. He and Stuart looked at each other – maybe the fight was coming to them? Dusk was in its full, deepening throes, but there were no headlights accompanying the rough growl of engines. They hunkered down in the shelter, heart rates increasing with every mechanical growl.

Both men filled magazines with rounds, their eyes fixed on the bottom of the driveway. Nat prayed the engines would die away into the distance. When he began counting the trucks into the driveway, his heart sank. They came fast: one… two… three… four… five… six – each tailgating the truck in front, losing little speed around the sharp turn into the drive. All the vehicles were big 4x4s.

Nat handed Amber the .33 rifle. 'Get yersel in the tree line! They start coming up the hill, start shooting and don't stop until they're gone, okay? Go! Quick!'

She swung the weapon onto her back and ran towards the trees. The men set off to meet their visitors at the ruined farmhouse. As the trucks motored up the long drive, they ran down through the wet grass, its undulations testing their footing as the decline of the hill pulled them faster than their limbs could manage. Just as the convoy was pulling up outside the tumbled down building, they fell in behind the stone wall that extended from the northern end of the barn.

With his back flat against the wall, Nat looked across at Stuart, who knelt looking back at him for the next call. The engines cut out one by one and they heard the crunch of boots on gravel. Nat nodded to his friend and both men rose, leading with their weapons. They had them trained on the visitors, with the cold, wet stones of the wall tucked into their armpits.

The men who had just arrived scattered as the weapons came into view. They scrambled for refuge behind the trucks, skidding on the gravel, all arms and legs. All the fuss was unnecessary. Nat recognised the Toyota up front.

Rowell's youngest son called out, 'Nat, it's Matty!'

'What's going on, why so many of ye?' Nat responded bluntly. 'Can we talk?' No response.

'About Claire!' he said.

'We're listening!' called Stuart immediately.

Nat stared at him angrily.

Matty called back, 'ye cannae do it on ye own. It's crawling with NSO. They'll kill ye before ye cross the river! We're attacking tonight. What if one of ours shoots ye in the confusion?' Matty stepped out from behind his truck, and then a few paces closer. 'We've ower a thousand men down at Waters Meet. We're going to attack tonight, drive the NSO out of Tynedale and start the war proper – from the North. Word is, the Cornish and the Welsh are fighting. We have the backing from the Scots – money and hardware. All through the North of England, people will join us if we can show some force.'

'None of that means anything to me...' dismissed Nat.

Stuart tutted loudly, shaking his head.

'We want revenge for Esme, but I care about Amber as well. And a lot of these people joined the rebels because of what happened to you. Don't let them down. Don't let your daughter down. And don't let them win by committing suicide. We need leaders...'

'Listen, son... all we're interested in is getting Claire back.'

'Okay, okay. You stay up there living in a tree for the rest of your life. But you know... one night somebody'll come and cut your throat. Or they'll just burn you out, sooner or later...'

'Come on, Nat, you stubborn old bastard,' Stuart urged. 'We agreed...we'll be much mair likely tae get Claire safely with them.' He climbed the wall and jumped down the other side. He walked over to Matty and held out his spade like hand. 'I'm his brains. How are ye, Matt?'

Nat slumped back down with his back to the wall and looked back up the hill to his beloved woods. The smell of wet grass and rain was heavy in the air. His clothes sodden and the semi-automatic rifle was cold in his hands. His daughter was already halfway down the hill towards them.

He pushed himself off the cold, mossy stones, out from cover and back into the biting breeze, heaved his stiff limbs up over the stone wall. A few stones tumbled as he slid down the other side.

His old bones rocked as he stomped towards the car, resting his weapon on his shoulder as he walked. The young men ventured from the cover of their trucks and began to clap their hands for him.

'Don't you fucking dare…' he bristled, his grimace thickened, and he awkwardly waved a large hand for them to stop.

The clapping stopped abruptly. It was bigger than his farm, bigger than his life. He didn't want it. He wanted Esme to be the start and finish of all. But life had moved on.

He looked into young Rowell's eyes, and he saw that the lad feared him. Neither said a word as they shook hands. Amber joined them and greeted friends among the men. Nat stood aside, feet wide, hands in the pockets of his muddied wax jacket, his shining white mane wet and matted. His head was spinning as he watched his daughter move through the young people and finally reach Matty. She hugged him tight and exchanged some soft words. Nat looked to his left: there was Stuart next to him. Shoulder to shoulder, they would stand against the NSO.

Bill Ludlum was in pain. He sat in a dark room in a quiet corner of the police station. The journalist had broken both bones in his arm. They had brought in a doctor from Newcastle to put a cast on it. He had done as good a job as he could, but the pain was excruciating. He was waiting for his latest round of painkillers to kick in.

He heard a voice in the corridor telling him that Ben Baines's office was on the telephone. Everything else could wait. The man handed him the phone and Bill pressed the receiver to his ear. He didn't recognise the officious, nasal tone of the aide's voice at the other end. There were no pleasantries.

'Mr Ludlum?'

'Yes.'

'Your inability to contain the rural community in your region is a great disappointment to Mr Dart.'

'I've got one man on a killing spree and an untrained group of terrorists making homemade explosives. Once I get more men, I'll contain both –'

'The way we see it, the rebels destroyed the largest employment facility in the area. And this Bell character has become a champion of the rebellion. All this on your watch. You do understand, don't you, that our ideology is largely concerned with getting people working?'

'I'm fighting a war here with kids and thugs as my army. I can't do everything myself. Once I have the trained reinforcements in position, I will get the area secured and under our control.'

'Did you know about the rebel force congregating in Acomb? I understand that is about two miles north of where you are...'

Bill balked. 'What? Twenty farmhands with shotguns?'

'No, hundreds at least, maybe more. Armed by the Scots. This job has become too big for you. A gentleman called Beaston, Major General Anthony Beaston, will arrive this evening with more troops. He will relieve you of your command and find a role for you to fill.'

Bill opened his mouth to argue his corner but there was a calm click as the aide hung up. He was now out in the cold, wounded physically and mentally. Worse than being bottom of the pile, he had failed.

He put the phone down on the table in front of him and looked around the room: at the felt carpet, the toughened plastic chairs, the ancient metal filing cabinet that stood under a clipboard littered with police bulletins, guidelines and assorted rubbish. He pushed himself up from the desk and walked slowly out of the office. He strolled silently through the police station reception and through the door leading to the maze of corridors that led to the rear of the building and the cells.

The keys hung on the wall outside the cell door. He picked them off the hook with his weaker left hand and dropped them. 'Fuck it!' he spat, wincing with pain as he bent to retrieve them. He unlocked the cell door, and it swung open, allowing the bright light of the corridor to flood the room.

The woman was bloodied and swollen, squinting into the light, her hands tied, her head lolling with pain from her injuries. Opposite her was the journalist, shrinking into the corner, his arms covering his eyes as though he were about to be beaten.

As he crossed the room, he heard the woman's gasping breaths as she struggled against the plastic ties that bound her to the chair. He wasn't interested in the woman. He stood over the journalist. 'Get up,' he said.

'Please, no...'

'Get the fuck up! now!'

The journalist pushed himself slowly up the wall. His eyes were closed, tears streamed down his cheeks. He mumbled incoherently. Bill waited patiently while he caught his breath. The gasping stopped and the moaning quieted. As soon as he opened his eyes, Bill swung the elbow of his unbroken into the journalists face and he fell to the floor with a scream. Bill leaned against the wall and swung his boot into him repeatedly. He didn't stop until he was physically exhausted. His victim had stopped screaming, or moving, long before.

Bill moved to the cell door and flexed his left arm. It was painful now, but he felt a release. He left the cell and closed the door behind him, plunging the woman back into darkness. Before he turned away, he heard her shuffle in her chair.

'Rory... Rory, say something...' she mumbled through her swollen mouth.

They took the black estate car, the one driven to the farm by the men who had come to take Nat's life and followed the speeding convoy of 4x4s. Nat drove and did his best to keep up with the young drivers who were taking full advantage of the empty roads. Like the cars on a roller coaster, they wound down the steep bank from Oakwood onto the roundabout that linked routes to Hexham, Newcastle and Carlisle and then struck the long ramp onto the dual carriageway at pace. They were doing well over seventy as Nat mulled over the wisdom of using the main roads. The speed of the journey was unquestionable. The noise of the seven big engines, however, was like sending a signal rocket high above the still countryside. He was sure the NSO would notice the movement.

The convoy left the dual carriageway and onto the straight road leading into the quiet village of Acomb. They passed the bus depot, which was now ablaze. Nat knew the reason; the NSO had been appropriating its buses. Not anymore. Five of them burned where they stood.

The journey continued down the narrow road until they pulled up a good mile from the river. Nat bumped the car up onto the verge behind the pickup truck in front. There were cars and people everywhere, hundreds of them. Everyone carried weapons: some had shotguns and hunting rifles; most had shiny new automatic rifles or machine pistols; a few hefted heavy machine guns and rocket launchers. Nat felt Stuart nudge him.

'Scottish Army gear,' Nat mumbled.

'Aye, gifts frae God's ain country!' Said Stuart

As they climbed from the car, it was difficult not to be affected by the mood of resolved anticipation. There were no raised voices, just a hum of sober exchanges, a thousand boots on tarmac and the metallic clicking and grinding of weapons. The atmosphere was electric, simmering just below boiling point. The faces around them reflected determined alacrity. The rebels were fired up and itching for a fight.

Nat nudged his way through the throng, the heaving mass of men and women, young and old, marginalised by the regime and committed to insurgency. Stuart stomped along next to him, and Amber followed in their wake. As they went, Nat noticed the faces lifting to look at him and heard whispers spread from fighter to fighter.

He followed the young Rowell to he didn't know where. Matty threaded his way through the crowd down the muddy path towards Waters Meet: the beautiful confluence of the turbulent South Tyne and the languid North Tyne rivers, a spot to which Nat had been many times with Esme to swim across the frigid waters. Now, it was barely recognisable. The thickening crowd churned up the ground and as they burrowed their way further into it, recognition continued to light up the faces around them. The rebels parted before them at their approach and the reverential whispers hummed like an enormous beehive. Embarrassed by the attention, Nat simply kept his eyes lowered as they trudged on in silence.

Through the trees came the glow of lights and the sound of steel grinding, springs clicking, the metallic song of weapons being readied. Above it all, the drone of lowered voices was becoming louder, and Nat knew he was the subject. He couldn't believe that he was having such an effect on these people. He dropped his chin and avoided eye contact.

There were accents from all over the country, although Borders Scots and Northumbrian lilts predominated. Many of the voices marshalling smaller groups into units sounded Scottish and most of the fighters carried the SAR90, the standard assault rifle of the Scottish Army.

Nat caught a nod from Stuart. He had been right: the Scots military were organising and arming the Rowell's army. Nat should have felt a reassuring gratification that here at last was an orchestrated revolt against the regime, but he didn't care. He wanted to save his friend. Beyond that, there was the seething urge to kill the rest of the raiding party that had attacked and murdered his wife. Nothing else mattered.

They approached the tunnel under the disused railway line. A fire burned and the crowds within it glowed with a flickering orange and gold. Old Man Rowell sat to one side while his eldest son, John, belted out instructions to those around him. Nat and Stuart nodded to the ruddy, round-faced old man. They passed the dense circle of people surrounding the fire and absorbed the image of those – mainly young – men and women making their peace with the reality of the coming offensive. John Rowell raised his gun in the air to acknowledge the newcomers, then he returned to whatever homily he was delivering.

Nat, Amber and Stuart came to rest with their backs against the side of the tunnel. As if in the eye of a storm, they were still and calm, watching the human commotion around them. Amber checked her weapons: her assault rifle taken from the NSO, a handgun and her hunting knife – the tool Nat had painstakingly taught her how to use.

Nat lowered his head and spoke quietly. 'What d'ye think?'

'We go in, get Claire and fuck off,' replied Stuart.

'Think they'll win?'

'Maybe... whae kens? But I dinnae want to be in town when the air force arrives.'

'Aye.'

Nat looked down at his daughter; she looked so young for a moment. He put a big hand down on the auburn curls covering the back of her neck.

'Stay close to us, okay? If you're not next to one of us, you're low to the ground – in shadow. Got that?'

She looked up from where she rested on her haunches, and smiled, nodding briefly.

Nat looked around at the other faces in the tunnel, picking out those he recognised. There were farmhands, labourers, gamekeepers, even his postman. A few weeks before, this scene would have been inconceivable. Now these men and women prepared to fight as an army for the place to which they belonged and called home. It dawned on him that some would never stop fighting. The NSO would never contain them. They had no choice; this land was in their blood, and they had fought for it for centuries. They were exactly like him, one and all.

Calls came across the line and the army quieted down. They slowly began to file in. The procession bottlenecked its way up the steep bank and onto the disused railway above their heads. Calls of 'Stay off the bridge!' came from above, since the sheer weight of numbers could cause the old structure to collapse.

Nat, Stuart and Amber joined the army. It was now eerily quiet. The heat and smell of all the bodies and the electricity of expectation filled the air with a feral energy. As he climbed the slope up to the railway line, Nat heard the roar of powerful engines through the trees and headlamps danced between the branches. The Rowell brothers, or whoever had organised this army, had prepared vehicular support for the men on the ground.

As Nat watched the lights of the vehicles disappear through the trees, a short man whose head Nat was looking over caught his eye.

'That's John Rowell… great fighter but he's wild. Off to raid the food banks out at Whittonstall,' he said.

'What d'you mean *food banks*?' Nat asked.

'All the produce goes straight to Whittontsall. It's stored there and distributed throughout the Northeast. The NSO take it all now.'

'Do we not need him tonight?' Nat nodded in the direction of the departing vehicles.

'Divvent worry – if we need him, he'll be there. He blew the factory… he'll not let us down. He's like ye!'

Nat was caught off guard by this observation and had no idea what to say in return. His eyes moved on down the column without a word. They began the two-mile march south to Hexham as the convoy of vehicles rumbled off to the east. It was slow going as the column compacted and stretched like a concertina. There was little talk. Steam rose from the bodies, drifting into the trees above. Through the branches, the rain clouds had

220

parted, and the deepening night was as clear as a dark blue gemstone cut to a million points as the stars blazed.

After twenty minutes or so, Nat noticed that the column was becoming more congested up ahead. As he approached, he saw people dropping out briefly to the left before re-joining the army. He couldn't make out what was going on in the poor light until they drew up alongside an old hawthorn tree. Somebody had left a battered guitar with a note scratched onto the rosewood: I'll be back for this. Surrounding the guitar others had left their most treasured possessions, from wedding rings and necklaces to photographs and clothes. As they passed, Amber broke from the crowd. She hung her mother's necklace on the thorny tree and turned to look at him. He bit his tongue; he didn't feel or care for any superstition.

After an hour, they reached the river and crossed in single file over the ruin of the old railway bridge. All that remained of the iron structure were four massive stone pillars and two huge girders spanning the river, which, though neither deep nor raging, was a good twenty feet below. Each person gave the one in front plenty of room. As they stepped off the other side, the three rebels looked around. There had to be four or five hundred people on the bank, with as many behind them crossing or waiting to cross the bridge.

Teams ran along the banks, telling the force to fan out all along the river in readiness to sweep into town over the golf course. Nat tapped his two companions and began leading them off into the shadows.

He wanted to head due south past the clubhouse, down the main drive of the golf course to meet the Haydon Bridge road some three quarters of a mile west of the police station. He hoped the Government held Claire there. Since the first part of the plan seemed to resemble that of the main forces, they would stay with them, ready to slip away at any point.

Ben stood at the side of the room. Dart was making a call.

'Why aren't you on the ground yet, Beaston?' He yelled.

His cell phone lay on the desk in front of him, the persistent grind of the military convoy powering along in the background came through the speaker. The noise clearly distracted him. His face was bright red as he leant on his clenched white knuckles.

'Mr Dart, I do not intend to showcase our convoy of thirty-two military vehicles. As I understand it, the rebels have hundreds of vantage points along the valley. So, I took a rougher but far more clandestine route over the moors from Blanchland. We are two miles out from the school where we will set up camp.'

'Okay. okay. Just get your men on the ground and take control of the situation quickly! I've got the Cornish coming up my arse and the Geordies down my neck, we can't let this escalate. Do you hear me?'

'Loud and clear, sir! Don't worry… we will control this end. Do we have drone backup? And what are your orders for contact?'

'Yes, drones will be available from later today or tomorrow latest. You meet resistance… you use all necessary force. If you think you're meeting passive resistance – harbouring or human-shielding – you do whatever is necessary, you hear? Whatever you must do.'

Dart looked up, but Ben looked away, he felt his gut twist at the thought of this violence, but his yearning for revenge was too great.

'Roger! I'll report back at zero one hundred hours.' The phone clicked off.

Lucas was exasperated.

'Once we have control, we can soften our position,' Ben said.

'It's not that Ben, we should have prepared and planned earlier. These bloody rebels have us on the back-foot and it could be a bloodbath… if you had allowed me more room sooner, I would have had that border tighter than a duck's arse and we wouldn't be here now!'

The military convoy pulled into the car park and tennis courts of the local school. Beaston gathered the officers to his truck and spelled out his tactics for the day. He unfurled the map of Hexham that he had studied on the journey. It showed a town easily defended with the right organisation. The centre sat high up the valley side above the northern quarter of the town. It was in this location that Beaston wanted his troops to meet the rebels. It was here the battle would be open and the NSO training, however brief, would prove invaluable to his men.

'We need to stop the rebels entering the higher ground in the town. Set up blockades on the roads leading in. Make sure we have heavy guns on each.'

Beaston knew about street warfare having been a NATO commander before it fractured – he held the Russians in Eastern Poland and he had cut his teeth in the desert.

He knew that insurgents could amass and dissolve like a flock of starlings if his force allowed them into the narrow winding streets of their hometown with its sympathetic front doors.

'We must move quickly into the streets and occupy buildings. We must make the rebels stand and fight.' He turned to his advisor. 'Let's see how keen they are to slug it out toe to toe.'

His men totalled over five hundred at that moment, although Dart had seen to it that figure would triple in the next twenty-four hours. He looked up to the night sky for a while and then decided it was as good a time as any to cross a task from his list. He snatched his cell phone from the breast pocket of his woodland greens and waited impatiently while the phone repeated its monotonous burps. Finally, he heard a voice at the other end.

'Ludlum?'

'Yeah, who's this?'

'I'm your replacement. I have orders to shoot anyone or anything that disturbs my operation. So, I hope we are going to work well together. Now, tell me how many men you have at your disposal.'

In the ensuing silence, he heard Ludlum gulp. 'About one hundred,' he replied finally.

'Are you sure? Or have old men in tweed caps killed some more of them?' Beaston imagined Ludlum with his broken arm, overtaken by events and in no mood for witty retorts. 'No, don't answer that. I'll be with you in five minutes anyway. Where are you, the police station?'

'Yes.'

Beaston hung up and signalled to his force to move out. He ducked his head slightly and did his trademark half run, half walk to his armoured truck. His movement was that of a man with a mind that was always a few steps ahead of his current action. His mannerisms were awkward, eccentric and easily laughed at, famed by the troops who served under him.

But he was also a man revered by his peers. Whatever comedic value his quick mind produced, it yielded absolute attention to detail and unwavering commitment to his cause.

Nat could hear the engines of the military vehicles, a low growl floating across the otherwise still and peaceful night sky. At that moment, he understood that the NSO knew they were coming, and the vehicles they were moving in were not the cars and buses they had been running around in up to this point. He looked across at Amber, walking a few yards to his right, eyes firmly fixed ahead of her, concentrating on the hunt. Nat feared for his daughter. He looked across to Stuart, on Amber's other side, and the big Scot gave him a broad grin.

'And I thought you got me intae shit back in the day!' He looked ahead for a spell then turned again to Nat, his face more solemn now. 'Ye hear the reinforcements too?'

'Aye,' said Nat.

The rebel force had fanned out, sweeping over the whole width of the golf course, a distance west to east of about three-quarters of a mile. Nat was at the western end of the formation. As they walked silently through the night, they saw no movement, no lights and no NSO. When they neared the clubhouse, Amber broke away into the darkness and Nat and Stuart lowered their shoulders, keeping to scrub and bush for cover. The rest of the hundred or so men and women who were near followed suit, ducking into concealment or simply low to the ground, and there they waited for the farmers' next move.

The clubhouse was dark and silent and evidently had remained locked up for weeks. Nat supposed that the regime was not a fan of golf – *there were some positives*. He looked back towards the rebels who had followed them on an arc around the open space. He gestured to a man behind him, whom he presumed was in charge because he had seen him talking to Rowell's eldest. His rudimentary signal consisted of a palm held up, a point to his eye and a point to the driveway leading out to the main road running Northwest out of the town. The other man got the idea and spread the word for the small force to remain where they lay.

Nat and Stuart moved swiftly into the darkness. Neither was a stranger to the nocturnal world or to the disciplines of moving silently and hunting prey. There was no thought for the extremity of the circumstances because it was simply their reality; this was the here and now and they had to play out whatever lay ahead of them.

Nat felt the sharp stab of the wound in his shoulder, but it didn't bother him now. He felt strong and cocooned by the dark. He knew this place like his own land. He no longer had a conscious handle on his motivation - revenge, freedom, justice - all simple words to describe a torrent that had swept him up and would only let him go when the storm subsided.

They hugged the eastern flank of the stone wall that led down the driveway. The only sounds were the stirring leaves, the occasional stick snapping in the distance and the odd telling whistle as either the rebel force or the regime's troops communicated in the darkness. The two farmers both felt it though: the unnerving energy of unseen human presence somewhere ahead of them. It was in the air like a time bomb ticking and there was no escaping it. As they reached the end of the drive, Nat leaned back against the wall and turned his head to Stuart. 'Not a shot fired… good or bad?'

'Nae idea. But they must be somewhere. You heard those engines. That was heavy machinery.'

'Aye, but why wait?' Nat took a breath then poked his head around the corner of the wall. The road ran straight for half a mile in both directions. The fields banked upwards on the far side and the grass verge was thick with brambles. At first, the road looked clear, not a soul in sight; then as his eyes became focussed on the distance, a shape materialised from gloom. As he studied it, it took on the form of an armoured personnel carrier, parked across the road at its narrowest point. Nat thought for a minute then turned to Stuart. 'Wait here. Let me know if anything changes.'

Abraham Turner watched his breath rise above the cold steel of the armoured personnel carrier. It was cold and dark ahead of him. His heart pulsed with nerves. A trooper he had met that night, spoke to him. They were the only ones awake in their team. Turner could not see the trooper, as he was resting below in the doorway to the truck.

'What brought you here?' the trooper whispered.

'I was at Uni five months ago,' Abraham answered, softly. 'Been a party member for two years. I believe in Baines, but this... I dunno.'

'You didn't sign up then?'

'Nope. Conscript – three months before I was due to graduate!' Abraham checked himself as his voice raised a little. His eyes scanned the darkness ahead.

'Me, too. Not a student, though. Out of work.'

Abraham stood on the ladder leading to the top of the armoured truck, his arms and weapon rested on its roof, staring down his gun sights into the gloom.

'When the rich were getting richer and the rest were suffering a life of reality TV and lager, twenty-two-year-old economists weren't standing on top of army trucks pointing serious weaponry down dark roads expecting attacks by a load of angry farmers.'

His words were wasted, the trooper below him had fallen asleep. He returned to the lonely business of keeping watch. When a faint green glow appeared in the centre of his night sights, his heart began to pound – and he froze. As the dim glow became stronger and took a human shape, a tear came to his eye. He fell off the truck and scrambled over the tarmac to his sleeping colleagues, fifteen in total, who occupied whatever space they could in the truck.

'They're coming!' he whispered loudly, shaking the men awake 'Please wake up!'

The detachment moaned wearily into action scrambling for their weapons and pushing each other out of the way. Only two of the fifteen had experience of combat. The man in charge was an ex-infantry soldier called Terry Deelam. Out on the tarmac behind the vehicle he grabbed Abraham by the shoulders. 'How many Abe? What did you see?'

'There's one – only one that I saw. He's walking down the middle of the road and he's covered in weapons.'

'What? *ONE*?' Terry leapt up onto the truck. 'Stand to, lads! I'll fucking shoot you later, Abe!'

The men climbed aboard the armoured car and set their sights to their eyes. They had a split second to register the green figure around one hundred and fifty yards out: long thin legs, broad shoulders, rifle hanging by a strap off one shoulder. He had a small box shape on the other, which, at the same time its identity registered with Abraham, lit up like a firework in his sights. Abraham felt calm in that netherworld of milliseconds before impact. Then the lights went out.

Nat had scarcely believed his eyes when the boy had bolted. He'd been gambling on nerves ruining his aim. He had sent the rest of their group through the trees and behind the wall along the side of the road. As he fired the rocket launcher at the armoured truck, the rebels leapt over the wall and charged towards the NSO position. The impact of the rocket had blown the truck backwards. It ripped the armour on the roof of the vehicle up and backwards. The explosion burned and mangled the men who had managed to get on top of the truck. The vehicle had crushed those who hadn't. Gore covered the scene.

The rebels quickly counted fifteen bodies; two were still inside the truck on impact. Four survived the explosion. All the survivors were likely to die of their injuries. The full weight of the truck had smashed one young man who had been standing behind it when the rocket struck. Nat found his body thirty yards from impact. He looked like a rag doll and had a scolding shard of metal embedded in his cranium. He spluttered blood, conscious but oblivious. Nat shook his head as he looked into the young man's eyes. He took out his handgun and shot him dead.

He could hear fighting elsewhere in the town now. He checked his weapons so that he didn't look at the misery around his boots. He turned to the rebels with him. 'Take weapons and ammo. Leave everything else. They'll be coming! Get into shadows and gardens. We work our way down this road to the police station. Every road we pass leave ten men in wait at the entrance to it. Ambush any NSO coming up or down.'

The message spread down the line and the force split into two moving down each side of the road through the gardens of the houses. As the army passed Eilansgate, more rebels met them coming up the hill. They'd had small skirmishes but encountered no real resistance. He looked down the hill towards the police station, one of the few buildings still showing lights and now only eight hundred yards away. He took stock because the gardens in front of the houses stopped at this point and there was little cover. They would have to move en-masse and in the open.

The force sat low and quiet as gunfire rang out from a distance. Nat turned to the rebels close by. 'Who's in charge of you?'

A dozen faces stared back, shining and vacant in the darkness. Then, out of the shadows, appeared two men and a woman. Nat recognised a couple of them but had never spoken to them. The first was a stoical-looking man in work boots, jeans and a camo jacket. He wore his assault rifle across his chest as though he had been born with it. He looked assured and in control and spoke with a calm, soft voice.

'I'm Andrew. This is Jackie.' He indicated a rosy cheeked woman with messy hair and a stud in her nose.

'Aye… Jackie. Esme bought a horse off your father couple of years back. He alright?' Nat said.

'He's gone,' she said abruptly. 'Scotland.'

Nat nodded, but his attention was on the road ahead of them. It was empty and still.

'And that's Barty,' Andrew introduced a squat, bald man in military fatigues. He held his weapon ready and looked determined enough, but in an ideal situation he'd be a good four stone lighter for the fight ahead.

Nat nodded at Barty. 'Builders merchants in town, wasn't it?'

The man nodded and Nat shifted his focus to the empty street. 'Now then... How do we go from here? There's no cover down the road and we'll lose the surprise if we detour around the streets with this amount of people.'

'They're waiting for us, aren't they?' Barty looked down the empty street, the crack of distant shots echoing through the otherwise silent town.

'Aye, Barty, son... We have to assume that.'

'Every one of us knew we were going to fight tonight,' Jackie said. 'That we could *die* here tonight. We need to push on, keep the impetus.'

The three of them looked at Andrew.

He stood tall, unwavering. He studied the empty street ahead, then nodded solemnly. 'We came to fight. We take the road all at once... fan out as soon as we can and form some platform to attack from.'

Nat looked around the gathered faces. He saw the fear, but he also saw courage and commitment. They had to keep moving. 'Okay, get your people ready. But remember... this only works if we're a wave of bodies and bullets.' With the weight of their lives on his shoulders, he surveyed the street once more.

Brigadier Quentin Harris watched from his position as the rebel army advance down the hill. He had his cell phone to his ear. Beaston, two hundred and fifty yards behind him in the police station, was on the other end.

Harris had sixty men at his disposal against four hundred or so rebel fighters. So, he had half his men take up positions in the upper floors of the buildings either side of the road as it widened once more. The other half of his contingent lay in wait behind garden walls. Right now, he spoke quietly to Beaston.

'They appear to be having a bloody conflab! There are a lot of them.' He took a moment to think. 'I'd advise that you pull back to the school. Wait there for news, because if they overwhelm us here, they'll be on you like lions on a limping goat.'

'Ok. Remember reinforcements are on their way, including drones. If you can repel them this time, we'll smash them the second they come.'

'I'll see what these boys are made of.' Harris slipped the phone into his pocket. He looked up the street and saw the mass of bodies charging down the hill. They were roaring like a battle charge from centuries before. He stepped into the middle of the street.

'It's your ammo against their numbers!' he screamed into the night. 'Remember, men… I want them to meet a wall of lead!'

Then, he skipped back across the road to safety behind his men. He rested a heavy machine gun across the wall of a pretty garden and squeezed the trigger, pumping round after round of twelve-point-seven-millimetre shells into the approaching mass. All his men lit up, too, and they cut the rebel force down before they had any opportunity to fire back.

The noise was all consuming, sixty weapons firing at thirteen hundred rounds per minute into the narrow road.

The rebels who came within four hundred yards were shot down as they ran. The rest turned and ran back up the street from where they had come. Harris allowed himself a smile but knew the fluidity of urban conflict might only allow his troops a fleeting glimpse of victory. He commanded them to show no mercy.

As they began running down the road, Nat realised the mistake, but it was too late. He couldn't keep up with the younger people; both he and Stuart were left behind. When the shooting began, the horror of what lay before them was unimaginable. The storm of lead tore through flesh and bone with an initial thud and damp fizzing as the rounds ricocheted out of bodies as they took their last agonising steps. The howls of injured men and women lying helplessly in no man's land rose horrifically above the gunfire. This was the sound of war.

A volley of shots hit Jackie and her body convulsed with the pummelling of the rounds. She screamed as though her insides were on fire before wilting onto the hard tarmac of the road. Andrew, too, went down, although he could have known nothing of his final moment: whilst on one knee and firing aimlessly at the regime's positions, a round struck him in the eye and passed through his head.

Nat stared helplessly at the mayhem with the taste of blood in his mouth, the air laced with agony. He was unsure of what to do until a large hand grabbed his shoulder and pulled him sideways into a gated inlet behind which was a house and garden surrounded by high walls. The panicking rebels were crushing into the small turn-in between the road and the gate. The gate fell open under the sheer weight of numbers pushing up against it. The stunned rebel force fell over one another into the safety of the garden.

The force had split into three; those in the garden, those running back to where they had started from and those lying in the street. The NSO continued taking pot shots at the living. Nat looked at the faces around him, blood-soaked bodies with tears streaming from their eyes. It had been a massacre. But they had to counteract the reverse, or they would all perish in that street.

Some of the rebels had climbed the trees flanking the high wall and were firing down at the NSO positions. Nat looked around the yard and saw a shed. He ran quickly to it and yanked open the door. Among other tools and bits of garden equipment was a sledgehammer.

He hurried back to the wall, and he swung the hammer hard against the bricks. Within three strikes he had knocked out a good hole with enough scope and leverage from which to fire a gun. He walked a few paces along the wall and swung the hammer again. He moved systematically along the wall smashing small holes into it. Others began using the other tools, loose bricks or anything they could lay hands on to do the same.

Nat ducked and weaved as the hail of bullets cracked and whined off the wall that separated the rebels from the incoming NSO fire. He looked out over the carnage, the death, the people around him, young and old, breaking down with the horror. The incessant hammering of gunfire spelled out the danger, the all-consuming screaming foretold the nightmare of injury and insanity. The bodies were everywhere, inert, rushing with activity and rocking with madness, the living sent wild by their proximity to the dead. There was no time to reason, to calculate. Nat just kept screaming for people to fire their weapons at the enemy positions. The chaos was all-consuming.

Gradually, however, Nat, Stuart and Barty managed to bring the rebels under control. The men and women who could still face the fight took up better positions and the weight of numbers began to tell. The rebels started to contain the NSO bullets with suppressing fire of their own.

Once it was possible, Nat and Barty ran the gauntlet back up the hill. They met the rest of the force who were out of range and under cover and waiting desperately for a signal or an order.

Quentin Harris felt in good. The stalemate suited his plan, and he could sit like this for days. He knew the reinforcements would be here long before that. He moved away from his men, down the side of the police station. The high perimeter wall and the station itself cocooned him. Behind him, the back of the station and a car park, similarly enclosed. Rubbish blown in on the wind littered the alleyway and there was an overturned salt bin. It was here that he turned and planted his backside. He had a view of his troopers' positions and could see the rebel bullets puffing in dusty clouds off the brickwork. The insurgents were keeping his fighters' heads low, but they were not winning. If the insurgents were to try another charge, he would be able to repeat the massacre.

He wiped the dust from his face as he perched on the bin then he crossed his legs and picked at his boot where a scalding hot shell had slightly melted the sole. He took out his cell phone and called the General.

'Tell me,' Beaston answered.

'We have them locked down for now.'

'How long can you hold them?'

'I don't know. It depends on what they do next.'

'Well, a few hours and we'll have reinforcements.'

'They're not going anywhere. We just decimated their numbers. If they try and move now, it'll be the same result. Just make sure no one gets through to help them and –' Harris broke off, distracted for a second. He looked behind him. The alley was empty. He shook his head and turned back to face the road.

'So, if we can…' His words drifted as he sensed something again, a presence. Before his brain registered the feelings, he felt warm air – breath on his ear, right next to the phone – and a soft but certain whisper.

'You'll never win here…'

He felt a thud in the side of his neck like a hammer blow, but no pain to speak of. He staggered to his feet, the phone still to his ear.

Beaston's voice came down the line. 'What? What was that? Who said that? …Harris?'

The brigadier could only gurgle. He sensed his heart pumping harder and harder to send blood to his brain, but the vital fluid wasn't arriving. Instead, it sprayed from the deep would in his neck. As he held his free hand to the wound, the blood covered his face and body. His eyes began to cloud over, and vertigo set in, Harris looked up at his assassin: a young woman with auburn hair and vivid green eyes, her face smeared with mud. In her hand was an oozing, bloody hunting knife fresh from its most recent kill.

The geyser of red began to wane, and the enemy commander fell flat on his face at Amber's feet. The mobile phone had already skidded across the ground. She picked it up and hung up on whoever was on the end of the line.

She put the phone in her pocket next to that of the spy then turned and ran back into the car park. Moving like a cat, she pounced up onto the armoured car parked next to the wall and over the top, vanishing in silence.

Beaston glanced at his phone, his mind racing. This was a concerning development. He had a bad feeling.

'What? What's happened?' Ludlum demanded.

Beaston looked at him and didn't hide his contempt. He couldn't stand private security like Bill Ludlum. Military trained, yes, but too selfish or weak to commit to the forces and too vain to give up the 'tough' life. 'This is what happens when one is rushed into conflict ill prepared.' Beaston responded.

Ludlum threw his good hand in the air. 'Thank you! I've been telling them this for weeks!'

'Shut up. I need to think.'

The enforcer shook his head and got to his feet. 'Well, I'll leave you to your little think then,' he said acerbically.

'I don't recall dismissing you,' Beaston said curtly. 'You'll take thirty of my men together with your own and defend this position. Hold it until reinforcements arrive. I'm moving back to the school.' Beaston saw the look that Ludlum gave him; he'd seen it many times before when giving orders. It was fear.

'You've finally got the fight you wanted.' He smiled thinly at Ludlum, allowing the glimmer of enjoyment to show in his face. 'This isn't a few hicks on their farms anymore.'

The two men looked at each other for a long moment, but Ludlum did not offer any argument, resignation taking hold. Beaston stood up from the desk, straightened his fatigues and strode over to the door. 'You've got a real war on your hands now, tough guy.'

'Don't worry Anthony, I'll hold the police station, and when you're sent off to some other shithole to fight some other fire, Tynedale will be mine again.'

Beaston stared at him, 'another idiot and another poisoned chalice, the spark that lights the fuse… you have to give it to the glorious deputy, he chose the right man for the job.'

Ludlum stepped towards Beaston, standing over him, 'you're an empty vessel, your high rank and power… When you die, what will you have? Nothing personal, just rich men spouting bullshit words at your funeral, and all those people that knew you, saying you were a great soldier, but really you were just a cunt.'

He said the last word slowly, and he noticed the sting in the military man's eyes.

'I'll see you on the other side son.' Beaston snarled, before he nodded at his men that it was time to leave.

The rebels charged again, only this time they had the covering fire of those in the garden suppressing the NSO positions. The NSO appeared in disarray now. Their return fire was sporadic, as they ducked the lead that flew both from the rebels in the garden and from those charging down the hill.

Stuart was dug-in behind the wall and had Nat's hunting rifle. He could take down a regime soldier with every shot he made. Rebel fighters continued to fall in the charge, but they broke the regime's line. Rather than bullets, the rebels were soon beating those who had massacred them hours earlier with the butts of their weapons.

The sheer weight of numbers left the NSO no chance. The rebels flooded into the houses on either side of the road to clear them of NSO fighters. The endless mind-bending chaos of gunfire now quelled to short bursts as the rebels emptied the surrounding buildings. As they looked back up the hill, it was obvious that the victory had come at great loss to them. This was no cause for celebration. They had routed a few dozen NSO troops but lost well over a hundred of their own.

The despair of seeing the piles of mangled bodies heaped in the narrowest part of the road, hit the rebels hard. Streams of red trickled down the tarmac towards them. The air carried the stench of death and gunfire. Nat staggered through the carnage as a stunned silence fell over the force. He heard the wounded scream in agony and fear and saw survivors break down in tears. Others wandered like him through the battle zone trying to comprehend the misery.

As the survivors re-grouped, many seethed with hatred towards this enemy, and it was not long before they were desperate to attack the police station.

Nat and Stuart had caught up with each other now amid the simmering crowd.

'Now, we get in there, get Claire, and get the fuck out of this chaos. Okay, Nat?'

'Aye,' Nat nodded 'Let's get this done and get back to the country where we can see these bastards coming.'

The rebel army surrounded the police station and began by peppering it with ineffectual gunfire. Whoever commanded the regime troops was keeping them within the main body of the building, only risking shots at those rebels who ventured too close. The tactic worked, and the battle became a siege.

Beaston was now organising his remaining troops half a mile away at the school. Word filtered through that the rest of the rebel force had broken the NSO lines and they were in control of the town. The rebels were running the retreating NSO soldiers down through the streets.

Beaston had taken a frantic report from a dying commander on the eastern flank of his force. The story was that John Rowell had returned to the battle from the east. He was late, but his tardiness meant the NSO had concentrated their forces on the northern attack. He had been able to swan into town and attacking the NSO from behind, almost wiping out the government troops in the chaos.

With word of his force's collapse, General Beaston led the rest of the NSO Troops to a quick retreat up the steep banks of Causey Hill and Eastgate. These were two narrow country roads edged by high hedgerows. The government forces beat up the steep tarmac with fear powering their tired legs and occupied the old racecourse.

Beaston fanned his thinning force out along the high limestone ridge just north of Causey Hill Road. The ridge cradled the town, and the position allowed Beaton's army an elevated position with a view over the whole of Hexham. If they were going to hold off the greater numbers of the rebel force, it was this position that would afford them the best chance.

SIXTEEN

Matty and Phalen Rowell sat side by side on the stone wall of someone's front garden. The residents would not recognise their house now: bullets had peppered the sandstone building – it looked as though acid had been thrown at the house; the pockmarked facia seemed to be melting away; the windows gone, and expensive curtains hung in rags which blew in the breeze.

They were about three hundred metres from the police station. Phalen stared at the bloodbath that beset the street. Matty watched the rebels try to tighten their noose around the police station.

He had a necklace in his hand that he had found in the dirt. He worked it through his fingers like a string of prayer beads. He questioned himself, like many leaders who had come before him. He was examining his judgment, observing the loss of life, questioning the decisions he had taken and even the worth and value of the cause itself. He knew it wasn't only his decision that brought all these people to this point. He knew he was a figurehead for a movement that would have taken shape sooner or later and in some form or other. As his train of thought ventured towards thoughts of fate, freewill and destiny, his brother nudged him.

'You want some biscuit?' Phalen held out a ration pack biscuit in his grubby and bloody hand.

Matty looked at it as if he had been offered arsenic. 'No, I divvent want any of your biscuits. How can ye eat, Phalen?' He didn't wait for an answer though, turning his eyes back on the bloody hand. 'You hurt?'

Phalen looked at his hand, he bent and straightened his arm a couple of times. 'Nah, I'm okay. Just a bit of stone or something caught me on the arm.'

Matty nodded towards the siege, 'We have t' get this done fast, and shore up our positions. They'll counterattack in the morning.'

'I saw Mark die tonight. And Jennifer – an' that guy from the petrol station... the one who never shut up when all you wanted to do was buy some snacks.'

Matty chortled as he reminisced – and then his head fell. After a spell, he turned to his brother and put a hand on his shoulder. 'A lot of folk died. It's down to us to make sure that doesn't happen again. We need to dig in inside the buildings and do to them what they did to us in this street tonight.' He was as sure as he could have been about his plan. 'Did you call Dad?'

'Aye. He's coming with a truck t' help pick up the bodies.' As he spoke, four men approached them, striding confidently, a slight spring in their steps that was out of place in this hell. Three of the men dropped back, leaving John to approach alone.

He wore black fatigues but looked as though he had been in an explosion: his clothes were ripped; his hair was a mess and singed; his eyes bloodshot and face bloody; but he was smiling and walking without apparent injury. His eyes had an intensity that those of his bothers lacked.

'What's happening, Phalen?' He gestured at their positions on the wall. 'There's no time to sit. We need to push on – take Causey Hill.'

'There's been enough bloodshed for one night,' Phalen said. 'We've got most of the town. We just need to swallow up the last pockets of resistance – fight in small groups, appearing and disappearing. We'll grind them down like that.'

John's face fell. Matty could now see that he was exhausted – just running on adrenalin.

'That's ridiculous!' John shouted. 'Why let them regroup, re-arm and re-organise?'

'Because *we* need to regroup and stuff,' Phelan said. 'We're out on our feet. I don't even know whether this lot can carry on tonight. And we have more men arriving in the night. Hundreds, I'm told – coming in from Haltwhistle way.'

'My men will fight,' John said. 'Anything else would be a big mistake. The NSO are broken now... they might not be in the morning.'

Matty sympathised with Phelan's position. He understood the momentum was with the rebels but, as he looked around, their force seemed not only decimated but exhausted. When he had watched them lay siege to the Police Station, he had asked himself the question: if they were struggling to take that building, how could they be pushed to take Causey Hill in another fully fledged battle?

'No.' Phelan said. 'I've made my decision. We rest, we eat, we regroup and attack at dawn – hopefully with reinforcements. What do you say, Matty?'

Matty looked wearily up at his brother. 'They need some time, John. A few hours won't jeopardise our upper hand.'

General Beaston spoke to Baines and Dart over the satellite phone. He sat alone in the back of a dimly lit personnel carrier, He curled over with the phone between shoulder and ear and rubbed at some dirt on his hand as he spoke, his mind racing for a way out of this fix. He rarely spoke so slowly. 'Look, don't ask for positives. There aren't any. We've taken heavy losses. Harris is dead. And they pushed us back out of the town.'

'What about Bell – have you got him?' asked Ben.

'Forget fucking Bell!' Dart snarled. 'What are you going to do about it, Beaston? You said you could deal with it! What went wrong?'

'Numbers. We were swamped. They attacked from three sides and at different times – the men on our eastern flank got sucked into the northern attack and then more rebels came in beh –'

'Forget it! I'm not looking for a review! I need to know that you have a plan – a route back to taking this town!'

'I've more men in transit. If I get them, we might be saved. But let me tell you… if we're attacked again now, we're finished. I'll die here along with all these men. They're ragged, inexperienced and traumatised. We're two hours off getting the artillery. We're exposed.'

Phelan looked around at the forlorn figures looking for loved ones among the dead. The injured tormented their ranks with their howling and wailing. The hardiest souls ate morsels of food or cleaned their weapons. He could see they were out on their feet. Then he looked up the hill, at the glow in the sky from lights in the far distance, a mile or so away. A chill ran down his spine as he thought of the NSO being given time to regroup and set up a new offensive. He looked back to his brothers.

'A few hours…then we'll attack,' said Phelan.

John shook his head with resignation. 'Okay, two hours. Hope you're right on this one...'

SEVENTEEN

Nat grabbed Stuart's forearm. The Scot looked at him with wild eyes.

'You're shooting at bricks, man!' said Nat. 'It'll get us nowhere.'

'Cannae just sit here. Claire's in there. An' wi' all this, she's in danger…'

Nat nodded and looked away, but he didn't let go of Stuart's arm; wasting ammunition was pointless. The Scot finally pulled away, turned his back to the wall he'd been firing over and slumped against it, his hair falling over his face.

Shortly after, Nat got to his feet. Bent double behind the wall for cover; he crept along it and looked towards the back of the police station. Without so much as a nod, he set off up the road. It was only when he was twenty odd yards away that he ushered his friend to follow.

As they turned into Hellpool Lane, Nat pondered how aptly named it had now become since the end of it was where rebel losses had been heaviest. Then they entered a small street lined by Victorian terraced houses with pretty gardens enclosed by stone walls. Fifty yards along this street, the road brought them out to the rear of the Police Station. They knelt behind the bushes where other rebels had taken up positions.

Nat pointed to a single storey extension attached to the back of the building. 'See there?' It had a flat roof and small windows.

'I ken what ye're gonna tell me,' said Stuart.
Nat nodded.
'The cells…' they said in unison.

'Aye, I should know,' Nat said. 'I've spent a few nights in there myself. Long time ago, mind – when I used to hang around with the likes of you.' He slapped his old friend on the shoulder.

'Bet ye that's no' a concrete roof. These places weren't designed for any breakouts, I'm sure.'

'Aye, that's what I was thinking,' replied Nat.

'Now? In the dark?'

'Aye. We'll have a go.' He looked up to the sky. 'It'll be light soon. Let's get a move on.'

In the final hours before the morning light broke the darkness, the rebels cleared the dead from the streets. They held the regime troops at bay with suppressing fire on the police station, and they prepared for another day of fighting. The Rowell brothers began to organise their forces.

Reinforcements were trickling into Hexham from the West.

At the racecourse, Beaston was sipping hot coffee, his fatigues open at the collar. He looked at a street plan of the town he was planning to smash and tapped a sharpened pencil off the table. He snatched up his mobile phone and hit the green button. He listened to the dial tone for three rings before the call was answered.

'Boyce, where the hell are you?'

'Sir, we are now in a village called Tow Law, thirty odd miles out from your position.'

'Good, good. See you on your arrival.' He sat back in his chair and heaved a deep contented sigh. For the first time, things were looking up. He had been preparing himself to try and hold his position with the men currently at his disposal.

Still, it was nearly an hour before the rumble of slow-moving machinery could be heard. His mood transformed immediately. He leapt out of his chair and grabbed a sergeant by the shoulders. 'Those stupid bastards *had* us! I want the artillery ready to fire in fifteen and troops mobilised and in position immediately.'

As the military convoy rolled into the racecourse, Beaston could see that Dart had not let him down. The top table was serious about quashing this rebellion and for once they had given him the right tools to complete the job.

He now had at his disposal two units of heavy artillery, twenty-three mortar squads, three drone teams and nine companies of infantry. The tables had turned dramatically in terms of both weight of numbers and firepower.

He deployed his men in an arc that curled around the high ridge south of the town from Gallowsbank Wood in the east to the Allendale Road in the west. Tactically, it was a superb position: at least a hundred and fifty metres above the town with a clear view of the whole theatre. He sent the drone teams out into the dawn. They flew high over Hexham with heat imaging equipment recording concentrated areas of heat. Then the artillery and mortar squads would target these areas for the initial attack.

Beaston paced around his makeshift command centre, itching to begin high on the anticipation of total victory. He had been in this position many times before; he knew the insurgents didn't stand a chance. He looked forward to showing his troops how winning could be easy. He couldn't understand why the rebels hadn't carried on the rout when they'd had the opportunity.

'We'll be having a brandy with lunch today,' he said to his team as the data from the drones filtered in. It showed a line of heat images running across the foot of the ridge and another concentrated around the police station.

'Make sure your gun bunnies overcompensate on their AOR's,' he commented quietly but firmly to his artillery commander. 'I want them legless and mentally ruined.'

As the Rowell brothers sat under the stars, the grunt and groan of heavy vehicles engaged in massive activity rumbled down the hill to Hexham. Matty knew John felt betrayed by their caution.

He watched as Phelan spoke, 'I don't think we can attack. We need to dig in and hold the town. We cannot send these people up that hill.' He nodded towards the rumble of an army preparing for war. 'Not with all that waiting for us at the top.'

'Agreed,' Matty said. 'We won't match them now, and they have the higher ground. We'll hide ourselves in the town and fight in the streets.'

'Make small sniping attacks on their lines? Suck them back into town and take on smaller groups' street to street.' Phelan was desperate.

'That's the way I see it,' Matty added.

He felt John's eyes burning down upon him, but he didn't look up. They appreciated the opportunity missed in not pushing on up the hill when the chance was there, but this was no time for reflection or accountability. Now, with the new sun came the dawning realisation that war was a constant. The enemy didn't just run away; they would always return, a little more knowledgeable, a little harder, and a little more desperate. There was no control over events now. They had started something they could not have imagined before. They had led their peers into war, its very nature one of suffering and tragedy. When he allowed a moment of reflection, all he felt melancholy and doubt.

Whether they won or lost this day, there would be no excitement or glamour in the tales of battle, only sadness and a hollow in the souls of those who experienced it for all those whose lives were obliterated by the madness.

Nat and Stuart could hear the reinforcements. Both knew the next battle was going to be worse than the first. The clangs, the engines and the yelling of orders echoed through the trees and houses. Nat spat in the dirt as the chill crawled down his spine like icy fingers. He looked at his friend, whose face registered the look immediately; he knew this was it.

'Let me go alone.'

Stuart looked around him as though he had been transported to an alternative universe. 'Fuck… off…'

Nat's smile and the faint shake of his head betrayed his resignation to his friend's will, but it also disguised his relief.

Stuart grabbed Nat's jacket. 'For Es… For Claire…' he growled.

Nat nodded, then looked around at the rebels, searching their faces.

'She'll be waiting when we get back,' said Stuart.

Nat's eyes met his friend's again. He decided it was better that Amber wasn't with them now. He gripped his weapon. It was time.

The two men crept towards the red brick community hall that stood alongside the police station. It had a drive running along its flank leading to a car park at the rear. A low wall bordered the drive, and they used it as cover. The wall stood roughly a metre on their side but two and a half on the police station side, dropping into the car park, which remained full of cars. If they could get over the wall unnoticed, the rest was straightforward.

They were on all fours behind the wall, their legs and backs cramping up.

'I'm gonna go,' whispered Nat, with a pained expression. He raised his head slightly above the wall and a single shot rang out from the police station. Before he had registered the noise, Nat fell back as dust and concrete shards stung his skin. Lying on his back he looked at Stuart, eyebrows raised, stunned.

Then the Scot's face clouded. He took his weapon off his back and checked the magazine. He looked solemnly at Nat and without a word shrugged his shoulders and leant on the wall, unleashing the contents of his magazine on the building.

The regime troops returned fire, hitting the wall and sending bullets fizzing over their heads. When Stuart started shooting again, however, the whole rebel contingent followed suit and the building was shrouded in dust as bullets rained down on it.

Stuart took his chance and leapt over the wall. Nat followed, and they found themselves sheltering behind a car as the shots cracked above their heads. They ran crouching under the deadly storm, moving across the car park and up hard against the windowless single storey wall.

They waited there for the rebels' firing to wane. Then Stuart leapt onto the roof of the car next to him and up onto the roof of the single storey extension. Lying on his belly on the flat roof, he hung his hand down and pulled Nat up behind him.

In the middle of the extension was a square lightwell. It stood over a yard where prisoners could be brought in or taken out of the cell block. The walls were built up higher than the roof, like a turret. The two rebels used it to obscure them from the view of the regime troops within the building.

Rounds had chewed up the roof and they could see gnarled lead roof curled and torn. They were in business, but the plan would only work if Claire was this side of the yard. They looked at one another, nodded and each shifted to the nearest hole where they began pulling and beavering the lead away, exposing the plasterboard of the ceiling below. They worked systematically across the roof creating small holes, calling out quietly, hearing nothing and moving on.

It was the fourth opening that Nat broke through. He made short work of the roof. He looked through the small hole as tracer rounds flew over his head, momentarily lighting up the sky. He saw a whisper of ivory skin in the darkness below. It was just a flash, but it was enough. As his size elevens smashed chunks of roof and plasterboard away, he caught Stuart's attention. Without a word, he dropped through the hole he had made. Stuart dived onto the gap and peered blindly into the blackness below.

Nat landed hard on the concrete floor. Although the ceiling was fairly low, the darkness had extended the drop, and he couldn't prepare his landing. He rolled on the floor in a heap, a deep throbbing pain rising through his feet and shins. As his palms touched the cool, smooth floor his fingertips brushed another object alien to the flat surface. He reached for it and felt a thick woollen sock covering a bony little foot. Attached to the foot was a denim-covered leg and a soft wool covered body that smelled of Patchouli.

Nat knew Claire was hurt; she was limp and dazed, hardly reacting to his sudden presence in the darkness. He felt the pulse in her neck, which was strong enough, so he began to tap her cheek but stopped immediately when he touched her swollen face, not least because she recoiled in agony. He moved quickly to cut the plastic ties binding her hands. He whispered in her ear, as softly as his gnarled vocal cords, would allow. 'Hold on now, lass. I'm gonna pass you up to Stu, okay?'

Her arms wrapped themselves tightly around his neck and he crossed his forearms under her bum and lifted her smoothly and easily up off the floor. His foot kicked something in the darkness and the familiar screech of a metal chair leg on concrete rang out. He stopped and looked about, expecting a door to swing open and guards to rush in, but nothing happened.

He used his foot to guide the seat under the flashing hole in the roof, as Claire gripped him like a fearful child. Once in position, he stepped carefully onto the chair. The plastic bent and the metal legs gave a little, but it took their combined weight. He lifted her as gently as he could and pressed her dead weight over his head. Stuart's hands, like the grabbing claws of a crane, took her wrists and guided her through the jagged hole and into his arms.

Moments later, Stuart's head reappeared at the hole. 'She says there's somebody else – a Rory?'

'Okay,' Nat whispered, and he called out quietly in the darkness. 'Rory? You in here, son?'

A murmur came from his right, and he found the curled-up frame of a man pressed against the cold concrete wall. Nat pulled him to his feet. 'You injured?' he asked.

'I can't' he moaned.

'Get up lad, pull yourself together. I can't lift you out of here.'

The broken man stumbled to the chair and, with Nat's pushing and Stuart's pulling, he too rose up off the chair and through the hole in the roof.

Moments later a hand came back through the roof and Nat could see Stuart's head silhouetted against the flashing dawn sky.

'Come on – let's move!' he called down.

Nat clapped his old friend's palm with his own. 'I'll see you back at the farm!'

'Dinnae be fucking stupid!' snarled Stuart, exasperated, 'I'm not leaving you!'

'You will,' Nat said. 'You'll go now and get them and Amber safe on the farm. I've got business here with these bastards. Then it's over. I'll be back before the sun's out.'

Stuart looked around at the rising sun and flashed him a cynical look. 'There's plenty of time for them later. Not now.'

'Go! Get Amber. *Go!*' Nat was resolved.

Stuart growled in frustration as he looked at Claire, shivering with fear, her back against the wall that separated them from the NSO guns. Then his silhouette disappeared from the hole in the roof, leaving Nat in the relative silence of the cold cell.

Nat stood for a short while in the darkness. He could almost taste the damp concrete. His heart pumped blood through his body like the fire in an engine. His muscles ached but his mind was as clear as crystal, lucid and focussed on what was to come.

He walked across the empty room until he hit the wall. From there he moved left, hands flat on the smooth painted concrete, damp with condensation. It wasn't long before his hands fell away into a gap and struck the steel cell door. He felt around the edges and found the hinges; the door would open outwards, forcing whoever might come in away from him. So, he moved to the other side of the door, and with his back to the wall he readied himself. He strapped his assault rifle tight across his back, took out his handgun and changed the magazine to a full one. Then he slipped his hunting knife from its sheath.

He took deep breaths as he thought about the best way of getting someone to open the cell door. He had time, so he opted for a lure rather than an alarm. He turned his gun around, holding the barrel he began to tap it against the concrete of the doorframe – not loudly, but enough to resonate through the steel door. He hoped that someone would be passing and at best think Claire was trying to escape, at worst become inquisitive.

The minutes passed, and Nat was becoming impatient when suddenly the viewing slot in the metal door slid open aggressively. Torchlight beamed into the darkness and waved around the empty space. It settled, for a moment on the empty chair, then it moved up to the hole in the roof.

Nat pressed tightly against the wall at the side of the door, his scalp rested on the cold plaster and his breathing was slow and steady. He heard voices.

'She's only gone through the fucking roof!'
'Open the door… let me see…'

Nat stood calm as he heard the clink of keys, the metallic grind of the lock turning and the clunk of steel sliding over. There was a wash of light as the door cracked open and his grip tightened on his hunting knife. The two men entered, their attention fixed on the chair and the roof.

'She must have been helped.'

Nat took one step forward and swung his right foot with all his power. His boot met the man on the left, a full, unadulterated kick in the groin from behind. His boot connected with such force that the guard was lifted off his feet and was thrown painfully on the chair, sending it flying and his torch skidding across the floor. Before torch or man had come to rest, Nat plunged his knife into the second man's side. He ripped it out in a slicing arc, shock took the man before death closed in. He staggered and slumped against the side wall of the cell, his life draining away in the blood that flooded the floor.

Nat moved back to the first man who was wailing from his belly, fighting for breath between waves of pain. Nat knelt beside him and sunk his blade deep between the ribs, silencing his racket.

As two lives in the cell ended, the third stood tall, breathed the cold air laden with the smells of war: hot copper, nitrate and dust. Nat had rarely felt more alive, his every sense burning for the next confrontation, his focus purely on hunting down the leader.

He darted his head into the corridor and snatched a glance in both directions, it was empty. He thought about where he was in the building and guessed that left would lead him to the central courtyard and on into the middle of the station. He turned that way and moved quickly, his back to the wall.

He reached a closed door and opened it slowly.

A voice came from the other side, 'tunnelled under the wall, has she?' There was sniggering from the guards who mistook Nat for their colleagues who had gone to investigate.

Nat shifted from slow motion into fast forward. He threw the door open. Three figures sheltered against the walls in the small open courtyard. Nat's handgun flashed with a metallic thump three times in quick succession and the three men remained where they lay. He searched the bodies, taking three grenades and a set of keys.

As he turned, he heard a heavy metal ball rolling on concrete. He recognised the rat-sized lump coming through the open door on the far side of the courtyard as a grenade. Nat scragged the man who lay at his feet by the scruff of the neck, heaving him up off the ground like he had done to ten thousand bales of hay on the farm. Then he hurled the dead weight across the yard with all his might. The limp body landed belly first on top of the grenade. The farmer had seconds but managed to throw himself against the wall while pulling another body over his own. He lay as flat as he could when the courtyard turned into an instant pressure cooker.

Even through closed lids, Nat was dazzled by the white light, then his body felt crushed in a wave of pressure, and he felt his skin burn in an instant. His ears felt as though they were plugged, and a high pitch ringing was the only thing that came through. His eyes registered a white light speckled with black, but there was no time to waste acclimatising; the person who had thrown a grenade through the door, would surely follow it.

Without moving the mangled corpse that had taken the brunt of the explosion, Nat loosened the strap of his assault rifle. He pulled it around to face forward across the courtyard and towards the door. Although his eyes were settling once again, the room was cloaked in a thick soup. As he saw dark blotches appear in the smoke, he opened fire, some of his bullets hitting their targets as the shadows fell to the floor. In return, the thumping bloody corpse that lay on him took a couple of rounds on his behalf.

He had to move. He threw the body to one side, jumped to his feet and skirting the side of the courtyard around to the open door as the smoke began to clear. The three fresh bodies lay in the doorway, where he found more grenades. Wasting no time, he took two more, pulled their rings, counted to three and threw them in either direction down the hall inside the door. He waited, counting the seconds. After four more, there were two ear-splitting bangs in quick succession.

He followed the explosions, looking blindly left and right, choosing right this time he hugged the wall in the smoky darkness. He tripped over a body as he approached yet another door. He cursed. He knew he could only ride his luck for so long.

He pulled another grenade from his pocket as he looked through the small rectangular window in the door. It was reinforced with wire, little squares that disappeared as he focussed on the corridor beyond. The lights were on, and it was empty – as far as he could tell; it turned to the left after ten or fifteen yards. Nat wasn't going to chance it. He repeated the action of clearing the passage with two more grenades. As he rounded the bend in the corridor, the walls were covered in gore. There were three people: two dead, the furthest dying. Nat put her out of her misery and moved to the set of double doors that gave access to the main central hall in the station.

He slipped through them and into the dark space. The tough lino floor squeaked slightly under his feet. At first, the dimly lit area seemed empty. Notices spanned the walls, and a large varnished wooden desk ran to his right, behind which were metal filing cabinets. The room still smelled clean and clinical.

Nat immediately calculated the risks: the door behind was not going to produce any surprises; the one at the far end of the hall led to the foyer then the street; there were two doors behind the desk. He edged towards the counter in silence broken only by a large clock ticking on the wall above the doors. The noise outside the station seemed to have stopped. He couldn't make out whether it was because he was deep in the guts of the building or because the fighting had slowed outside.

He stepped slowly, his weapon shouldered, eyes straight through the sights, index finger resting gently on the trigger. His breath was calm, his mind calculating, ready to react to an instinctive feeling that something was about to happen. He sensed that whatever was about to occur in this situation was most likely going to be at his expense. He sidestepped twice, turned quickly and slumped down against the desk so that it stood solid between himself and the doors.

His breath was faster but under control. He sat and looked at the pale blank wall opposite. There was silence other than the ticking of the clock and the occasional crack of firing outside and within the building, but all of *that* was outside his microcosm.

His tailbone ached on the concrete floor, and he shifted as he pondered his total lack of a plan. The red mist had undone him. How could he have entered this building on his own expecting to survive? He looked at the front door but the prospect of friendly fire on one side and NSO guns on the other did not appeal to him. Out of nowhere came Esme's smile and, as he sat in the stillness, he decided that he could make peace with death. He sat in the quiet. His weapon rested vertically between his legs, his forehead leaning against the hot metal of the barrel. The pain of losing Esme was at its least bearable in moments of calm and solitude. It would be a mercy to be released from this grief. Then he thought of Amber and his stomach turned; she was only eighteen.

The doors behind the desk opened with a slight metallic creak of the hinges and the squeal of wood against the floor. Then he heard the soft steps of many men entering the room.

He sat with his head lowered as eight men rounded the desk with their weapons trained on his head and body. They had torches mounted on their guns and his sight was compromised by the beams directed into his face. He kept his head down, figuring that somebody would kill him – or they wouldn't. Not just yet.

Bill joined his men in the hall where Bell was slumped on the floor in front of the desk.

'Looks like 'e's 'ad enough,' said one of the soldiers. Bill was not as quick to write the old farmer off. He kept behind his troops and their blinding torches – safer for him to be unseen – he had no stomach left for this enmity.

'Looks like we're all losing this one, eh Bell?' He spoke.

As he heard his voice, Bell's head rose. His white hair and teeth glowed in the bright lights. His sweating brow scowled around those cobalt eyes. The blood of many men was painted on his face.

Every one of the men trained their weapons on the farmer, whose eyes blinked in the blinding beams of the torches. He didn't speak, he just grimaced into the light, those dogged eyes searching for his prey.

'It's never quite as satisfying as you might imagine,' said Bill, 'this *'gotcha'* bit.'

Bill paused, he was about to give the order to shoot the man, but something was stopping him, it was a hollow feeling, a deep irrepressible sense of malevolence. As he paused to savour the moment, there was a deafening clap which resonated through the building. The sound was enough to drop the men to their knees. An instant later, flames leapt through the doors behind the desk and a wave of energy carried debris, bricks, rafters and steel beams through the air towards them. The ceiling collapsed and no sooner had dust filled their lungs than the weight of the building was on them.

Bill fell against the wall as the roof caved in around him. He saw the men in front of him disappear under the rubble, but he himself was encapsulated by the roof joists and the wall. Two of his men had found themselves in the same spot as him; although he couldn't see them through the dust, the torch beams indicated where they were. Bill's face, mouth and nostrils were caked in plaster and masonry obliterated by the blast. He tried to wipe it away and take a lung-full of air, but it felt as though he was inhaling cement. He choked violently as he pulled a rag from the shirt he was wearing under his coat and tied it over his mouth and nose.

He crawled through the gap between the fallen ceiling joists and wall. When he was able to stand again in the glowing, dust-ridden space, he saw nothing but carnage in front of him. As he registered the destruction, the earth shook again, and another deafening boom dropped him to his knees. As he began to get up again another explosion shook his world. Hexham was being flattened by artillery.

'You alive?' He called for any of his men. Two torch beams appeared from the wreckage, followed by the coughing and spluttering soldiers who carried them.

Bill looked up to the open sky. 'You bastard, Beaston,' he mumbled to himself. Then he looked towards the desk and moved urgently through the rubble, hoping to find a dead Bell. He approached the desk, wafting the fugg away from his face. His heart sank and his nerves peaked. The filing cabinets and desk had held to form a capsule just like the one that had saved him; there was a small crawl space where he imagined Bell had been, but now he was gone.

He spun around and signalled to his men: *eyes on.* They shouldered their weapons and flashed their lights through the gloom. It was a matter of seconds before one of the torches illuminated a huge dark apparition in the dust and smoke, but no sooner had it appeared then it vanished, followed by a blood curdling shriek and one of the torches fell to the floor.

Bill froze, there was silence for a moment, he looked at the last of his men but didn't even have time to warn him as the shadow came from nowhere behind the soldier. The second torch and weapon fell to the ground with a clatter, followed by the bearer. Bill thought he saw the farmer's blade glint in the shadows as he disappeared once more.

He gasped, his limbs leaden. He rubbed his eyes and craned his neck into the gloom. He was blinded by the smoke and dust as he felt around for a weapon. Then he looked at the door –Could he run? Could he make it?

As Nat melted into the ruins, he watched the stunned figure of the NSO enforcer standing, waiting to die. Then the bombs came again. The thought that the NSO might bomb the town had never crossed his mind. The gauntlet thrown down by the rebels had been accepted by the NSO in no half measure. War was upon them, and Nat realised he was in the eye of a storm that he had, in part, created.

As the building rocked under another explosion, he fell backwards, and the shockwaves stunned his body and mind. He sat slumped in the rubble, his gun across his legs. He stared at it vacantly as he pondered the indiscriminate killing, the unbridled death he had helped to unleash. As artillery shells boomed all around, he stayed on the floor, shivering and jumping with every explosion. Every boom and tremor snapped another thread of his sanity.

He noticed that one of the enforcers lying in front of him was coming to. First, he was dazed, then another explosion made him jerk with fear. He cried out in pain from all the bones broken when the building had collapsed around them. Nat watched him, lost in his own thoughts. The man was coughing and spluttering in the dust when he noticed Nat. Panic flashed across his face. He scrabbled in the dirt for his gun. When he found it, it was pinned under a rafter. He winced in pain as he pushed and pulled the weapon to get it free.

Nat moved his own gun slowly, without lifting it off his lap. When the barrel pointed at the injured soldier's face, he pulled the trigger.

Another bomb landed close by to send Nat sprawling across the floor. He lay in the ruins, the dust settling on his ripped and bloodied clothes. It was Stuart and Amber that suddenly filled his thoughts; *had they escaped?* He pushed himself, painfully, to his feet and checked for injury – nothing life threatening. He moved off through the wreckage and saw more of the NSO troops – mangled bodies, arms and legs sticking out of the bricks.

The heavy dust from the demolished building and pulverised masonry was thick in the air. The flames that roared from the impact zone created up-draughts that kept the particles airborne. The same flames gave off a flickering orange glow that afforded Nat some vision in the confusion. The stench of burning material and flesh hung heavy in the air. He was thankful that he could see the morning sky when he looked up. He feared he would have asphyxiated by now had the explosion not taken the roof off the building.

He climbed through the debris; it tore at his limbs. The splintered timbers were the claws of mythical beasts and the rubble the knuckles of giants beating at some part of his body with every step. He could see the white painted wall he had stared at earlier; now it was a Pollockesque masterpiece of charcoal black, dusty brown and blood red.

As he staggered through the bedlam of the ruin, he came upon a figure in the clouds. Ludlum was caked in a thick layer of dust. He appeared suddenly in the thick smoke, only a couple of feet in front of Nat. The barrel of his handgun was almost touching Nat's eyeball.

'You know, I thought you had m –'

Nat jabbed his right hand into the enforcer's throat. As he began to gasp, Nat followed up with an arcing punch that struck him square on the jaw, knocking him unconscious. Nat grabbed the back of his jacket and dragged him across the floor. He came round, groggy at first, his arms flailing at Nat's grip in a futile attempt to fight him off. As they reached some relatively bare ground, Nat threw the man against the same painted wall; Ludlum slumped against it, his eyes shining in the orange light. As he looked up at Nat, the fear reduced his years, Nat saw him as a little boy now, innocent and vulnerable.

'Those weren't the eyes that looked at me before,' he growled, 'when you took everything I had and replaced it with filth and misery.'

'You've had your time…' Ludlum attempted, but stopped as Nat lowered himself down onto his haunches and drew his hunting knife.

Without a word and without breaking eye contact, he raised it high above his head. The Enforcer screamed and covered his eyes with his forearms. Nat shouted over the din of pulverising mortars.

'Look at me!'

Ludlum's arms came away from his head – palms up and pleading for mercy. Their eyes connected once again, and Nat brought the blade down hard into Ludlum's knee as though he were stabbing the knife into a block of wood. The steel split the patella and tore through ligament and skin before hitting the concrete floor. The man screamed in agony.

He sat up and clenched his knee with both hands – including the one at the end of the plaster cast. As he came up, Nat grabbed his head and held it between hand and forearm, so his ear was close to Nat's mouth.

'You won't be leaving just yet,' Nat pulled the knife from his knee, and he screamed again.

'She was still alive when I got back,' Nat whispered – and drove his blade deep into the man's stomach.

'She was drowning in the blood that flooded her lungs after being shot in the back.'

Nat rested the man against the wall. All Nat's hatred welled up within him.

'Did you shoot her in the back before or after you raped her?' He spat the words in the dying man's face as blood flooded into his mouth.

Nat watched Ludlum's eyes dull as he writhed in agony, bile mixed with blood burning his insides. Even with access to the best medical teams there was no saving him from such a severe knife wound to the stomach. That didn't mean however, that he would bleed out quickly. Nat crouched next to him for eternal minutes. He grabbed Nat's coat. With the whites of his eyes shining suddenly, he pulled his killer closer.

'Pl... please... k-kill... me... finish...'

Nat didn't let his glare waver. 'You just keep looking at me!' he said, with a venomous snarl.

The man panicked and tried to move, but Nat's hand slammed against his throat, pinning him to the wall. Now the man lashed out with what strength he could muster; he scrabbled on Nat's clothes with desperate fingers and spat profanities. Nat held him down with ease until he passed out. But Nat slapped his face until he came around, far more subdued now, his breath shallower, faster, Nat knew he was on the way out; he couldn't feel pain anymore. He hated him more for that. His reality would be a blur of consciousness with little lucidity.

Nat stood up, and looked down at the sorry, crumpled figure. He wiped his bloody knife on the man's clothes and turned towards the entrance to the building, leaving the last of the men who murdered his wife to die and burn in the belly of the police station.

General Beaston stood on the ridge south of town admiring the carnage he had caused. He understood all too well that the insurgents could have won the battle had they carried on attacking up the hill through the night. Victories are won and lost on the margins, and as he watched with marvel the bloodbath that lay before him, he knew how close he had come to ruin.

It was a crisp morning. Flames leapt from piles of rubble along the centre and southern reaches of Hexham, where the rebel army had paused in their advance. The buildings were flattened; the town was unrecognisable. He was certain his men had decimated their enemy. His reverie was interrupted by his phone - it was Baines himself.

'How are you getting on up there?'

'I think we've seen off this little uprising already. The troops will be entering the town shortly, so consider the mission a success.'

'And the farmer?'

'Which farmer? Weren't most of them farmers?'

'Bell. The one that's been in the news...'

'I have no idea. We've just flattened the town with artillery. He could be lying in the rubble waiting for us or he could just be raspberry jam – who knows?'

'Well, you better put it on your list. I want a body. Get me proof he's dead. Or hunt the bastard down and bring him in, you hear me?' Baines seemed to have lost his usual calm. Beaston listened to the bare bones of desperation and anguish.

'I'll get him for you, sir.'

'I'll be waiting...' Baines hung up.

As Beaston looked out over the devastation he had caused, he mumbled to himself, '*Thank you, General Beaston, for solving our problems up north.*' He turned and walked as casually as he was able back to his vehicle. Climbing in, he picked up the radio and ordered the troops to enter the town. He explained that their mission was clearance of all rebels by whatever means. He also ordered the circulation of Bell's picture - he was their primary target now the battle was won.

He climbed back down from the vehicle and counted the minutes. Eight had passed in eerie silence before the crack of high velocity rifles signalled the snipers opening fire on rebel positions. It was fifteen minutes before the heavy diesel engines could be heard thundering into the ruins of Hexham. The intermittent rapid fire of his troops clearing buildings drifted up the valley sides with the thick black smoke from the bombardment.

He stood at the edge of the high valley overlooking the town. There were many people milling around him, mainly those who had escaped the rout during the night. Most sat or roamed, shocked and silent as the battle ensued below.

'Will we allow civilians to leave?'

Beaston looked to his right, where a man in his twenties sat looking back at him. He had a round face.

'The civilians are no concern of mine.' He looked the young man in the eye. 'The theatre of war is hell... a humanitarian conflict is a contradiction.' He turned back to the action, somewhat irritated by the interruption.

'But those people are not at war with us.'

Now Beaston turned to him again. 'What's your name, son?'

'Roland.'

'Well Roland, I take it you're... NSO militia?' Roland nodded.

'Let me teach you something...' He took a step closer to Roland. 'Everyone in the conflict zone is the enemy. The chaps with guns will use the chaps without them...'

'That doesn't justify killing them...'

Beaston tutted and shook his head. 'No wonder this region was in chaos.' He gestured down the hill, losing his patience with this upstart. 'No one down there is innocent. This is not normal life. This is war – it's about getting the job done.'

'Is this a war?' asked Roland bluntly. 'These people are English...'

The two men stared at each other for a long moment.

Nat's mind was now filled with thoughts of Amber. He was desperate to find her, to get her safely away from this hell.

He squeezed his way through the rubble and out into the bright morning. He found himself standing on the steps of the police station. He stood up to his full height and took in the scene. The pointlessness hit him as he stood there, his eyes panning across the devastation.

The town he had known all his life was gone. To his right, a terrace of houses had been levelled and burning debris was piled high in their place. In front of him, a lone facia remained standing but everything behind it had gone – and the same hell stretched off to his left. Where his view had previously been four-storey terraced houses from the station steps, he could now see over the piles of stone as far as Hexham Abbey, half a mile to the northeast. As his brain acclimatised to this new topographical reality, the details began to pounce like demons from the wreckage: the gruesome hand lying on the tarmac at the foot of the steps; an old lady staggering aimlessly through the rubble, covered head to foot in a coagulating mass of blood and masonry dust; the countless bodies strewn in the street. He thought about those who might survive in Hexham, enslaved by this destruction. His head fell and his heart sank as he realised that he had been part of this. He had no idea what war was until this moment.

His feet felt stuck to the hard concrete. His lungs felt like they were filling with a fine porridge as he inhaled the dust and smoke that hung thick in the air. Subconsciously, he moved to run his fingers through his hair, but found he could not push them through the matted mass. A thick white dust covered him from head to toe; he was as much a ghoul as the old lady who still wandered from nowhere to nowhere.

EIGHTEEN

Nat staggered through the remains of the street and the death that blocked his path, heading the same way out of town as he had entered. The going was just as difficult now, though instead of gunfire, he now had bodies, mangled cars and crumbled buildings to contend with.

Thick smoke wafted across the scene every so often, blanketing his view with an acerbic blackness. As one such cloud cleared, his boot caught on some jagged brickwork lying in the middle of the road. He struggled to keep his footing. His hands went down towards the ground where he saw the shock of auburn curls matted and spilling from a pile of rubble that banked steeply up to his right. He caught his breath as shock paralysed his muscles. He fell to his knees and began to rip the debris away to find the head that belonged to the locks of auburn hair, for the hellish confirmation that his daughter was dead.

His hand touched the back of the bloody scalp, and he froze, paralysed by terror. He searched the devastation around him. How could anyone have escaped? Long seconds passed before he resumed his dig – but it wasn't her. The hair belonged to a bearded face, bloody and unrecognisable but not Amber. Nat fell onto his backside, the trauma paralysing his muscles. He was dazed and tired, his mind close to shutting down.

A bullet fizzed past his nose and thudded into the masonry to his left. The velocity and size of the snipers round snapped him out of his darkness. He wasn't ready to give up yet – not now. He had to find Amber and then Esme.

The well-armed NSO troops were closing in – and fast. He rolled to his left, putting the bank of debris between him and the oncoming NSO forces.

With renewed agility and speed due to adrenalin, he traversed the rubble and found himself at the top of Westbourne Grove, a small, steep road that would take him down the valley side onto the flood plain of the river Tyne. Then it would lead into the industrial sector of the town. He hoped he would be able to find a car in one of the many garages there.

He ran down the middle of the street. He was not alone; there were other rebel and civilian survivors beating the same retreat, many wounded, others shell-shocked and crazy with the chaos. Nat was once more as focussed as a thrown stone, his trajectory pre-determined, his heavy feet stamping down the hard concrete.

He heard the crack of small arms fire behind him and realised the army was already coming down the hill, killing whoever stood before them. His heart pounded and his lungs burned as his legs kept pace with the incline. He had not run so fast in years, but the swarm of troops was too close for comfort. They were just out of sight up the hill, but he could hear rounds whistling through the morning air, and he could feel the Reaper walking by his side.

As he ran, his eyes darted left and right for an escape or at least a place to hide. Where the road began to level, a bullet hit him from behind and the impact knocked him off his feet. He could not catch his breath as his shoulder and chest began to burn. He pushed himself to his hands and knees, spat blood on the tarmac and coughed to find air. Then he was hit again, this time through his calf. His leg felt utterly useless, and he had to fight the shock as his brain told his body to give up. He felt the warm sticky ooze flowing freely from his chest, an inch or two above and to the left of his heart. He wondered whether the round had passed through his lung. He wondered whether he would live for more than a minute.

He heard shouts, whoops, and barbaric cheers as he balanced on his hands and knees. He looked up the street and saw the NSO soldiers running towards him.

He heaved himself up and ducked across the road. He fell over the wall and back into the burn which had been his escape route a few days earlier. The Cockshaw Burn went underground again after about twenty yards. As he disappeared into the shadows, the NSO guards hit the wall above him. They sent a couple of shots after him, but he realised none were keen enough to jump into the icy water behind him. He dragged himself through the dark tunnel, fighting his need to rest with every movement before he finally reached daylight and was able to leave the freezing water.

After what felt an eternity of staggering through the deserted streets, he was behind the wheel of a thirty-year-old Toyota in a deserted garage. He had tied off his calf roughly with a strip of material cut from the car's seatbelt – he had tried the same for his chest but without success, so he left it to bleed, preferring to escape first and worry about his injuries later.

He took his knife and prized off the access cover underneath the steering column. Bent double with knees around his ears and wincing with the pain, he grabbed the wiring harness connector and pulled it out giving access to the wires behind the ignition. Taking the two red wires he stripped the ends and wound them together. Then, he took the brown wire and touched it to the end of the reds and the engine fired. He revved it a few times and let it turn over as he pulled the dead agent's telephone from his pocket.

He brought up the dialled numbers. There was only one, so he pressed the green button and put the phone to his ear. He listened to the dial tone: three… four… five rings and then someone picked up.

'Yes?' It was Baines. Nat could hardly hear his voice over the drone of the engine. He could imagine Baines wishing, praying that he was dead already. He could imagine him hoping that this might be an NSO operative calling the number he found in the phone on the outlaw's body. But it wasn't...

'I thought you were supposed to be different,' said Nat, his voice a whisper even though he tried to disguise his laboured, shallow breaths with a guttural growl.

'You will pay for what you have done...' screamed Baines.

'One of us will pay. You took everything from me...'

'It appears we are in the same place, you and me, I will not rest until you are brought to justice...'

'Justice... power decides that doesn't it?'

There was no answer from Baines. Nat waited in silence, but neither man spoke again, he looked in the mirrors and saw men behind. He pressed red, threw the phone onto the passenger seat and gunned the old Toyota out of the car park.

On the approach to the bridge out of Hexham, he saw two large trucks parked across the road and a heavily armed contingent watching the out-of-town approach. He didn't notice whether any troops saw him as he veered left off the main road about half a mile short of the roadblock. He raced along Tyne Green, parallel to the river, pushing the old Toyota, aiming to cross back over the river at the point the rebel army had the night before.

The road ran out, but he gave little on the throttle as the car bounced up and lurched over the uneven surface of the golf course. The road tires struggled for traction on the wet grass, but he pushed on, bleeding and in pain. He was a good eight hundred yards short of his destination when he lost control of the vehicle. The car aquaplaned over the grass and fell sideways into a bunker. It rolled onto its roof and wet sand oozed through the smashed windows. Nat fell from his seat, landing on his injured shoulder. He groaned with pain then curled up, as the delayed effect of having the wind knocked out of him took hold of his abdomen.

Once he regained his breath, he pushed himself out of the car and made sure nothing was broken as he sucked air into his lungs. His calf was agony, but he had to walk on it now. He banished the pain to a remote corner of his mind and began the walk back to the rebel cars at Waters Meet. It took agonising minutes to cross the ruins of the railway bridge and his injuries heightened his sense of vulnerability. He was exposed to attack as he crossed the metal girders of the bridge and he struggled to balance on the relatively narrow metal with his wounds making him lame and his left arm almost useless.

Noise of the rebel slaughter echoed out of the town like the howls of ghoulish beasts, overwhelmed only by explosions and the rumble of falling buildings.

He staggered on down the path – he was dragging his leg behind him now. His lung gurgled, filling with blood and the wound was debilitating – but he would not stop. He told himself there'd be a car with the keys ready where the rebels had met. There may even be a doctor... first aid. Was Stuart dead too? Just a little further...

Then something caught his attention in the morning light. He stopped in front of it and stared blankly for a moment. His head shook almost imperceptibly, betraying the melancholy and regret that ate away inside him. As Nat looked at the shrine of personal belongings left by the rebel soldiers, he saw the necklace that Esme had given to Amber. He snatched it up and buried it deep in his pocket. A tear rolled from his eye.

NINETEEN

The earth moved just as Amber's foot had touched the ground. She was stepping out of the transit van that they had used to escape Hexham. She turned and stood stiff as the bank of fire erupted high above the town. It was like the walls of hell ripping through the air in a churning billowing mass of flames and smoke. The ground trembled under the barrage that thundered down on the town. The shock wave reached them a few seconds before the crack, which rolled and rumbled on after its initial percussion. Amber fell to her knees as she saw the carnage. There wasn't a square inch of the southern side of Hexham that the flames did not appear to engulf. She couldn't imagine any shelter in the pulverised streets.

She felt Stuart's hand on her shoulder, and the deep voice she knew so well spoke softly. 'I'm sure he'll be long gone, child, dinnae you fear.'

'Can you swear to that?' She looked up into his bearded face and dark eyes.

'Naw, Amber, love. Naw, I cannae.' His eyes searched the middle distance as if for more words, but there were none. He put his hand gently on her head.

Twelve of the rebels had escaped the fighting in the transit van that now stood on the gravel at Carlins Law. Claire lay battered in the back of the van. A woman – another nurse – was tending her injuries with a rag and some water. Stuart turned to the people who had spilled from the van to watch the carnage unfold in the valley below.

'We need to get back on the road north… does nae look like they're taking prisoners. We have to beat them to the border!' He clapped his hands, bustling the forlorn gang into the back of the van. His hand ran across his whiskers as he looked pensively at Amber, still kneeling, and facing away from him – towards Hexham. He moved over to her and lowered himself to her level. He rested a hand on her shoulder again.

'C'mon, lassie. We have tae go. We cannae stay here.'

'I'm staying here. This is my home – me mam, me dad... where will I go?'

'Wi' me, lass. 'Til we find your Da... C'mon, please. I cannae leave ye.'

'I'll be okay. I'll stay in the woods, like Dad. He'll come back. He'll find me.'

'Naw, it's no' happening that way. You come with me now, then in a few days when the dust settles, we come back and catch up with him.'

'I know what you mean, and I understand. But if I leave, I won't know – won't be able to help. He might need me – he might be injured...'

'I know.' Stuart raised his head and looked over at the others. 'But look at these people – they cannot survive in ye're woods. If ye stay, I will too, and they'll hunt us all down. If we go, we get them safe. We escape this army.' He nodded towards the burning town. 'And we can come back. Ye ken your father... he'll either find us or he'll be here when we get back.'

'Sounds like what *he* said when we left the last time – and then me mam died.'

'Dinnae do this to them! Dinnae make the same mistakes your father's made!' The grit showed through in his voice as time began to fray his patience.

Amber's head dropped; she knew he was right. She got slowly to her feet and closed the back doors of the van with a hollow metallic slam. Then, she climbed into the front passenger seat. Stuart ran to the driver's side and wasted no time in speeding away from the farm.

Nat's foot was flat to the floor along the military road. He hit the roundabout at the Errington Arms at seventy-eight, his tyres screamed on the tarmac. Out of the corner of his eye he saw a white van heading north – fast. There were no other cars on the road. It worried him to think there may already be NSO troops in the countryside or maybe it was some lucky rebels making a dash for the border. He didn't slow the car. He took the next turn off the roundabout and carried on hammering the engine.

He was back at his ruined home within ten minutes of leaving the roundabout. He smelled diesel in the air and his instincts kicked in. He scanned the surrounding rubble, buildings, and landscape for signs of life, signs of an ambush.

Had somebody been dropped off to await his return? He tasted the air and studied the places that a hunter would choose, and he knew there was nobody waiting, nobody watching him. For now, he was alone.

He went to the barn and grabbed some towels. There was a bottle of whiskey there – it was half empty, he remembered sitting out on the crag sharing it with Esme – he shook the memory from his mind and grabbed the first aid kit.

His head pounded, so he drank from the tap to slake his thirst. He slumped stiffly down in the dusty light of the barn, his back against the cupboard under the sink, and took stock of his injuries. He was no doctor, but he was relieved to see that both bullets had passed through him. The pain beat through his body like a drum. The wounds burned as though a red-hot poker was stabbing his flesh. His internal organs ached and shooting pains were whipping through his body. His muscles were limp and his mind dizzy. He had to fight both the shock and his desire to give up.

He ripped off the beaten-up wax jacket and his sodden clothes. Taking the hose from its circular rack he turned the stiff tap until a jet of icy water tightened his clammy skin. He washed himself down quickly then towelled himself off. The towel was damp but did the job.

From the first aid kit, he took strong painkillers and crudely sewed his wounds shut as best he could. Then he tied them off tight with bandages. The painkillers gave him some relief, but he was disoriented. He stuffed the first aid kit into his pack. Then he grabbed some fresh clothes that had been sitting in the dryer since the day his life had been turned upside down. He thanked Esme for insisting the washing stuff was in the barn. He took another wax jacket, and he took some comfort from the feel of clean, dry clothes on his skin.

Warm and drugged against the pain, he moved back to his supplies. He strapped his hunting rifle across his back once more, put a handgun and his hunting knife into his belt, stuffed his poncho, a few items of clothing and some tins of food into his pack. He picked up an old crook that leaned against the wall and walked quickly towards the door, gritting his teeth against the pain. With an energy-sapping limp, he spilled out into the open once more.

He hobbled up the hill towards the woods where he would decide his future. His mind was cold and focused on survival.

He dug in close to the edge of the tree line overlooking the approach to the farm and pulled his poncho over him – like a hide. It was a mild morning, thick acrid smoke billowed high up above Hexham and he could hear the murmur of small arms fire drifting up the valley. In the fields below him, his sheep grazed across the pasture, and he knew the weather was going to remain fine. He noticed a ewe in the bottom field that was lame. He could do nothing to help it, but it would feed him that night. He lined it up in his sights and watched it for a few minutes. Its front leg was broken or infected and it was tired, struggling just to feed. He imagined a fox would have it that night if he failed to get there first.

A twig snapped, drawing his attention away from the lame ewe. The broken stick was behind him. With the poncho covering him he was trapped at the mercy of his hearing. Any movement would betray his position.

He lay close to the dirt in a thicket of brambles. The rich soil filled his nose with earthy tones, and he could smell the sap of the foliage around him. He could hear something approaching him. The noises were small, quiet, but relatively constant; whatever was behind him was on the move.

He rolled slowly onto his back and concentrated on the direction of the intermittent rustling. A translucent spider danced across the sheeting, it captured his attention until the brambles to his right scragged and shook. His eyes darted and his head turned slowly. They were less than two yards from each other.

The Roebuck stood at around two and a half feet tall. He was beautiful with twelve-inch, four pointed antlers. His coat was almost black from the long winter, and he stared straight back at the hunters hide. The deer did not flinch, did not run, but he could sense a presence – he just couldn't see Nat or smell him. Nat was happy with his hide. If this wily old prey couldn't see him, it was unlikely humans would.

He relaxed the grip on his knife and slid it back into its sheath as the deer skittered away with long bounds through the undergrowth. He rolled back onto his front and his eyes settled once again on the ruin that was his farm.

They would often lie down in the thick grass and look down on the farm: Esme and him. They would talk about the business, about the neighbours and people around, as families do. They would talk about Amber's future, and Esme would be the reason to his anxiety. He had always been hard and capable physically, but Esme was his latitude, his liberalism and adventure.

The world outside the farm scared him; it was full of threat and deceit. It wasn't so much the physical threat to him that he had feared; it was fear for his daughter and his wife. He felt that society had created a greed that would always sell short those without power. It was his wife who had quashed this paranoia as she joked and reasoned with him. He missed her so much. He shook himself as he thought about his current predicament. Everything he had ever feared was now real.

As he pondered, it dawned on him that he had to move. He had to leave the farm or sooner or later they would find him there and burn every square inch until he was dead.

In that instant, he decided to make a break for the border. He got to his feet and left the safety of the tree line. He looked up to the vast sky and sucked the fresh air deep into his ailing lungs. He hobbled down the hill, labouring with his lame leg. The pain from his wounds defeated the painkillers, but the open air of the middle of the field gave him a freedom he hadn't sensed for a while. He felt the breeze in his hair, on his face.

There was hope.

TWENTY

'He does have a certain capacity to survive...' General Beaston spoke urgently but calmly, delivering the bad news. He kept his sentences short, '...but we are turning his land over now.'

'He bloody well called me! He's taking the piss out of us!' shouted Ben.

'Well, we'll catch him – that's all I can say now.'

'Just make bloody sure you do!'

Ben put the receiver down. He understood all too well that Beaston didn't have anything to go on, but that was not his problem. He would make sure that the soldier spent the rest of his days hunting Bell down, if that was what it took. He pushed himself up from the desk and marched decisively out of the room.

He tapped on Dart's office door before entering. His friend, colleague and adversary was hunched over his desk, lonely as a bull squashed into a stall. The only light in the room was his desk lamp; it was dim, and the shadows were long.

Ben walked into the room and slumped casually in the seat opposite his old ally. 'Tough at the top, eh?' he said jovially.

Dart's head rose from the papers he was poring over. 'What can I do for you? I've got a lot to get through.' He lifted the articles slightly from his desk.

'What's that?' asked Baines.

Dart looked at him, like a poker player looking for a 'tell'.

'What d'you want?' The Deputy's eyes narrowed, and his gaze didn't waver from Ben, who slouched in the chair across his desk. Ben sat up and leaned towards Dart. He smiled and raised his hands.

'I want you to know…' Ben smiled, '…that when you screwed me…' He let his smile fade. '…you made things very complicated.'

Dart was evidently surprised but said nothing. Instead, he sat back briefly, then pushed himself up and walked the couple of paces to a side table on which stood a decanter and two glasses. He raised the decanter in Ben's direction. Ben nodded, preserving the silence, as he allowed Lucas to pour two drinks.

Lucas took his time, calculating - Ben imagined, while the tinkling of cut glass and the warming sound of flowing spirit filled the silence. He returned with the glasses and put them either side of the desk, all the while looking searchingly at Ben, and sat back heavily into his roomy leather desk chair.

'There are many ways I could shut you up.' he said.

'But you won't.'

'Give me one good reason why not.'

Ben leaned forward slightly. 'Trevor Eastman,' he said softly.

The colour fell from Lucas's face and Ben saw the fear in his eyes as he processed the information. Ben really had no idea why this name would produce such a reaction in Lucas, but he made sure he did not give away his ignorance. He had gambled and it had paid off.

Finally, Lucas appeared to collect himself. 'I never thought you would betray us…'

'I haven't… But I'll do it if it's in the people's interest. We're gonna have to get along for a while.'

'For a while?'

'Until this mess is sorted,' Ben stood up and looked down at his deputy, sweating. 'And then we'll see where we're at…'

They were interrupted by an urgent knock at the door and Lucas jumped to his feet. Ben couldn't help but smile. The door cracked open, and an aide's head edged through it. He addressed Ben.

'Sir, we have located the insurgent, Bell. The helicopter is on standby as you requested.'

Ben looked at Lucas. 'As I said, nothing is definite. Let's sit down when I'm back. The madness must stop, but we could rescue this situation.'

The deputy raised his arms in a shrug. 'As you wish.' He nodded towards the door. 'Go on. I'll be here.' As Ben turned to leave, Lucas said, 'I'm sorry about your brother. A ruddy mess and a great man lost.'

Ben nodded to Dart. 'Was going to happen sooner or later. Luck was with him for forty-odd years.' He looked down at the floor. 'The reality of death is that life doesn't even skip a beat. If I stop to grieve, we lose ground.' He looked up and at his deputy again. 'And we can't lose ground now, Lucas.'

Lucas walked over to Ben and held out his hand. At first Ben just stared at him, unsure that the gesture was sincere, but his friend's hand stayed there. And they shook. Lucas grabbed his shoulder, his face solemn. A shiver ran down Ben's spine; he felt Lucas was about to share something serious, something important.

'What is it, Lucas?'

'I never wanted it to happen like it did. I never wanted...' He looked away.

'You never wanted what?'

Lucas pushed away and turned his back to him.

'Tell me Lucas...'

'No, it's nothing... I just meant I didn't want to hurt you. We were once so close, you and me...' When he turned around, his eyes were filled with emotion.

'You sure, there's nothing you want to tell me? You *can* tell me.'

Ben paused but as the seconds ticked away, he felt the moment pass. Until he turned and left the room without another word.

Lucas listened until he was sure that Baines had gone. His heart was beating so hard that his chest hurt. He slipped a mobile phone from inside his pocket and waited the excruciating seconds as it turned on. He pressed the green button and held it to his ear. He paced around his office. Then he heard the gravel voice that he despised so much.

'Yes...'

'You fucked me! You think I'll just lie down!'

'Hey, hold on... *Hold on!* You better back up and give me a damn good reason why you're starting fights you can't win, son.'

'Baines! He gave me your name. Are you playing *everyone* now?'

Eastman chuckled, a hoarse smoke-filled cackle. 'You are too much. He's bluffing. I met with him – he didn't want to know.' Eastman was silent for a moment. 'He was fishing. Did you give anything away?'

'Of course not.'

'Did you?'

'No! No, I didn't. But he took me by surprise. He smelled something...'

'Well, you'd better get a grip – or it's Plan B...'

'No. I won't have that. You've had everything from me! Not that... we agreed.'

'Well pull yourself together then and get it sorted.' The line went dead, and Lucas was left alone with his thoughts once more. He sat down on the big, comfy sofa, he closed his eyes and leaned back. He rubbed his chest as he tried to catch his breath.

TWENTY-ONE

The walk back down the hill was hard going on Nat; his calf muscle was next to useless. Every time he put weight on the leg, the pain was fierce. That was painful enough, but he had no idea of the damage the wound in his chest had done or was doing. He needed medical attention, and he needed it fast.

He staggered towards a car. No sooner had he touched the door handle, he heard the distant engines. His heart sank as his head turned to see seven or eight military vehicles snaking along the narrow country road below his farm. He watched for a second or two then turned to his wood. The land he knew so well was his only chance of escape. It was not enough to give him the upper hand – not against these numbers – but if he could get into the trees he might disappear.

Jumping into the car, he fired the ignition and the engine sparked first time. He slammed his foot on the accelerator and pulled off the clutch; the car leapt into action, tearing for bite in the loose gravel. As the tyres chewed at solid earth, it lurched forward, and he spun the wheel to point the car at the gate leading into the field and up to the woods. He clattered through the wooden gate that had crossed the gap to the top field for all those years. He kept his foot flat as the car revved in second gear up the steep incline. The land was not too boggy, and the tyres gripped enough to push up the hill. The engine whined as he approached the gate to the wood. He drove straight through it then veered into the ditch with a violent rocking thump. He shook off the impact and rolled out of the car.

Scrambling through the undergrowth, briars tearing at his skin, he fell on the top of a knoll just behind the stone wall that separated the wood from the field below. He had a clear sight of the farm; the trucks were stopping, lining up on the gravel parking area and the drive. Troops jumped down from them. They must have seen him driving up the hill, since they were being directed to fan out across the field and approach his position.

He laid his head in the soft wet grass. He was desperately cold and tired. He had three full magazines for his rifle. He could drop some of the men who wanted him dead now or he could run and leave them guessing where he was.

He raised his head to the telescopic sights, and he lined up his first hapless victim. He settled his breath... in... out... calm and steady then squeezed the trigger. He felt the kick, heard the *pfft* of the silenced shot and the distant figure fell.

He rested his head in his hands. He had little stomach for killing faceless men anymore. He looked again at the approaching soldiers and beyond, picking out the NSO commander by the trucks. Without hesitation, he put his eye to his weapon and fired twice. The target was a long way off, but he hit the man in the shoulder, and he watched him scramble out of sight behind the vehicles.

It was less than a minute later that he saw the black dot parting the smoke over Hexham with its violent downdraft. He listened for a second for confirmation of what he already knew. There it was: soft, almost inaudible, the pulsating throb of rotor blades beating a course for his position.

He wanted to lie there forever but he had to move. Digging into the depths of his resolve, he pushed himself through the pain and onto his feet. He limped as fast as he could into the thickest part of the wood. He didn't stop; he knew he had many acres to lose himself in.

Ben had been strapped into the back of the Gazelle helicopter for an interminable two hours. His head was pounding, dehydrated from the whisky. He chugged at a bottle of water, but it wasn't having the desired effect.

When he had received the call from Beaston to say they had reports of the farmer on his land, he had the impulse to see this one through personally. As they approached Hexham, he decided that the whisky was probably to blame for that impulse, but now he was here, he was looking forward to seeing this bastard fall.

'We'll be over Hexham in three minutes sir.' The pilot's voice fuzzed in his headphones, tinny and distant. He shifted in his seat to get a view out of the window. He craned his neck, eager to see the battlefield. As they entered the thick plumes of acrid black smoke, the rotor blades parted the vapour in arcing valleys, and he caught site of the town below. He pressed his face to the window, transfixed by the scene - a hellish vision of utter desolation.

He felt lightheaded and sick. He blinked and shook his head to try and regain his composure. It was not the buildings reduced to rubble, nor the personal belongings strewn, blown and hanging in the wreckage, or even the NSO troops brandishing and firing their weapons as they picked through the debris that had turned his stomach.

It was the bodies that lay like they were sleeping, and the red hue that spotted the ground which revealed their horror. He wept as the image cut through his heart.

He glanced across at the others in the chopper, they were all pinned to the windows as well; they hadn't seen his tears – except Pierre. The Frenchman stared at Ben; Pierre's face was full of anger. Ben couldn't hold his gaze; he had reverted instead to the privacy of the window and the devastation he had wrought. It took a supreme effort to suppress the urge to be sick. He felt stupidity – *what had he expected*, then he felt disgust.

No sooner had they hit upon Hexham then they were over open country once more.

'Nearly there sir,' said the voice through his headset.

'You have thermal imaging on board, yes?' Beaston spat over the radio to the pilots in the helicopter. 'Find him and relay the location to me.'

'No problem, we'll call it in.'

'I want to see the whites of this bastard's eyes.' Beaston put the receiver down. He sat on the tailgate of a truck, his shirt pulled down off his shoulder. Bell's bullet had passed through his shoulder-blade shattering it into fragments. A medic worked quickly to stem the blood and make the injury stable. He winced as the medic worked on this painful and infuriating dent to his pride.

As the chopper roared overhead, he brushed the medic away and barked at his troops to re-form. There was no time to lose. Now was the time to rid the dog of his tick.

Nat scrambled through the thick coniferous wood. The bare branches close to the ground level were hard as bone and snagged at his clothes and the scent of resin filled his nostrils. He ignored his injuries as best he could, but he knew that his movement was laboured and that he was still losing blood – he was dizzy. He focussed on surviving the next hour. His goal was to reach a certain outcrop of rock that would give him shelter from the searching helicopter and some elevation from the approaching NSO men.

He was about two hundred yards from where he wanted to be. To his left were the deepest darkest coniferous trees in the woodland. To his right was the edge of the steep ravine that gave passage to where

Esme lay buried, her grave remained like a testament to this chaos. He hugged the edge of the drop because the going was much easier than in the thick of the trees.

As he clambered, disoriented and chaotic, he tried to duck a fallen tree trunk, but he caught his back on the bow. It knocked him off balance and he veered over the edge of the ravine. He threw out a hand instinctively and grabbed a thick branch from the fallen tree. He hung there, his legs scrambling on the steep unstable slope. His hunting rifle slid from his shoulder to hang on his wrist on his injured side. He had no strength to swing it back up onto the flat ground, so he wriggled it free and let the weapon slip away down slope.

The thud-thud-thud of chopper blades were loud in the air now and he was a sitting duck.

As Ben caught sight of Nat Bell in the flesh for the first time. He squinted for the murderer, the beast, the monster. But all he saw was a man, hunted and fearful, dying at the hands of a far more powerful force. Seeing things for what they were now, as he rested his forehead against the window and watched the indestructible Bell hanging over the edge of a precipice, one side of his body limp and bloodied, his legs kicking in the dirt for some purchase. Chased like a lone wolf that had ventured too close to the herd, the dogs closing in.

He had won. The farmer had lost.

He glanced at Pierre again; his friend still glared at him, refusing to be a spectator to this sport. He leaned forward, close enough to speak to Ben over the din of the engines.

'It is never how you imagine – this part. A life is a life.'

Nat's good arm held his weight, but he had to move, to get back onto the path. He swung himself up and grabbed with his left hand. Excruciating pain shot through his chest as he grasped another branch, and he screamed out as his weakened body took the strain. He was then able to walk his legs up to the top of the incline. His calf was also hurting but nothing like the pain in his chest. He blinked and breathed heavily as he contemplated moving his sound arm.

Finally, he took the full weight of his body on his left arm and grabbed the next branch with his right. The rough bark tore at his hands, but he was there, able to use his uninjured arm to lift himself up and onto safe ground. He lay for a brief time to catch his breath and collect himself. All composure had gone. He began to understand that his injuries made it impossible to keep running. One thing was certain, however: he had to get up onto the rocks or he didn't have a chance.

TWENTY-TWO

The white van trundled over the blind summits of the North Northumberland highway. Few places on earth offered a sky vaster and a landscape wilder. Amber sat staring out across the browns of the moorland as it stretched off for miles before hitting the blue sky with its huge billowing clouds. Stuart didn't look up from the horizon. They hadn't spoken since leaving the farm.

He swung the van off the road at Catcleugh Reservoir and followed the rough woodland track through Castle Crag Forest to hit the border a few miles further north. It was a crossing the Scots had opened for the retreating rebels. They had travelled a short distance when he skidded to a stop. Coming the other way were several vehicles that pulled to a stop in front of the van.

The door to the first truck opened and Matty Rowell jumped down from the driver's side. He ran to Stuart's window.

'You made it! I was worried about you. You okay?' He looked through to Amber and smiled warmly.

'Aye,' she replied distracted. 'The border shut up ahead?'

'No, it's open. We're going to get your da.'

'*What?*'

'Friendlies in the NSO gave word he's on the run… Carlins Law…'

Amber grasped the door handle without a second thought. 'I'm coming with you, then!'

'Whoa, lassie,' said Stuart. 'We'll *both* go. But we have tae get these safe first.' He pointed to the back of the van.

'No time,' Matty butted in. 'Word is they have men in numbers combing the land to flush him out. We need to get down there and meet them head on from the north.'

Stuart looked across at Amber, thinking for a moment. 'Okay, we'll come with ye if there's room.

Somebody in the back can take this one on to the border.'

'No problem. Let's go.'

Stuart and Amber jumped into the flatbed of the truck. It was cold, but they were joining ten other bodies huddled in there. The convoy moved out to save the farmer who had become much more than a mere fighter in their struggle against the regime.

The helicopter flew low, almost over his head, and the trees rocked wildly under the downdraught of the rotor blades. The noise was deafening. Nat couldn't think. Undergrowth slapped him across the face and filled his eyes with specks of dirt. He clenched his fists and beat the earth pushing himself to his feet. He staggered towards the rocky knoll and slid between the crags. To his dismay, the helicopter hovered low above his position, and he knew that it was guiding the men on the ground to where he was.

The chopper turned slowly, about fifty feet above his head. He wondered whether a bullet would pierce the windshield. Then he looked at the tail as it came around. He had a clear shot straight up below the tail and he judged that it was moving slowly enough. He had no idea whether the rounds from his handgun could penetrate the metal or affect the mechanics, but it was worth trying.

The helicopter rotated and Ben glimpsed Bell looking up at them. With every revolution Ben lost sight of the farmer for interminable seconds before the view was unobstructed again. Each time Bell came into view, his eyes remained fixed on the helicopter. *Was he looking at him?* He shook the thought from his head. He turned away from the window, sat forward and rested his elbows on his knees. His head fell into his hands as he heard Pierre's voice again.

'Is this what you wanted?'

Ben didn't look up. His emotions were choking him, the pressure building inside. He felt that he was about to explode.

Nat brought up the handgun and aimed at the tail of the chopper. He followed it as it turned slowly. He gently increased the pressure of his finger on the trigger. He was unsteady; his eyesight was blurred and his hand shook. He tried to stay calm as his grip tightened and the gun fired.

Ben lifted his head suddenly. 'I've seen enough!'

'Sorry sir! What was that?' the pilot replied through their headsets.

'Let's go. Enough of this…'

'But sir… General Beaston –'

'I said *enough!*' Ben yelled. He would have jumped from his seat had he not been strapped in. 'Turn this fucking thing around and fly away! *Now!*'

The helicopter banked sharply away from the crag and away from Nat Bell. Ben looked around at the other men in the helicopter. They glowered at him; but when he looked at Pierre, he received a barely perceptible nod.

Ben buried his face into the corner between the seat and the window.

No sooner had he taken his first shot than the helicopter banked sharply to the right and sped away south. He stared at it as it flew off. At first, he thought he'd damaged it. When it didn't go down, his eyes concentrated on the surrounding woods. It had done its job and the men on the ground had to be onto him.

The wood fell silent, peaceful. Nat lay against the rock, his breathing shallow and blood oozing from the wound in his chest. Right then, he felt that he would never move again. Through the trees came the faint rustles and snapping branches of the approaching soldiers. He lay prone against the cold stone, slumped and lifeless. He was shivering and struggling for breath, concentrating on the necklace that Esme had given to Amber. He waited.

The convoy took a sharp left off the A68 and sped along the narrow country lane running along the northern border of Nat's land. The vehicles pulled up hard where the road ran parallel with the Fairspring Burn and the rebels leapt down onto the lush grass verges.

They were about two miles north of Nat's position. They could see the helicopter hovering low above the trees.

'I know where he is!' screamed Amber. 'Follow me, follow me!' She leapt the stone wall into the next field. They were in no formation, just running as fast as they could, trying to cover the ground between themselves and the cornered farmer as quickly as possible; it was like an infantry charge of old. There were about fifty of them sprinting en-masse and in silence towards the woodland, the whisper of rye grass under their feet.

Nat waited. His beloved trees surrounded him, enveloped him with nature and made him feel safe. He could feel Esme and Amber there with him. He could see mist ahead of him – or was his sight failing? Though he felt heavy, there was no pain. He could make out dark figures as they began to emerge from the trees.

They stopped and fanned out in a ring around his position. Nobody fired and nobody spoke.

Nat sank as low as he could, but he was confused by the hesitation. In full view, lying in the undergrowth, he understood now that he didn't stand a chance. The first few drops of rain pattered down through the foliage, soon followed by a deluge that beat a tattoo through the wood. Nat stayed in his nest, the water beating off his poncho, watching the men who had come to kill him and listening to the drumming of the rainfall. It was a good few minutes before he heard the voice.

'Bell? Can you hear me?'

Nat could identify the figure that spoke but shaded by the trees, he couldn't make out any features. The voice came again.

'Well… I'm going to try again! I want to parley with you! We need to have a conversation before whatever happens here, happens.' The General's voice seemed strained a little as if he was in a measure of pain. Was this the man he shot at the farm?

Again, the wood went quiet. Nat listened to the drops of rain landing on leaves, a cough from one of the enemy and then he decided.

'I can hear you sqwark!' he snarled.

He saw the figure step a little closer, into the light. 'You stamped on a nest of hornets, Bell. We have no choice, you understand?'

Nat looked at his hands. They were black with dirt, cut and bleeding from injuries he had not even registered.

'I'm done running! I've got nothing left!'

'I can see that. I reckon you've got about fifteen minutes at best. It comes to us all, son. War is lost when you have nothing left.' Beaston took a few careful paces towards Nat and the two men looked intently at each other.

'I was very unfashionable for a while. You know why? Because I know that you can't win a war with hearts and minds. War is about stopping hearts, enslaving minds and crushing hope. That's what I do very well.'

Nat shifted painfully on the wet ground. As he moved, he heard the soldiers shoulder their weapons and train them on his body. He mustered all his strength to sit up slightly, to face Beaston.

'They were innocent people who died in Hexham.'

'There are no innocents!' Beaston's voice was raised, irate. 'I never understand you people. It always baffles me people in this country... I don't know why you're surprised. I mean we've spent the last three centuries fighting wars in other people's countries. That's war... winners and losers. Don't blame me, I'm just the instrument – effecting the will of others.'

Beaston's words made Nat sick with hatred. As he listened, he carried on edging up the stone, his arms spread, his poncho flapping in the breeze.

Amber cut through the trees far quicker than the others. She could hear nothing over the padding of her feet on the wet soil and the swishing of twigs in her face and across her body. Then the rain began to fall and mask even those sounds. She could see the craggy outcrop and was sure her father would be holed up on the other side.

She stopped momentarily, to see where the others were. She was reassured by movement through the trees behind her as though the forest were coming alive, so she turned again and moved on. She still had about three hundred metres to cover. She skimmed through the tightly packed trees like a roe deer on the hoof. She cocked her weapon and pushed herself harder to cover the ground.

'Stop right there, Bell!' Beaston called out from behind the shady bough of a great oak tree. He pointed a bony finger at Bell, who was almost to his feet.

Bell's face was ashen, the lines deep and pronounced by the pain. The calf of his left leg was sodden; a dark burgundy soaked the material. The left side of his bloodstained poncho betrayed a chest wound. His beard hung wet and limp, as did his hair. But his eyes, shone azure and sharp.

After a few moments, Beaston pushed himself off the tree and walked slowly towards him. He tried not to show his vulnerability, but it had become impossible. Nat stiffened, trying to conjure some strength as he watched Beaston approach. The General now had a pistol in his hand, which he swung freely. Nat's eyes narrowed in on the weapon. Blood showed through a field dressing on Beaston's shoulder. His brown hair was wavy, verging on the foppish; his military greens were well worn but clean and well pressed. He wore black boots, and he covered the ground with a clear contempt for its nature. Its uncultivated beauty was an irritation to men like Beaston. Nat hated him the more for it. He came within ten yards.

'That's better,' Beaston said. 'I can look you in the eye now.' His face had seen many hard years and the life he had lived was written in his skin. His flickering eyes were dark and intense. 'You remind me of those damn jihadis. You've got your own set of ideas and to hell with the rest of us, eh?'

Nat said nothing, but his heart still pumped enough blood for his brain to function.

'You know…When I was young, I was like you – not young teenage, I mean – really young. Anyway, one day we had a big family lunch, and my father wanted us all to play some damn game. Well, I didn't want to play inside – fucking charades or some such – I wanted to play outside with my cousin. But my cousin was too scared of my father, so I went out alone. I was playing with a ball in the garden when my father came out. He took me to the greenhouse. I was a little scared at this point – I knew I was in trouble. The old bastard took me by the neck and pushed my head down into the water butt. I thrashed about and pushed and pulled but… My God, man, I was only eight or nine. I was no match for his power. I remember the cold. It made me gasp, made my headache.' Beaston waved his pistol around his temple. 'He held me underwater until I passed out.' He nodded at Nat as if to affirm the veracity of his story.

'When I came to, my father told me that the first lesson in life is that other people are in control. You might not want to do what you must, but if you don't do it, the whole system fails.' He paused again, nodding, letting the point sink in. 'I think you could have done with a lesson like that, Bell. I'm the hand holding you under, son. But I'm afraid there's no let up here. You went too far.'

Beaston's face hardened and the troops behind him pricked at the flashpoint of unspoken energy.

Amber was sprinting as she rounded the outcrop. Her father came into view and her heart rolled over as she saw him leaning against the rock, visibly wounded and about ten feet from another man. An officer of sorts. She aimed her weapon but, registering the NSO troops in the trees behind, she waited for the others to arrive.

She had paused for no more than a second when her brain unscrambled the situation. Her mouth opened to scream, and her finger squeezed the trigger as her father moved like lightning to draw a handgun from his belt. He fired once, hitting the soldier in the head. With a short shrill scream, the soldier fell backwards to the ground.

Her father stood tall, his gun outstretched, as all hell broke loose from the trees. The rounds pumped into him for what seemed like an eternity. Amber watched as his body convulsed, absorbing round after round. The stone behind him splintered as the bullets ricocheted off it. His blood misted the air in front of him and he fell sideways into the bracken, his blood flowing free into the land.

Amber was struck dumb with grief and horror. It was like being in a desperate, visceral nightmare. She screamed a banshee's wail and fired wildly at the NSO troops, but the shots flew into the tops of the trees. Stuart was next to her, holding the burning barrel of her gun high to ruin her aim.

'*Enough!*'

She wrenched the gun from his grasp and made to charge down to where her father lay, but a huge arm ensnared her waist and pulled her back to safety leaving the other rebels to fight the regime troops.

Something dark flushed through her veins. She kicked and thrashed and smashed the butt of her weapon into Stuart's face. She screamed and wailed and cried and spat, a heavy mist descending in her soul. Hatred blackened her heart, and she fought the Scotsman's grip until both stood exhausted.

As the rebels overwhelmed the regime's soldiers, the pair stood in the leafy clearing. The rain beat down upon them and upon her father's forlorn body lying in the scrub.

Amber seethed, breathing hard. Her fists were clenched, hanging like wrecking balls, waiting to smash everything. She gazed at her father. He looked pitiful and broken, tamed finally by death. The weight of her suffering dragged her to her knees.

'C'mon, lassie. We have tae get out of here…'

She looked up at Stuart, his dusky eyes full of pain and worry. She pushed herself up to her feet and pulled her weapon across her chest. She watched the rebels fight and die for their cause. Then she turned again to Stuart and straightened her back.

'I'll never leave this place again.'

Printed in Great Britain
by Amazon

59860792R00167